# DRAGONS—ASSORTED

All Dumery had to do was to get into the hatchling cage, steal two of the dragons, and run. But the cage's latch was a black lump in the dimness. Dumery poked it in growing frustration. But when he pushed two thumb-sized stubs together in the middle, he heard a clank, and the door swung open.

A dozen little dragons stared up at Dumery from inside the cage, their gleaming eyes unreadable. The colors were harder to distinguish in the gloom than he had expected.

Dumery was just about to step inside the cage for a closer look when he heard the growl. He found himself looking directly into another, much larger pair of draconic eyes.

One of the big dragons was loose and standing not ten feet away, with its long neck extended—and with a wide open mouth and fangs ready for him!

By Lawrence Watt-Evans
*Published by Ballantine Books:*

# THE
# BLOOD
# OF A
# DRAGON

## Lawrence Watt-Evans

A Del Rey Book
BALLANTINE BOOKS • NEW YORK

A Del Rey Book
Published by Ballantine Books
Copyright © 1991 by Lawrence Watt Evans

Library of Congress Catalog Card Number: 91-92108

ISBN 0-345-36410-4

Manufactured in the United States of America

First Edition: November 1991

Cover Art by Darrell K. Sweet

Dedicated to
Marian
and Tom
and Gordon

# CHAPTER 1

*The boy stared eagerly down into the Arena, chewing his lip* in anticipation. The horse races were over, and, as a foretaste of what was to come, the sands were being raked smooth by magic.

The rakes themselves were the same perfectly ordinary wooden rakes that had been dragged back and forth across the sand by perfectly ordinary people before each race. Now, however, the rakes were moving by themselves, as if held in invisible hands, and the slaves, or servants, or whoever the people were who were responsible for the Arena's maintenance, were nowhere to be seen.

Dumery wondered whether the rakes had been animated somehow, or whether they were being wielded by sylphs or sprites or demons, or whether the servants had been turned invisible. Magic could do so many amazing things!

The rakes were all painted bright blue, and he wondered if that was important. Did the magic in use here only work on blue things? He knew that magic could have peculiar requirements. Or were the rakes blue because the Lord of the Arena had taken blue and gold as his colors?

Or perhaps had he taken his colors from the golden sand and the blue rakes and other fittings?

Or was there some other reason entirely?

There were so many things that he didn't know! He had read everything he could find about magic, but that wasn't much; he had asked questions of everyone he knew, but he knew no wizards, nor witches or warlocks or sorcerers or any other other sort of wonder-worker. He had occasionally met a magician or two and had always asked questions, but he hadn't always gotten answers.

The rest of the time he just asked whomever was handy, even though they weren't magicians. Sometimes they had answers anyway, sometimes they didn't, so he just kept trying.

"Dad," he asked, "why are the rakes blue?"

Startled out of a contemplative half doze, Doran of Shiphaven let the front legs of his chair drop heavily to the floor of the family box, rattling the gold chain that draped across his velvet-clad chest. Rings clicked against wood as he gripped the arm of the chair and turned to stare at his son.

"What?" he asked.

"Those rakes out there," Dumery said, pointing. "Why are they all painted blue?"

On his left, Dumery's sister Dessa, a year older than he, giggled into her hands. Their two older brothers, noticing the noise, peered over from their father's right side to see what the fuss was about.

"So they won't rot, I suppose," Doran said, puzzled. "Or to keep down the splinters."

"But why *blue*?" Dumery persisted. "Why not red, or green? Brown wouldn't show the dirt as much, or if they *want* to see the dirt then white would be better. Why blue?"

After a baffled pause, his father admitted, "I don't have the faintest idea."

Derath leaned over, smirking, and said, "It's to match your eyes, Dumery!"

"My eyes are green, stupid!" Dumery retorted. "Maybe you'd better have an herbalist check *your* eyes if you don't know that!"

"Oh, *I* know that," Derath said sweetly. "But the Lord of the Arena doesn't!" He turned and grinned triumphantly at the eldest brother, Doran the Younger, who snorted derisively.

Dessa giggled harder than ever.

Dumery felt his cheeks redden slightly and he turned his attention back to the Arena floor, pointedly ignoring his siblings. He didn't think Derath's joke was funny, since it really didn't even make any sense, but he knew from long experience that if Derath and Doran and Dessa once got started mocking him it would last for hours. Retorting wouldn't stop it; ignoring them might.

The raking was finished, Dumery saw, and the Arena sands

gleamed smooth and golden in the afternoon sun. The crowd quieted in anticipation.

The silence grew, and a certain tension grew with it, until suddenly a cloud of thick yellow smoke appeared, swirling out of one of the many gateways that opened into the Arena from the labyrinth below. The smoke did not dissipate, the way any natural smoke or vapor would, but instead hung together in a spinning globe, something like a miniature whirlwind but far denser and ball shaped rather than the tapering cylinder of a normal whirlwind.

Dumery caught his breath and stared. Beside him Dessa stopped giggling. On the other side of the box Doran the Younger and Derath fell silent, as well.

The seething ball of smoke drifted out into the Arena, moving across the sand at about the speed of a brisk walk, until it stood in the exact center, its base just barely disturbing the neatly raked lines.

The smoke was a paler yellow than the deep gold of the sands, a sickly, ugly color, like the belly of a snake. Dumery stared at it, utterly fascinated.

Thunder boomed from nowhere, and lightning flashed, almost blinding him; he looked up, startled, but the sky was still clear and blue, and the sunlight was still sweeping across the stands.

When he looked back, the yellow smoke was gone save for a few fading wisps, and in its place stood the wizard.

Dumery leaned forward eagerly.

The wizard was a plump fellow of medium height, wearing a gleaming ankle-length robe of fine red silk. Dumery was no good at guessing ages, but this man was clearly no longer young—his face was weathered and his jowls sagged. His hair was still a glossy black, though, without a trace of gray.

The wizard thrust his hands up in the air, fingers spread, and cried, ''Behold!''

The vastness of the Arena swallowed his voice, and it was obvious that only those in the best seats could hear what he had said. Dumery felt a twinge of disappointment at that. Surely a wizard's voice should have enough magic in it to overcome such inconveniences.

Then he forgot about the voice as streams of colored smoke

poured forth from the ten spread fingers. Each spouting plume was a different color: crimson, violet, ochre, lizard green, and pale blue spewed from the left hand, while magenta, indigo, copper, forest green, and midnight blue streamed from the right.

The wizard waved his hands, crossing them above his head, and the rising hands of smoke braided themselves in intricate patterns, each remaining pure and discrete.

Then, abruptly, the smoke stopped, and the wizard dropped his hands. He took a step forward, and then another, and with the third step Dumery realized that his feet had left the ground. He was climbing up into thin air as if it were solid stone steps!

When he had ascended to a height of about eight feet above the ground, the wizard stopped and stood calmly unsupported in midair. He waved a hand again, and a trail of golden sparks glittered behind it.

"Behold!" he cried again.

Behind him, the sands of the Arena rose up into a column, sweeping away the last traces of the colored smoke. The column rose to a height of perhaps fifteen feet, then burst apart into a flock of white doves that flew quickly away, scattering in all directions and fluttering up out of the Arena. A single snowy feather fell from one bird's wing, unnoticed until the wizard turned and pointed at it.

The feather grew and changed and became a white cat that fell to the sand, landing, catlike, on all fours. It did not run away or wash itself as an ordinary cat would have, but instead began chasing its tail, spinning faster and faster until Dumery could no longer make out anything but a blur.

When it suddenly stopped, the cat was black, from its whiskers to the tip of its tail.

It sat back on its haunches, and the wizard waved at it.

It grew, and became a panther.

The wizard waved again, and the panther was gone, leaving only a cloud of smoke that rolled up into the sky and dissipated.

Dumery stared, enthralled, as the performance continued.

To his right, Dessa was somewhat less impressed. Dumery could hear her humming quietly to herself.

When the wizard conjured a naked man out of a seashell Dessa giggled; Dumery ignored her.

To his left his father was dozing off in the bright sunlight. Beyond him Derath and Doran were loudly whispering crude jokes to each other.

Dumery's lips tightened.

How could they fail to appreciate such marvels? How had he ever been born into such a family of clods?

Finally the wizard finished his performance, bowed, then began climbing up that invisible staircase in the sky again. He mounted higher, and higher, and higher, while behind him the blue rakes emerged again—guided, this time, by merely human hands.

Dumery paid no attention to the rakes, nor the servants wielding them, nor the scenery being hastily erected for the play that would conclude the day's show. He watched the wizard as he climbed upward into the sky, out over the side of the Arena, passing fifty or sixty feet above the family of Grondar the Wainwright two boxes over, eighty feet above the outer wall of the Arena, and on into the distance until he vanished.

Once the wizard was really, truly gone Dumery waited impatiently for the play to be over, paying no attention to the clever dialogue—after all, even when he could make out the words, half the time he didn't understand the jokes, which usually seemed to involve sex. His knowledge of sex was still very limited and entirely theoretical.

The sun was scarcely above the western rim of the Arena when the actors finally took their bows and the crowd called out polite applause.

As they were marching down through the stone corridors, on their way back to the street, the elder Doran remarked, "Well, Dumery, I hope you enjoyed that. Seemed like a good way to mark your birthday."

Dumery nodded, not really listening, and totally unaware of the annoyed look his lack of enthusiasm received.

"When *I* turned twelve," his father continued a moment later, "I didn't get any trip to the Arena, let me tell you! I spent the day in the hold of a ship, cleaning up the mess where a storm at sea had broken open a dozen crates of pottery and herbs."

Dumery nodded. "You own that ship now," he pointed out. He had heard the story before—several times, in fact.

"Damn right I do!" Doran replied. "I was lucky, and I worked hard for it, and the gods blessed me—I own that ship. And if she's still afloat when I die, she'll go to your brother Doran, because *he* was lucky, and was born into the right household. You boys don't appreciate what you've got, because you've always had it, you didn't have to work for it."

"I appreciate it, Dad," Derath interrupted.

"No, you don't," the elder Doran snapped. "Maybe you think you do, but you don't really, because you've never been poor. Your mother and I saw to that!"

Derath and Doran the Younger exchanged glances.

"You've never had to work for anything in your lives," their father continued, and Dumery wondered whether he was complaining, or boasting, or both.

They reached the street and turned north in the golden twilight, joining the loose-packed throng that was strolling up Arena Street, a hundred sandals slapping the hard-packed dirt in a patter like falling rain. Shopkeepers were lighting their storefront torches, and the familiar, friendly scent of burning oil reached Dumery's nose. As a rule he never noticed the city's ubiquitous odor, which had been a constant in his life since the day he was born, but the smoky smell of the torches seemed to emphasize that distinctive mingling of spices and ordure that always flavored Ethshar's air. As he remembered the wizard's performance, the fading light and that complex odor suddenly seemed magical, transforming the familiar avenue into something exotic and wonderful.

"Never worked a day, any of you," his father muttered suddenly, breaking the spell cast by the sunset and smoke.

"And *they* never will!" Dumery said, annoyed, jerking a thumb at his brothers.

Doran of Shiphaven looked at him, startled, then back at Doran and Derath, and then at Dumery again.

"No, they won't," he agreed. "And I don't suppose Dessa will, either, if she's careful."

Dessa threw him a startled glance, but then went back to watching the shops as they passed, ignoring the rest of the conversation.

"Just me," Dumery said, trying to sound flippant, rather than resentful.

"Well," his father said, "I don't know. We could find you a way out of working, I'm sure."

"Oh? Like what?" Dumery replied, making less of an effort to hide his bitterness. "Doran's getting the ships, and Derath's getting the money, and Dessa's getting the house—what do I get, if not an apprenticeship fee? What else is left? And every apprentice I ever heard of works hard enough!"

"Maybe we could dower you . . ." Doran began.

Dumery made a rude noise.

"As far as I know," he said, ignoring his father's annoyance at the interruption, "I don't want to get married, let alone like that!"

Doran said, "You'll want to get married when you're older . . ."

"Oh, I suppose I will," Dumery interrupted. "But I don't want some fancy arranged marriage where I don't have any say about who or when or what we'll do afterward."

Doran nodded. "I can see that," he said. He kept his eyes straight ahead, not looking at Dumery.

They walked on in silence for a few moments. Doran and Derath dropped back a bit, slowed by their horseplay, and Dessa dawdled, as well, looking in the shop windows, so that Dumery and his father were able to talk in relative privacy, without being overheard by the rest of the family.

"Maybe," Doran suggested, "we could arrange for you to stay with the family business—not as an owner, of course, because we've already settled it all on Dorie, but as a manager, perhaps. Something that would pay well."

"And wouldn't have me hauling on ropes? Thanks, Dad, but I don't think so. It's bad enough being the younger brother now; I don't think I want to spend the rest of my life being Dorie's kid brother, and having to do what he tells me or starve."

"You always were stubborn," Doran said, "and too damn proud to take orders from anyone."

They walked on, and a block later Doran shrugged and said, "Then I can't think of anything except an apprenticeship."

"I know," Dumery said, "I've been thinking about it for

weeks myself and I couldn't think of anything else. And I don't really mind that much. I'm still lucky, just as you said—it's just Dorie and Derath and Dessa were luckier.''

Doran could think of no reply to that.

After a moment Dumery added, ''I'm not afraid of work, anyway.''

''Well, that's good,'' Doran said, in a satisfied tone. ''Have you given much thought to what sort of an apprenticeship you want? I'm sure we could get you aboard any ship you like, if you'd care to be a pilot, or to work toward a captaincy.''

''Thanks, but I don't think so,'' Dumery replied. ''I'm not that interested in going to sea.''

''Well, there's bookkeeping, or chandlery, or we could apprentice you to a merchant of some sort. Had you thought about any of those?''

''I've thought about them all, Dad,'' Dumery said, stating what he considered to be the obvious. ''I know what I want to do.''

''Oh?'' Doran was slightly amused by his son's certitude. It was a trait the boy had had since infancy, always knowing what he wanted and being determined to get it, no matter what it took. ''And what's that?''

Dumery looked up at his father and said, quite seriously, ''I want to be a wizard.''

Doran stared at his son in shocked disbelief.


# CHAPTER 2


*Doran of Shiphaven had not given his son an immediate* answer. When pressed, he had limited himself to a noncommittal, ''We'll see.''

In the days following the show at the Arena he thought the matter over carefully.

There could be no doubt at all that the boy was serious.

Dumery had never been one to take things lightly; when he asked for something he meant it, it wasn't just a passing whim. And he had been obsessed with magic for years now.

That wasn't unusual, in a boy his age, and somehow Doran hadn't realized just how obsessed Dumery was. The child didn't just want to *see* a wizard, he wanted to *be* one.

That took some thought.

In theory, wizardry was a perfectly respectable profession, and Doran should have no objection to seeing his youngest son pursue it, but somehow he just wasn't comfortable with the idea. Wizards were such strange people, either showy braggarts or ill-tempered recluses, from what he'd seen. And wasn't magic supposed to be dangerous stuff? All that messing around with unseen forces simply didn't seem safe.

It could be worse, of course, it could easily be *much* worse. The boy might have wanted to be a demonologist. Now *that* was dangerous work, dealing with the forces of evil themselves and trying to wring good from them!

Or maybe not trying to wring good from them, for that matter; Doran had certainly heard plenty of rumors about demonologists performing assassinations and the like. And nobody ever denied that they laid curses on people. And every so often demonologists would disappear, leaving only the most bizarre and fragmentary evidence behind, and nobody really knew whether they'd lost control of their demons, or lost out in a dispute with other magicians, or maybe been struck dead by the gods for their tampering in places where humans weren't supposed to meddle.

At least Dumery wasn't interested in *that*!

And he wasn't interested in witchcraft, which was such a peasantish sort of magic, or sorcery, which still had a rather unsavory reputation even though the Great War had been over for centuries, or warlockry, which was new and strange and whose practitioners all seemed to make everybody very nervous.

Theurgy, though—that was respectable enough, and nobody ever heard about theurgists getting a spell wrong and vanishing in a puff of purple smoke. Talking to gods seemed a lot healthier than messing around with runes and powders and so forth.

He suggested it at dinner one night, and Dumery sat silently for a moment, pushing his greens around his plate with his fork.

"Well?" Doran demanded at last.

"I don't know, Dad," Dumery replied. "I mean, it just doesn't interest me the way wizardry does. None of the other magicks do—at least, not the ones I've heard of."

Doran was baffled. "What's so special about wizardry, then?"

"Oh, I don't know," Dumery replied, "It just . . . I mean, it . . . it just *is*, that's all."

Doran sighed. He knew he couldn't argue with that. It rarely did any good to argue with *anything* Dumery said.

"We'll see what we can do," he said.

He tried to think of an alternative, or an excuse for delay, but nothing came, and three days later he and Dumery slogged through muddy streets in a steady spring downpour, hats pulled down tight on their heads, on their way to an interview with Thetheran the Mage.

"Spoiled," Doran muttered under his breath as yet another puddle turned out to be deeper than it looked. "I've spoiled the boy. Wizardry—ha!"

Dumery could hear that his father was muttering but couldn't make out the words, and took it for curses directed against the gods of weather.

He didn't mind the rain, not really—the important thing was that he was going to be a wizard! He really was!

Oh, he'd start out as a mere apprentice, of course, and he'd have to work harder than he ever had in his life and study night and day and practice, but after six years—or nine, or twelve, depending—he'd be a wizard! A real wizard!

They were on Wizard Street now, and Dumery pushed his hat back a little, so that he could see the signboards better as they walked along. He didn't want to miss Thetheran's place.

"There it is!" he called, pointing.

His father looked up. "Yes," he agreed, "that's it."

As they approached the little shop the door swung open; Dumery felt a tingle of excitement run through him and he shivered with anticipation.

A tall, gaunt man in a midnight-blue robe appeared in the

doorway, then stepped back to make room for them as they crossed the threshold.

Something Dumery couldn't see snatched their hats away, sprinkling his face with cold rainwater spilled from the brim.

"Come in," the tall man said. "Come in and dry off."

Dumery looked up at him expectantly, thinking that their clothes were about to be dried magically, but the wizard—if this was he—performed no magic, he merely gestured toward a half circle of velvet-upholstered chairs arranged around the hearth, where a fire was crackling comfortably.

Mildly disappointed, Dumery followed along and slid onto one of the chairs. His father took the next, and the tall man the one beyond.

"So you're Dumery," the tall man said, staring at him intently.

Dumery stared back but said nothing.

"I am Thetheran the Mage, master wizard and master of this house, and I bid you welcome," the tall man said.

Doran discreetly prodded his son with an elbow. "I'm Dumery of Shiphaven," Dumery said, remembering his manners. "Thank you for making us welcome."

"I understand that you wish to apprentice yourself to me, to learn the wizardly arts," Thetheran said, still staring him in the eye.

Dumery threw his father a glance, then looked back at the wizard. "That's right," he said. "I want to be a wizard."

Thetheran finally removed his gaze from Dumery's face, looking instead at Doran. "If you will forgive me, sir, I must speak to the lad in private to see whether he has the makings of an apprentice. You may wait here, or go where you will and return in an hour's time." He raised one hand in a peculiar way, the wrist twisted in what looked to Dumery to be a very uncomfortable fashion, and added, "Should you choose to stay, you will be brought food and drink, if you wish. Simply call out what you want; I have *oushka*, if the rain has chilled you, and ale, to wash the *oushka* down or merely to slake your thirst, and a well of clear water that I keep pure by my magic. To eat, I fear I have little to spare at present but good bread and a fine wheel of Shannan red cheese."

Doran nodded politely and was about to say something, when the wizard stood, staring at Dumery again and obviously no longer interested in anything the boy's father might have to say.

He reached out, and Dumery stood as well.

The wizard started to lead the boy toward a curtained doorway in the rear wall of the shop—if a shop it actually was, with no merchandise or displays of any kind, but only the furnishings that one might find in an ordinary parlor.

"Wait a minute," Doran called.

Thetheran turned back toward him.

So did Dumery, and for a moment the boy thought his father looked uneasy, though he knew that couldn't be true; nothing ever bothered Doran of Shiphaven, master of the sixth-largest trading fleet in the city's harbor.

"Just call?" he asked.

Thetheran nodded.

"Call *whom*?" Doran asked.

Thetheran sighed. "What would you like?" he asked.

What Doran really wanted was to take Dumery and go home and forget all about any involvement with wizards or magic, but Dumery wanted to be here, and it was pouring rain outside, which made the prospect of strolling about for an hour extremely unappealing.

He didn't understand what the wizard was talking about, telling him to just call for what he wanted, but right at that moment he thought he could use something warming to drink. *"Oushka,"* he said. "I'd like *oushka.*"

Thetheran nodded. *"Oushka!"* he called in a firm, clear voice, pointing at Doran.

With a sudden swirl, the curtain hiding the back room was swept aside, as if by a strong wind, and a silver tray sailed out into the room, unsupported and rotating slowly. Upon it stood a brown earthenware jug and a small crystal glass.

It sank gently onto the chair next to Doran, who stared at it—fearfully? Distastefully? Dumery wasn't sure.

Then Thetheran took Dumery by the hand and led him through the doorway, and he saw no more of his father or the magical tray for quite some time.

# CHAPTER 3

*At Thetheran's behest Dumery seated himself on a tall stool* that stood close beside the wizard's littered workbench. He sat there, staring at the room around him, while the mage puttered about with various mysterious objects.

This room was as large as the front parlor, maybe a bit larger, but far more crowded. The parlor had held six chairs around the hearth, a few small tables, and a divan, with a few assorted knicknacks and oddments here and there; the walls had been mostly bare. In this workshop Dumery couldn't even *see* the walls, behind all the clutter!

A stair leading to the upper story ran along one side, and an incredible miscellany of pots, pans, and boxes was jammed under it, stacked every which way. On the opposite side several hundred feet of shelving were piled high with books, scrolls, papers, pouches, boxes, bottles, jars, jugs, and other wizardly paraphernalia. The great stone workbench ran down the center of the room midway between these, and while half of it was kept scrupulously clean and clear, the other half was strewn with scraps of paper, spilled powders in every color of the rainbow and several colors of more doubtful origin, bits of bone and bent metal, and other arcane debris.

At either end of the room a curtained doorway led somewhere—one to the front parlor, the other the gods knew where. The walls around both doorways were plastered over with diagrams and sketches and outlines, none of them making any sense at all to Dumery.

Something small and green was staring at Dumery from behind a jar; he stared back, and the thing ducked down out of sight before he could get a good look at it. He wasn't sure what it was, exactly; he'd never seen anything quite like it. Some of his brothers' friends had been telling stories about strange little creatures that had been stowing away aboard ships from the Small Kingdoms and then getting loose around the docks; maybe the stories were true and this was one of them.

Wizard Street wasn't anywhere near the docks, though. Maybe it was some magical creature, like the sylph, the air elemental, that must have brought his father's *oushka*.

Or maybe it wasn't a sylph, maybe the tray was enchanted— wizardry was so varied and wonderful!

He sat there, surrounded by the artifacts of wizardry, and stared at it all in amazement.

Then Thetheran was back, holding a small black vial and a pair of narrow silver tongs. He put them down on the workbench and turned to Dumery.

"So, boy," he said, "you want to be a wizard?"

"Yes, sir," Dumery said, nodding enthusiastically. "Very much indeed."

"Aha," Thetheran said. "It's not your father's idea, then?"

"No, sir; I believe he'd much rather I do something else. But *I* want to learn wizardry!"

Thetheran nodded. "Good," he said, "very good."

He drew a dagger from his belt, and Dumery tensed, wondering if some sort of blood ritual of initiation was involved.

Thetheran reached out and touched Dumery's forehead with the tip of the dagger, very gently. "Don't move," he warned.

Dumery didn't move. Not only did he want to make a good impression, not only was he worried about magic spells, but that knife looked very, very sharp.

Thetheran muttered something, and Dumery, looking up as best he could without moving, thought he saw the blade of the dagger glowing first blue, then purple.

Thetheran blinked, then pulled the blade away. He looked at it closely.

Once again it looked like perfectly ordinary dagger to Dumery.

Thetheran muttered something again, then said, "Hold still."

As before, Dumery froze.

Thetheran reached out with the dagger again, but this time he touched it to Dumery's black velvet tunic, directly over the boy's heart. He held it there for a moment, and then ran it lightly down Dumery's breastbone and across his belly to his navel.

Dumery held his breath until Thetheran finally pulled the knife away. As Dumery exhaled, the wizard held the blade up in front of his eyes and studied it closely, his expression at first puzzled, then annoyed.

He put the dagger down on the workbench and picked up the vial and tongs.

"Here," he said, gesturing, "watch very closely now. *Very* closely. I'm going to do a simple little spell and then ask you to try to do it."

Dumery nodded, almost trembling with anticipation. He leaned over and stared intently.

Thetheran opened the vial and fished out its contents with the tongs. He held up a roll of white fabric for Dumery to see.

Dumery nodded slightly, keeping his eyes on the little cloth bundle.

Thetheran put it on the bench and unrolled it with the tongs.

Inside lay a sliver of grayish wood roughly the size of a man's finger, a tiny glass bottle half full of a brownish-red substance and a wad of brown felt.

Thetheran spread the wad of brown felt to reveal a lock of hair. He plucked out a single strand with the tongs and held it to one side.

Then, using his other hand, he pried the black rubber cap from the miniature bottle.

He dipped the single hair into the open neck of the bottle and drew up a single misshapen drop of the substance within, and as he did so he said something, speaking very slowly. The words sounded to Dumery like "Fulg the walkers nose arbitrary grottle."

He moved one hand in a circle while the fingers of the other seemed to dance madly about, then he lowered the hair with the drop of stuff down to the piece of wood.

The instant before it touched, he said what Dumery took for "Kag snort ruffle thumb."

When the stuff did touch, a white spark appeared. Thetheran dropped the tongs and let the hair fall—except that it seemed to Dumery it fell in the wrong direction, and when he tried to follow it with his eyes he couldn't find it. Then the wizard reached down and picked up the glowing spark between his two index fingers. He brought his thumbs down to it, hiding it from sight.

Then he announced, "Behold, Haldane's Iridescent Amusement!" He drew his hands apart, and there in the air between them, stretching from one thumb to the other, was a string of gleaming polychrome bubbles the size of oranges, each joined to the next at a single point, colors shifting eerily around their surfaces almost as if they were somehow alive.

Dumery stared, delighted.

Then the bubbles all silently popped and were gone, without leaving even a trace of moisture. Thetheran smiled a tight little smile, then touched his hands together and drew them apart again, and there was a new string, the bubbles even larger this time. Where before the commonest hues had been blues and reds, now green and gold predominated.

Then these, too, popped, and once more the mage drew out a new string, this time milky and streaked with purple.

When those vanished there were no more.

"There," Thetheran said, "now you try it."

Dumery blinked and reached out for the tongs.

The hair had vanished, along with the drop of stuff, so Dumery picked up a new one from the felt. He was unfamiliar with the tongs, so it took several attempts before he managed to pick up one, and only one, strand.

He dipped it in the little bottle and drew up a drop of the reddish gunk. He announced, "Fulg the walkers nose arbitrary grottle."

He waved one hand in a circle while wiggling the fingers of the other.

He touched the hair and goo to the piece of wood and said, "Kag snort ruffle thumb."

Then he waited for the spark to appear.

Nothing happened; the thick stuff on the hair dripped onto the wood, but that was all.

He waited, but his hand quickly grew tired, holding the tongs steady like that, and at last he had to put them down.

"It didn't work," he said.

Thetheran was staring at him.

"My boy," he said, "you are a phenomenon. A curiosity, really."

Dumery blinked. "What?" he asked.

"You are a fluke, an aberration. You have absolutely *no* talent for wizardry whatsoever!"

His previous blink had been from startlement; this time he blinked to hold back tears that were suddenly welling up. "What?" he said again.

"Lad, I tested you first with a simple spell with that dagger," Thetheran explained. "It should have glowed green, at least, when I touched you with it. If you had the talent strongly, it would have been golden, and if you were destined to be one of the great wizards of the age, it would have glowed white-hot. You saw what it did—a flicker of blue, no more, and it stayed as cold as iron."

Dumery stared up at him, uncomprehending.

"I thought perhaps I'd misspoken the spell, or something else had gone wrong," Thetheran continued, "so I tried again, with your heart instead of your head, and still got nothing. Well, I thought, perhaps you're a special case. So I gave you a chance to show me a spell. I took the hair and blood of a beheaded murderer, and a piece from the scaffold he died on, and I worked one of the simplest little spells I know, one that can't go wrong easily, if at all, and then I let you try—and you got *every single step* wrong! Not one word of the incantation, not one gesture, was right! You didn't even speak the second stanza until too late in the procedure. And with some of the most potently charged ingredients I have on hand, short of wasting dragon's blood, you raised not a single spark of eldritch energy. Not one little twinge. *Nothing.*"

"But . . ." Dumery began.

"It's amazing," Thetheran said, shaking his head.

"Let me try again!" Dumery said, "Please! I'll do it better this time, I swear I will!"

Thetheran stared at him for a moment, then shrugged. "Go ahead," he said.

Eagerly, blinking away tears, Dumery picked out another hair with the tongs.

Maybe, he thought, the power wasn't there because I didn't know what these things were. The hair and blood of a beheaded murderer—gods!

He trembled slightly at the very idea.

He dipped the hair in the bottle of blood and drew it out, and Thetheran coached him. *"Pfah' lu gua' akhar snuessar bitra rhi grau k'l,"* the wizard said.

"Fall oogah acker snoozer bid rory grackle," Dumery said. He watched closely the gestures Thetheran made and tried very hard to imitate them.

*"Khag s'naur t'traugh f'lethaum,"* Thetheran said.

"Cog sonar to trow fill them," Dumery said, just before he touched the drop of blood to the bit of scaffold.

Again, nothing at all happened. Dumery stared at the bit of wood in abject disappointment.

When Thetheran started to say something, Dumery burst out, "Let me try a different spell! This one's too hard to start with; let me try another!"

"It's an easy spell, boy," the wizard said, and when Dumery started to protest he held up a silencing hand. "It's an easy spell. But we'll try another, if you like."

Dumery nodded.

He fared no better with Felojun's First Hypnotic than he had with Haldane's Iridescent Amusement. The ingredients were simpler—a mere pinch of dust from the floor—and the incantation shorter, being a single word, but still, Dumery failed utterly.

"Face it, boy," Thetheran said after the third unsuccessful attempt. "You have no knack for wizardry. Teaching you wizardry would be like trying to make a minstrel of a deaf man. There's no shame to it; it's just the way you were born. It's not just that you don't hear the words clearly, nor that you get the gestures wrong; it's that the magic doesn't *like* you. You don't feel it, and it avoids you. I don't know why, but it's true; I can sense it."

Dumery had run out of protests. When Thetheran jogged his elbow he got down from the stool silently; he followed quietly when the wizard led the way back through the curtain and into the parlor, where Doran was sitting, watching the fire.

"I'm sorry, sir," Thetheran said when Doran looked up expectantly, "but I'm afraid your son is not suitable for an apprenticeship with me."

Doran blinked in surprise.

"He seems like a fine lad," Thetheran explained, "but he has no innate aptitude for wizardry. It's just not in his blood. I'm sure he'd do well in any number of other fields."

Dumery stood, silent and woebegone, as Doran looked past the mage at him.

"You're sure?" Doran asked Thetheran.

"*Quite* sure," Thetheran said.

"Well," Doran said, "thank you for your time, anyway." He glanced at the silver tray, where the crystal goblet had clearly been used. "And the *oushka*, too; it was quite good, and just what I needed on a day like this."

"Thank *you*, sir," Thetheran said, with a trace of a bow. "And I'm sorry I couldn't take the boy."

"Well, that's all right, I'm sure we'll find a place for him." He gestured. "Come on, Dumery, let's go."

Dumery stood, not moving.

His father said, "Come *on*, Dumery!"

"It's not *fair*!" Dumery wailed suddenly, not moving from where he stood. "It's not *fair*!"

Doran glanced at Thetheran, who gave a sympathetic little shrug. "I know, Dumery," Doran said, "it's *not* fair, but there's nothing we can do about it. Now, come on."

"No! He didn't give me a *chance*! He said the words so fast I couldn't even hear them properly!"

"Dumery," Doran said, "I'm sure the wizard gave you a fair test. He's as eager to find an apprentice as you are to be a wizard and he wouldn't send you away without good reason. Now come along, and we'll go home and figure out what's to be done about it."

Reluctantly, Dumery went.

Out in the street, during a lull in the downpour, Doran called, "Well, now that wizardry is out, you'll need to give some thought to what you want to do instead."

"No," Dumery said, emphatically, "I won't. I want to be a *wizard*!"

His father glared at him silently for a moment.

"You *can't* be a wizard," Doran said. "You heard what Thetheran told us."

"That's just Thetheran," Dumery said. "He's not the only wizard in the World."

"No, he's not the only one," Doran agreed, "but he's a good one, and he knows his business. Don't be an idiot, boy; we'll find you something else."

"No," Dumery said again. "I want to be a wizard, and by all the gods I'm *going* to be a wizard!"

"No, you're not," his father said flatly. He could be stubborn, too.

Dumery didn't reply. He didn't want to argue any more.

At least, not right away.


# CHAPTER 4


*I*t took him a full sixnight to convince his father to try again.

This time, the master was to be a young wizard by the name of Zatha of the Golden Hair. Dumery was interested to see that she really *did* have golden hair—blond, his father called it. Dumery had rarely seen anything so exotic, even in Shiphaven.

Unfortunately, the results of the interview were no different from what happened with Thetheran. Simple analytic magic revealed no power at all in Dumery, and he utterly botched a few trial spells.

"I'm very sorry," she told Dumery, "but the talent just isn't there. It's something people are born with, like double-jointed fingers or green eyes, and you were born without it."

"But can't I *learn* it?" he asked, on the verge of tears.

She shook her head. "No," she said, "really, I'm afraid not. If there were any skill at all, it could be nurtured, I suppose, and a few spells learned—but there wouldn't be much point in it. For someone with only a trace of talent it would take years to learn what a real wizard, or an apprentice, or anyone with the knack for wizardry can pick up in an afternoon—and in your case, Dumery, I don't think there's even a trace. You're one of those rare people with absolutely no talent for wizardry at all."

He managed not to cry and didn't argue with his father on the walk back home.

At least it was sunny, with no rain soaking them through.

After that, his father was adamant. No third attempt would be made, and Dumery was to find some other career to pursue.

Dumery yielded to this, asked for time to think, and got it.

He then took all his carefully hoarded savings—birthday gifts, Festival pickings, money earned running errands, his winnings from the kid down the street who couldn't play the finger game but kept trying to learn, all of it—and very early one morning, while out playing, he "wandered off."

Once he was out of sight, he headed straight for the Wizards' Quarter, and started going door to door, looking for someone, *anyone*, who would take him on as an apprentice.

In doing so, over the course of a very long day and well into the evening, he spent all but a few copper bits in honoraria and testing fees, and learned that not only did he have no talent for wizardry, but that he had no talent for warlockry, demonology, theurgy, witchcraft, or any other form of magic—except possibly sorcery. The only sorcerer he dealt with had no tests to perform, but merely looked him over carefully and asked him a variety of peculiar questions, mostly dealing with numbers and unlikely hypothetical situations.

Finally she shook her head.

"I'm sorry," she said, "but you won't do."

By that time Dumery had given up arguing. He nodded, thanked her, and went on.

Twice, as he prowled through the Wizards' Quarter, he glimpsed Thetheran the Mage, going about his business. Both times Dumery tried to stay out of sight, ducking back into doorways; he was afraid that if Thetheran saw him he'd say something embarrassing.

Dumery felt he had been embarrassed quite enough already.

It wasn't fair, he thought, that Thetheran should be strolling about, so calm and collected and confident, after he had ruined Dumery's entire life! It wasn't fair *at all*.

If only there were something he could do about it! Some way he could get back at Thetheran for refusing him.

Couldn't the nasty old wizard have at least taken him on for a few days, to see if the talent might have *developed*, or something?

He was sure that it wouldn't do any good to go and ask for another chance; after all, the great man had stated his position. He wouldn't back down from it just because one spoiled rich kid asked him.

Of course, Dumery didn't consider himself spoiled, but he'd noticed that whenever he asked a grown-up to do something for him, the grown-up always seemed to think that Dumery was being a spoiled rich brat. He ascribed this to the fact that the adults concerned hadn't grown up rich and were jealous.

For himself, he thought he'd much rather have grown up poor—that would have eliminated the jealousy, and he'd be able to dress in comfortable old clothes he could get dirty instead of the fancy velvets that his mother always gave him. Sure, he'd have to live in a tenement instead of his father's house and he wouldn't have his own room, but so what? Sharing a room with his brothers might have been fun.

He wouldn't want to be *really* poor, living out in the Hundred-Foot Field or something, but a tenement apartment wouldn't have been all that bad.

Would it?

Maybe it would. If he were going to be rich, then, why couldn't he have been born to the nobility? Living in the Overlord's palace would be fun, wouldn't it?

Speculation was pointless, of course, He *had* been born the son of a successful merchant and he was stuck with it.

He sighed and trudged on.

When his funds, energy, and ingenuity were all largely exhausted, and most of the magicians had long since closed their shops, he headed wearily home, stumbling now and then as he dodged the ox droppings on Arena Street.

He reached home long after his mother had cleared away the dinner dishes, and in fact she would have been in bed and asleep had she not waited up for him. She was angry enough to refuse to feed him anything but the leftover heel of the loaf of bread that had been served with supper.

He ate that and drank water from a crystal goblet he got down from the kitchen cupboard himself. He consumed this sorry excuse for a meal while sitting morosely in his room, staring out the window into the courtyard behind the house and trying to think what he could do with his life.

Magic, it appeared, was out. Whether he really had no talent at all, of any sort, or whether Thetheran had a grudge against him and had somehow coerced all the others into turning him down, he wasn't sure, but at any rate, magic was out.

At least, if he stayed in Ethshar of the Spices, magic was out. What if he were to sail off somewhere on one of his father's ships? Might he find more obliging magicians in, say, Ethshar of the Sands, or Morria in the Small Kingdoms?

It wasn't likely. Everyone agreed that Ethshar of the Spices was the greatest city in the World, its merchants the richest, its wizards the most powerful, and its overlord the wisest.

And he wouldn't have his father there to pay his apprenticeship fee, if he went somewhere else.

Well, then, he would just forget about magic and try something else.

But what else *was* there? He'd wanted to be a wizard for as long as he could remember. He had never seriously considered anything else.

Well, now it was time to consider, so what else was there?

He could apprentice to a merchant, of course, or a pilot, either a harbor pilot or a ship's pilot. His father would have no trouble at all arranging those.

Or he could sign on as a sailor and try to work his way up

to captain. Commanding his own ship, sailing free across the waves—that sounded nice.

But it probably wasn't. The sea captains he'd met were mostly foul-tempered men who didn't seem to enjoy their work particularly. And there were storms and pirates, and while it was all very romantic and heroic to battle storms and pirates, Dumery remembered Captain Senallon, a big, robust, cheerful man who had rumpled Dumery's hair, taught Dumery a few interesting swear words, showed him how to tie a few knots, and who had never come back from an ordinary run up to Ethshar of the Rocks. His ship sailed out and was simply never seen again. A report eventually came that a pirate had caught him off Shan on the Sea, but that was never confirmed.

And Daddy had been furious about that, not because Captain Senallon was dead and his widow and children bereft, but because the cargo was lost and Doran of Shiphaven was out goods valued at some seventeen pounds of gold.

Sailing anywhere didn't sound very appealing after all, Dumery decided as he swallowed the last stale mouthful of bread.

Maybe he should just wait and join the city guard, then.

One had to be sixteen to join the Guard, of course, and Dumery's family was sufficiently well known that lying about his age probably wouldn't work, at least not for long, so that would mean a four-year wait. And after that four years, it would mean living in the barracks under the city wall or over in Camptown, spending his time marching back and forth or standing guard at a gate somewhere or going up and down the streets collecting taxes for Lord Azrad. That was not really a very exciting life, when one actually sat down and thought about what was involved; it was no wonder that the Guard got most of its recruits from failed apprentices, boys who had been kicked out by their masters for stealing or disobedience or incompetence, or whose masters had died before the apprenticeship was completed.

Of course, life in the Guard could be exciting if there was a war or something, but Ethshar hadn't been in a war for over two hundred years—not a real war, anyway. The Great War had ended back in 4996, or maybe 4998, or something—Dumery wasn't really very good at history, particularly not remembering dates—and he wasn't sure if there had been any little wars since then.

A war would be exciting but dangerous, too. And while Dumery didn't think he was really all that bothered by danger—he *certainly* didn't consider himself a coward—he didn't care to depend on the chance of something as dangerous as a war to make his life interesting.

No, not the Guard, then.

What did that leave?

Well, there were ship chandlers and ropemakers and coopers and sailmakers and shipwrights and shopkeepers of every sort, and none of them looked very appealing. Most of them involved a lot of standing around haggling with customers and hauling dirty, heavy objects around, and they didn't pay all that well, either.

The brothels in Shiphaven made plenty of money, and the gamblers and gamers, but Dumery didn't think one got into those trades through apprenticeship. He really wasn't very sure.

Being a gambler might be interesting—but it had its risks. What if you lost? The gods of luck could be fickle, everyone knew that. And losing opponents could be hostile; Dumery had seen a sailor knifed over a stupid little game of three-bone once. The stake had only been about four silver pieces—Dumery had spent more than twice that in testing fees today.

The sailor had lived, and in fact his wound really wasn't very serious at all, but any occupation where one ran a significant risk of being stabbed wasn't quite what Dumery had in mind.

As for running a brothel—well, now, at age twelve, he was embarrassed just thinking about it. And surely, one didn't get into it through an apprenticeship.

He sighed, and gulped the last of his water.

He'd have to find *something*, but right now he couldn't think of a single possibility.

Maybe he would do better in the morning.

He left the goblet by his bed for his mother to pick up, and went to sleep.

# CHAPTER 5

*W*hen the sunlight poured through his window the next morning, thick as honey and warm as a purring cat, Dumery still hadn't thought of any nonmagical occupation he cared to pursue.

He told his mother that at breakfast. He couldn't tell his father, because Doran had left early to make sure an outgoing ship caught the morning tide without leaving any of its cargo behind on the docks.

"You can do anything you like," Faléa the Slender told her son as she poured herself tea.

Dumery started to contradict her. "Except wizardry," she added hastily, cutting him off.

He glowered silently for a moment, then said, "But I don't know what I like."

Dessa snickered; Dumery glared at her, and she turned away, smirking.

"Look around, then," Faléa said as she picked up her cup. "See what you can find."

"Look where?" Dumery asked.

She lowered the cup and looked at him in mild exasperation.

"I've *looked* all over Shiphaven," he explained.

"Then look elsewhere," she suggested. "It's a big city. Why not go to the markets and look around?"

"The markets?" Dumery thought that over.

So did Faléa. She remembered, perhaps a little later than she should have, that Shiphaven Market was the recruiting center for all the crackpot adventurers and ax-grinding lunatics in Ethshar, and that the New Canal Street Market was the center of the local slave trade.

She didn't particularly want her youngest son to run off on some foolhardy attempt to unseat a usurper in the Small Kingdoms, nor to sign up as an apprentice slaver. There was something distinctly unsavory about slavers—she had always had her suspicions of how they acquired and handled their merchandise, despite the official claims that the whole business was closely regulated by the city. As a merchant's wife she knew how easy it was to bribe the overlord's harbor watch and she didn't doubt it was just as easy to bribe other officials.

There was a certain romance to undertaking desperate adventures, and even to buying and selling slaves—just the sort of romance, unfortunately, that might well appeal to a twelve-year-old boy. Particularly to a twelve-year-old boy who had been interested in magic, rather than any safer and more sensible occupation. Faléa decided that it would probably be a good idea to distract Dumery before he investigated either of the markets in Shiphaven. If he once got it into his head to sign up for some half-witted expedition—well, Dumery could be incredibly stubborn.

"Why don't you go down to Westgate Market," she said, "and take a look at the people there, both the city folk and the customers who come in from beyond the gate. Maybe you'll see something of interest."

Dumery, who was familiar with the recruiters in Shiphaven Market and had been wondering whether that could really be what his mother had in mind, considered her suggestion.

There was a charm to the idea, certainly. He hadn't been in Westgate in months, maybe years. He remembered it as being full of farmers smelling of manure, but surely there was more to it than that; he'd been a little kid when he went there before, not yet old enough to apprentice. He'd be looking at it with new eyes now.

"All right," he said, "I will." He served himself an immense portion of fried egg and stuffed it in his mouth.

His mother smiled at him, glad that she had successfully diverted her son from New Canal Street and Shiphaven Market, and not particularly concerned about what he would find in Westgate. She rarely went there herself, and then only to buy fresh produce when the courtyard garden wasn't doing well, but it seemed like a wholesome enough place, where the boy wouldn't get into any serious trouble. There were no slavers or recruiters there.

Dumery finished his breakfast, then went up to his room and pulled on his boots. He took a look out back, where his mother was feeding the chickens and chatting with one of their neighbors from the other side of the courtyard.

If he ever got as rich as his parents, Dumery thought, he'd hire servants or buy slaves and let *them* feed the chickens. His mother seemed to enjoy little chores like that, but Dumery was quite sure that *he* never would.

He turned and hurried downstairs and out onto the street. Two blocks from home he turned right onto Shipwright Street. The avenue was already crowded with people hurrying in both directions, and Dumery quickly fell in with the southbound stream.

He stumbled and almost fell once, near the corner of Sea Captain Street, when something small and green ran between his legs, but he caught himself in time. When he turned to see what had almost tripped him it was gone.

He wondered if it had been the same sort of creature he had seen in Thetheran's workshop, but he couldn't spot it anywhere.

He shrugged, forgot about it, and marched on.

Twenty minutes' walk brought him to Wall Street and into the northeast corner of Westgate Market, where the morning sun shone brightly on the vividly colored awnings of half a hundred merchants' stalls, and even turned the somber gray stone of the great gate towers cheerful. Farmers in brown or gray homespun jostled against city dwellers in blue and black and gold, and a freshening sea breeze had worked its way through the streets and over the rooftops to send the tunics and robes and striped awnings flapping. The snapping of fabric provided a beat for the shouts of hawkers proclaiming the superiority of their wares.

"The finest hams in all the Hegemony!" a man shouted almost in Dumery's ear as he passed a wagon beneath a red-and-white striped awning, and for a moment the pungent scent of smoked meat pierced the more general overlay of dust and sweat.

"Peaches, sweet peaches!" called the woman in the next stall, gesturing at her own fruit-heaped cart.

Dumery looked, then walked on. He had no intention of becoming a farmer or a butcher, nor anything else so mundane.

The market was not over-large—certainly smaller than Shiphaven Market—but it was very crowded, so it took some time for Dumery to see everything.

He passed stalls selling apples and pears and plums, beans and broccoli, beef and mutton. He passed churns of butter and shelves of cheeses, all fresh from the farm—or so their sellers swore. Fine wool and spun cotton, felts and velvets, silks and satins, all, proclaimed a cloth merchant with an unfamiliar accent, the best in Ethshar, and at bargain prices.

Dumery didn't believe that for a moment. He knew that the best fabrics were sold in the Old Merchants' Quarter, not in the open-air markets.

Most of the goods sold here were the products of local farms; that was Westgate's specialty, after all. Anything that came any great distance came in by ship and went to the markets of Spicetown and Shiphaven and Newmarket. Anything that could stand to sit unsold on a shelf for any length of time was more likely to wind up displayed in a shop somewhere, rather than hawked in the market square. That foreign cloth merchant was an anomaly, probably some ambitious fellow from the Small Kingdoms who had hoped to get around the Ethsharitic shipping cartels. Westgate Market was a place to find pumpkins, not a career.

All the same, it was pleasant to stroll about, taking it all in. The sun was warm, the colors bright, and the smell of manure much less than he remembered.

As he strolled, there was a brief disturbance on the far side of the market, and Dumery heard a cry of "Thief!" He stood on tiptoe and craned to see, but could make nothing out through the intervening crowds.

He shrugged and wandered on.

After a time it occurred to Dumery to look behind the carts and wagons and stalls of the vendors, at the permanent buildings that lined the east side of the square.

They were all inns, of course—the Clumsy Juggler, the Gatehouse Inn, half a dozen in all, squeezed into the hundred

or so feet between Shipwright Street and High Street, each with
its signboard and open door. Dumery paused and considered.

He knew that scores of other inns did business in Westgate,
in addition to this row on the square, and there were many
more elsewhere in the city as well, a few at each gate and
several scattered along the waterfronts—though, of course,
Westgate had the largest concentration.

Dumery thought about inns. Could he become an innkeeper,
perhaps?

How *did* one become an innkeeper? Did innkeepers take
apprentices?

It might be interesting, meeting new people all the time,
listening to travelers' tales—but on the other hand, an innkeeper probably heard more about account books than adventures, more complaints than chronicles. And really, he'd be
little better than a servant. It wouldn't do.

All the same, he looked over the row carefully, admiring the
artistry of the signboards.

The Clumsy Juggler, with its red-clad fool dropping half a
dozen multicolored balls, was the most whimsical of the six;
most were fairly straightforward. Two, the Gatehouse Inn and
the Market House, had their names spelled out in runes, while
the others relied, sometimes mistakenly, on illustrations to
convey their names. The sign two doors from High Street,
showing something green and wiggly on a field of irregular
blue and gold stripes, seemed particularly incomprehensible.

Dumery was staring at that one, simultaneously trying to
figure out what it was supposed to be and wondering who
painted the boards and whether there was a potential career
there, when two figures emerged from the door below the sign.

He glanced at them, then stared.

The lead figure, a big man wearing scuffed brown leather, he
had never seen before, but the other, following a step behind
and looking very irritated, was Thetheran the Mage.

Dumery blinked in surprise, and then, without really knowing why, he turned to follow the pair.

They were marching straight across the square toward the
southern half of the huge pair of towers that bracketed the city
gates. The man in the lead seemed cheerful and lighthearted;

Dumery glimpsed a smile on his face when he turned to look back for a moment. Thetheran, on the other hand, seemed very annoyed about something; he was frowning ferociously and stamping his way across the hard-packed dirt.

Dumery wondered whether he would hurt his feet, walking like that. Maybe there was some sort of magic in it.

Curious about what could possibly annoy the wizard that way, Dumery continued to follow even after his initial impulsive action. He hurried through the crowd, dodging around clumps of haggling tradesmen and farmers, at one point ducking through a display of melons and almost toppling a pyramid of the great pale fruit.

The man in brown reached the base of the south tower, where a guardsman in yellow tunic and red kilt was leaning comfortably against the gray stone beside a small wooden door. He spoke to the guard; the guard rapped on the door and shouted something that Dumery couldn't quite make out over the noise of the crowd.

Thetheran, Dumery noticed, looked quite impatient about all this.

The door opened, and the man in brown stepped inside, out of sight; Thetheran started to follow, but the guardsman stopped him with an outthrust hand against the wizard's chest.

Thetheran exploded into a bellow of rage, but the guardsman bellowed back, and the wizard subsided.

Dumery stared. He had expected Thetheran to pull out a magic wand and blast the guardsman to dust, or something, not to simply back down like that. He wondered what in all the World could possibly make Thetheran behave this way.

Of course, even wizards, he supposed, must fear the power of the city's overlord, Azrad VII. And the guards were Azrad's direct representatives.

Then the leather-clad man emerged from the tower, one hand held high, clutching something that looked like a peculiar sort of bottle. It wasn't particularly large, perhaps the size of a big man's fist, and it gleamed purplish red in the sun.

Thetheran reached for the bottle, but the man in brown turned away, holding it out of the wizard's reach.

Dumery had now crept close enough to hear when the man

in leather said, "That'll be six rounds in gold, in advance."

Dumery's jaw dropped.

Six rounds in gold!

That was six *hundred* pieces in copper—more than a laborer earned in a year!

What was *in* that little bottle?

"I'll pay five, after I weigh it," Thetheran said.

"No," the man in leather said, "you'll pay six, now."

"Forty-four gold bits, then, but I weigh it first."

"Forty-*eight* bits. Six rounds. I told you."

"All right, all right, if it's full weight I'll pay the six rounds!"

"Fair enough," the seller said. "They'll have a balance at the Dragon's Tail; we'll weigh it there."

Thetheran nodded. "All right, then. A quarter its weight in gold, then, as we agreed—for the blood only."

"Counting the flask, of course," the other said, grinning.

Thetheran began to protest again, but thought better of it.

"All *right*, damn it," he said. "Counting the flask."

"Good enough, then," the man in brown said. "Come along." He marched back toward the inn they had come from, and Thetheran followed in his wake, fuming.

Dumery stared, then ran over to where the guardsman was once again leaning quietly against the wall of the tower.

"*Hai*," he called. "Guard!"

The soldier stirred and looked down at him.

"What do *you* want, boy?" he asked mildly.

"That man," Dumery asked, pointing. "What did he sell that wizard?"

The guard glanced up at the retreating back of Thetheran's midnight-blue robe. He grinned.

"Oh, that," he said. "That was dragon's blood. We guard it for him."

Dumery blinked. "Dragon's blood?" he asked.

The guard nodded. "Wizards use a lot of it. It's one of the most common ingredients for their spells. Without dragon's blood they couldn't do half what they do."

"Really?" Dumery stared after Thetheran and the man in brown.

"Really," the guard said. "Or at least so I've always heard."

Dumery nodded. It made sense. He'd always heard how wizards used strange things in their spells and he'd seen himself that Thetheran had shelves and shelves of such things, like the hair of a beheaded man and all the rest of it. Dragon's blood would fit right in.

He ran after the two men, back toward the inn with the strange signboard, the one that really didn't look much at all like a dragon's tail, regardless of what anyone said.

They were inside. Dumery didn't enter; he leaned in through the doorway, looking for them, and waited for his eyes to adjust to the shadowy interior of the taproom.

It took him a moment to spot them, among the thirty or forty people in the room, but at least he saw them, seated across from each other at a small table near the stairs; Thetheran's dark-blue robe was fairly distinctive, and the man in brown was tall enough to be easily noticed, taller than Thetheran—who was no dwarf—by half a head. The pair was not far away at all, merely in an unexpected direction.

Dumery leaned in farther, listening intently.

The transaction was under way; Thetheran was counting out coins, and the man in brown was testing each one, making sure they were all real gold.

He looked up. "I haven't sold to you before," he remarked, loudly enough for Dumery to hear, "but I hope you know that if any of this gold turns out to be enchanted, you'll regret it."

"I know," Thetheran said, almost snarling. "I've heard about *you*. It's all real, you'll see. I didn't enchant anything."

"I hope not," the man in brown said, "because if you did, the price goes up for everyone, and you know your guild isn't going to like that."

"I *know*, I said!" Thetheran snapped. "Gods, all this just for dragon's blood! You'd think the beasts were extinct, you make this stuff so precious!"

"No," the other corrected him. "*You* make it precious, all you wizards who use so much of the stuff. Dragons aren't extinct, but they're damnably dangerous—if you want dragon's blood, you have to pay for it."

"I know, I know," Thetheran said, rummaging in his purse for the last gold bit.

Dumery stared, silently marveling.

Dragon's blood. Thetheran had let himself be humiliated for a flask of dragon's blood. He had paid *six rounds of gold* for a flask of dragon's blood—as much as Dumery's father would earn from an entire trading voyage.

And dragons were big; a dead dragon, just *one* dead dragon, even a small one, would surely fill a dozen flasks easily.

Dangerous, the man said. Well, yes, dragons *would* be dangerous, that was obvious. Even if the stories about breathing fire and working magic weren't true, and for all Dumery knew they were sober fact, dragons still had claws and teeth. But all that gold! And to have wizards humbled like that! To have *Thetheran*, who had refused him and insulted him, forced to pay any price he asked!

It was irresistible. Now Dumery knew what he wanted to do with his life.

He wanted to be a dragon-hunter.

# CHAPTER 6

*It occurred to Dumery that in all likelihood not a single full-*time professional dragon-hunter lived inside the city walls. It was not an occupation that could be practiced in an urban environment, or that would be in great demand on the streets of Ethshar. In order to ply his trade a dragon-hunter would naturally require the presence of wild dragons, and the only dragons in the city were baby ones kept as pets or showpieces by rich eccentrics, or for the Arena by magicians and show people.

No wild dragons lurked in the streets and courtyards, Dumery was sure. Not even in the sewers or the Hundred-Foot Field.

So no dragon-hunter would live in the city.

That meant, Dumery realized, that his father wouldn't be able to arrange an apprenticeship for him. Doran's contacts in the city were extensive and varied, but elsewhere, outside the walls, as far as Dumery knew all his contacts were with other merchants.

To the best of his knowledge, the only person Dumery had ever seen, since the day he was born, who might be a dragon-hunter, or at least might know where one could be found, was the man in brown leather, right there in the Dragon's Tail, pocketing Thetheran's gold and gloating shamelessly over it.

Furthermore, the odds of Dumery finding another dragon-hunter—if the man in brown actually *was* a hunter, and not just a middleman of some sort—before he was too old to apprentice to *any* trade except soldiering looked rather poor. After all, he had gone twelve years without ever noticing a dragon-hunter before; even when looking, he suspected that he might easily go two or three years without seeing another.

This, then, was it, Dumery told himself. This man in brown leather was the key to his entire future, an opportunity he could not afford to waste.

An overhasty approach might bring disaster; Dumery decided against simply marching up and presenting himself.

As the boy reached that decision, Thetheran rose, haughtily ignoring his supplier. As the mage stalked out of the inn into the sunlit market Dumery ducked back out of sight, behind a wagonload of tanned leather.

Of course, there was no real reason to hide from Thetheran; he had done the wizard no harm and had no real reason to think the man wished him ill—Dumery didn't really believe in his own theories of a conspiracy created by Thetheran for the express purpose of preventing one boy, himself, from learning magic.

All the same, Dumery preferred not to be seen.

When the magician had grumbled his way around the corner onto High Street, out of sight and sound, Dumery emerged from behind the wagon and hurried into the Dragon's Tail. He looked at the corner by the stairs.

The man in brown was gone.

Dumery stared, horribly disappointed, at the empty table where the wizard had bought the flask of dragon's blood. The boy turned, quickly scanning the rest of the room, but he saw no sign of his target.

How had the man slipped away? Dumery had never turned his gaze from the tavern door for more than a couple of seconds. He looked around the taproom.

There was the hearth, and a door to the kitchens, and a long wall adorned with a strip of scaly green hide—from a genuine dragon's tail, perhaps? Then came a broad, many-paned window, and the door to the square, and then the stairs.

The stairs. Dumery finished his circuit of the room, past the curtained booths below the stairs and past an open door that appeared to lead to the cellars, and back to the hearth.

Unless there was a way out through the kitchens or the cellars, or behind one of the draperied private booths, none of which seemed like anywhere an ordinary customer would go, the man in brown had probably just gone up to his room.

Of course, if the man in brown thought that Thetheran was angry enough to try some dire revenge, then perhaps he *had* gone out through the kitchens or cellars or booths—thoughts of secret passages and ancient crypts and hidden tunnels came to mind.

That didn't seem very likely; Dumery was old enough to know that most of the more romantic tales he had heard were exaggerated, and that as a general rule everyday life did not include many hairbreadth escapes or mysterious passages.

All the same, this was a man who dealt harshly with wizards. If anyone might anticipate a need for a secret departure, he might.

"*Hai!*" Dumery called, waving to a young woman in a white apron, carrying a tray under her arm.

She saw him and sauntered over.

"What is it, boy?" she asked. "Aren't you a bit young for a traveler?"

"I'm not a traveler," Dumery said, concocting a lie on the spot. "I'm a messenger. My master heard that there was a man here selling dragon's blood, and as it happens, he has need of a pint or so."

The woman frowned. "Oh? And who would your master be?"

"Doran of Wizard Street," Dumery improvised.

"And the name of the man he sent you after?" she asked.

"I don't know," Dumery admitted. "A tall man in brown leather, I was told. My master said I'd be sure to know him when I saw him. But I've looked, and I don't see anyone here like that. This *is* the Dragon's Tail, isn't it?"

"Of course it is!" she snapped. "You saw the signboard, and there's the skin of the tail itself." She gestured at the hide stretched on the wall.

Dumery nodded. "Of course. Well, maybe he's stepped out, then, this man I was sent after?"

"No," she said. "I know who you mean. He's upstairs, settling his bill and packing his things; he's been three days here, and he's done his business and is ready to go. I don't think he's got a drop of that stuff left, but if you want to ask him, he should be down again any minute."

"Oh," Dumery said. "Thank you."

Someone called, and the woman turned away, lifting her tray. Dumery sat down on a nearby chair and waited.

While he waited, he tried to figure out just how he wanted to approach the situation.

Perhaps fifteen minutes later, when Dumery was beginning to wonder if he'd been tricked, two people came tramping noisily down the stairs. One was a plump, elderly woman wearing a white apron and carrying a plump purse—the innkeeper, presumably—while the other was the familiar man in brown. The man had a large pack slung over one shoulder.

Dumery waited until they passed him, then got quickly to his feet.

The innkeeper turned left and headed for the kitchens; the man in brown turned right and headed out the door.

Dumery followed the man in brown.

The man marched across the market square, Dumery staying close behind, watching his every step. It appeared he was heading for the south gate tower once more.

Sure enough, he stopped and exchanged a few words with the guard; Dumery was not close enough to catch the words this time. He worked his way through the crowd and emerged a pace or so away just as the man in brown turned away and marched on—out through the city gates and into the wide World beyond.

A sudden irrational terror struck Dumery at the thought of following him.

Never, in all his life, had Dumery left the protection of Ethshar's city wall. Venturing out of the streets into the wilderness beyond—or at least, comparative wilderness—was truly frightening. Dumery knew that the real wilderness didn't begin for a hundred leagues or so, but *anything* that wasn't city seemed dangerous and alien.

Still, this was his one chance at becoming a dragon-hunter.

*"Hai!"* he called, running after the man.

Even as he ran, Dumery was surprised to see that the market continued outside the gate. The city did not; to either side of the bare packed dirt of the highway lay open green fields, rather than streets and shops. Even so, wagons lined the sides of the highway, and farmers were selling their wares to a milling crowd of city-folk just as if they were all safely inside Westgate Market.

"Hello," he called, "dragon's blood! In the brown leather!"

The man in brown heard him and stopped. He turned, startled, as Dumery ran up to him.

"Yes, lad?" he asked.

Dumery had to catch his breath. Furthermore, he was disconcerted to find himself actually outside the wall, and the broad expanses of open space, dotted with trees and farmhouses, were so strange that his eyes kept being drawn away from the man's face. By the time he could gather himself sufficiently to speak, impatience showed in the man's features.

"Please, sir," Dumery said, "I'm of an age to begin an apprenticeship and I saw you selling dragon's blood, and I thought that you must be a dragon-hunter, and I can't think of anything I'd rather do than to become one. A dragon-hunter, I mean."

This was not the careful explanation and appeal he had tried to plan out while sitting in the Dragon's Tail, but rather a rush of words that got out before he could stop them. He shut his mouth, cutting the flow off, and bit his lip nervously, trying to think what he could say or do to improve the impression he was making.

The man stared coldly down at him, and for the first time Dumery really got a good look at him.

The man's hair and beard were dark brown, almost black, and both were long and thick and not particularly tidy. His eyes were brown and sunken, beneath heavy brows. His nose had obviously been broken at least once, and three scars ran parallel across his right cheek, as if something had clawed him badly once. He was big, well over six feet, probably over six and a half, and he was broad, too—his chest and shoulders looked as if he'd have to turn sideways to fit through most doors. His hands were gnarled and scarred and looked strong enough to crush stone.

He wore a heavy brown leather tunic, cut longer than was the fashion in Ethshar, and matching breeches that were stuffed into the tops of his heavy brown boots. A wide brown belt held three knives of different sizes, an ordinary purse, and a larger pouch. He carried a pack on one shoulder that was roughly the size of Dumery.

He did not actually look like very pleasant company, but Dumery had committed himself.

"Ah . . ." the boy said, "my father can pay all your expenses, if you take me on . . ."

"Boy," the man said, interrupting him, "I don't want an apprentice, and if I did, it wouldn't be a runt like you. Go home and find something else to do."

Dumery's mouth opened, but no sound came out.

Runt?

The man had called *him* a runt?

He wasn't terribly big for his age, but he was no runt! He was maybe a little over average height, even. Perhaps a little thin, but he'd fill out, he was sure, in a few years.

"I . . ." he began.

The man held up a silencing hand.

"Forget it, kid," he said. "I don't need an apprentice, I don't want an apprentice, and I won't *have* an apprentice, and

I certainly won't have *you*. I don't care if your father's the overlord himself and you're Azrad the Eighth to be, I'm not interested. And quite aside from any apprenticeship, I won't tell you anything about dragons or hunting or anything else. I don't want anything to do with you. Don't argue—just go away.''

Dumery blinked, but could think of nothing to say.

The man in brown—or the dragon-hunter, as Dumery thought of him—turned away and marched on down the road.

At first Dumery simply stood there, watching him go, but something inside him refused to give up that easily.

The man had called him a runt and had refused him—but what if he showed that he wasn't a runt, wasn't as scrawny as he might look? What if he proved he could handle the wilderness and wasn't just a pampered rich city kid?

*Then* maybe the dragon-hunter would take him on!

After all, even Thetheran had tested him. He had failed that test, of course, but he wasn't going to fail this one.

Maybe the man in brown was even doing it *deliberately*! Maybe he really *was* testing Dumery, to see if Dumery had what it took to hunt dragons.

Dumery had to follow him.

He began to hurry after the man in brown, but then he stopped, considering.

If it *wasn't* a deliberate test, and maybe even if it was, he didn't want to be spotted too easily. He ducked off the highway, cut through the line of farmers' wagons, and set out, traipsing across a muddy field, paralleling the road, trying very hard to keep the man in brown in sight.

Maybe, he thought, I can find some way to help him out somewhere. Then he'd *have* to accept me as an apprentice, if I saved his life from a rampaging dragon or something.

Awash in dreams of glory, Dumery marched on through someone's cotton field, stumbling over plants and ditches. He kept an eye on the man in brown, but he didn't try to catch up; instead he deliberately hung back. He didn't want to be spotted.

Once they were both well past the outermost fringe of the market, though, Dumery did return to the highway. Pushing through the fields was just too much work.

They marched on. Or rather, the dragon-hunter marched, while Dumery kept up as best he could, maintaining the distance between them. He had to run occasionally, to make up for the big man's much longer legs, and he often thought he was about to collapse from exhaustion—but each time he reached that state the man in brown would settle down for a rest.

When the dragon-hunter rested, Dumery rested, stopping fifty or a hundred yards away, where he wouldn't be easily recognized. He would sit, massaging his feet and nervously watching the man in brown, and when the dragon-hunger rose, Dumery would snatch his boots back on and leap to his feet and set out anew.

A brief afternoon shower almost discouraged him, but after some initial dismay he hunched his shoulders and resolved to ignore it. The man in brown pulled a hat from his pack and put it on, but other than that he, too, ignored the rain.

The rain ended in less than an hour, and the sun reappeared, clean and bright. Through it all, Dumery marched on, westward and then northward along the highway as it curved, keeping the leather-clad man in sight but never drawing near.

Only when the sun finally reddened and sank low in the west, and the skies began to darken again even though the clouds continued to dissipate, did Dumery realize just what an incredibly foolish mistake he had made.

# CHAPTER 7

*H*e was only twelve years old. He was wearing an ordinary cotton tunic—velvet hadn't seemed practical for a morning visit to Westgate Market—and woolen breeches and soft leather boots. He had a cheap belt knife with him. He had a purse with a few bits in copper in it and down at the bottom a few scraps of string and an old and somewhat dusty honey drop he had never gotten around to eating and not much else. He had no blanket, no flint and steel, no enchanted bloodstone, no sword, no pads for the blisters that had formed on his feet—none of the supplies a sensible traveler would have.

And he was about ten leagues outside the city wall, and it was almost full dark, and he had never been outside the city before, not for so much as a ten-minute stroll.

The man in brown was still walking, though, still marching on, just as he had all day.

It was too late to turn back. Dumery knew he couldn't possibly make it back to the city gate until long after midnight, even if he didn't lose the road in the dark, and even if he didn't meet any wolves or bandits or demons prowling along the way. He wasn't sure he could make it back at all. His feet and legs ached; he had never before walked anything near this distance. The soles of his boots, which he knew were really still perfectly sound, felt paper-thin and soggy with sweat; every pebble seemed to jab him.

He saw a low ridge ahead, and at the point where the ground began to rise the road forked, the right branch going up across the ridge, the left fork paralleling the slope; a glance at the sun's fading glow told him that the right fork ran north, the left fork west.

Nestled in the fork was a good-sized building, and with a start Dumery realized that it wasn't a farmhouse. The farmhouses he had passed all day were never built so close to the road.

Most of them weren't so large, and most weren't built entirely of stone, either. This structure ahead had wooden shutters and doors and a thatch roof, but the walls were all stone, right up to the gable peaks, and peculiar-looking stone at that. Even the attached stable was stone.

There was no signboard, but all the same, Dumery guessed it was an inn. The fork was certainly a logical place for one, being not merely at the junction of two highways, but just exactly a full day's walk from Ethshar.

The man in brown marched directly up to the front door of the inn and entered, opening the door without knocking. Dumery hurried after him.

By the time he reached the building the man in brown was inside, and the door was closed again. Dumery hesitated, unsure whether to knock or just walk in—this place, with no signboard and its door closed, and so big, was not like the inns he was familiar with in the city, and he was uncertain of the etiquette. The dragon-hunter hadn't knocked, but did that mean nobody did? Or was the man in brown privileged somehow?

Just then the door opened again, and a man stepped out holding a torch. He was fairly tall, brown-haired and heavily built, but nowhere near the size of the dragon-hunter. He was wearing an ordinary woolen tunic and a white apron.

"Oh, hello," he said, noticing Dumery. "Welcome to the Inn at the Bridge." He turned and reached up to place the torch in a bracket over the door.

"Bridge?" Dumery asked, looking around and seeing no bridge. There were meadows, and the inn, and its attached stable, and the highway, but no bridge.

"Other side of the hill," the man in the apron said, turning back and jerking a thumb toward the north fork of the highway.

"Oh," Dumery said.

"Come on in," the man said, and he led Dumery inside.

The main room of the inn was spacious and comfortable, with a plank floor and stone walls. At one end was a huge fireplace with a nondescript sheathed sword hanging above it;

doors here and there led to the kitchens and stables and other such places. A score or so of customers were scattered at various tables.

Something small and green scurried along the floor; Dumery tried to get a look at it, but lost sight of it among the chair legs.

He'd been seeing a lot of those things in the last few days, where he had never seen any as of, say, two months before. He wondered what they were for a moment, then turned his attention to more important matters.

The man in brown was seated at a table near the kitchens, chatting with a young woman who was standing beside him; Dumery turned his face away hurriedly so that he wouldn't be recognized if the man happened to glance this way.

The woman turned and bustled away, into the kitchens, and Dumery saw she was holding a tray—one of the serving girls, obviously. The man in brown looked up when she had gone, and Dumery did his best to not be noticed.

The man in the apron, presumably the innkeeper, told Dumery, "Make yourself at home, and someone will be right with you." Then he, too, headed for the kitchens.

Dumery looked about for a chair where the man in brown wouldn't see him, and as he did the thought occurred to him that although he was ravenously hungry and utterly exhausted, he couldn't stay here.

He couldn't afford it.

He had all of six bits in copper, as best he could recall, and that probably wasn't enough for a meal and a bed. He didn't know how long it would have to last him, either. If he spent it all here and now, what would he do tomorrow?

If he had any sense, he told himself, he'd go back *home* tomorrow. He wasn't equipped for anything else.

Well, he replied mentally, he obviously had no sense, because he wasn't going to go home, he was going to follow the dragon-hunter to *his* home, even if it took a sixnight.

And that meant he didn't dare spend all his coins. He might need them later.

Accordingly, when another serving girl, one who looked scarcely older than he was, came and smiled down at him he said, "I'm sorry, but I don't have any money. Can I work for room and board, perhaps?"

The girl's smile vanished.

"I don't know," she said. "Let me ask Valder."

She turned and hurried to the kitchen.

A moment later the man in the apron emerged and crossed directly to where Dumery sat. The boy glanced over at the man in brown, hoping that he wouldn't notice anything out of the ordinary, anything that might draw his attention to Dumery's presence.

"Asha says you told her you have no money," the innkeeper said, without preamble.

Dumery nodded. "I can work, though," he said.

The innkeeper shook his head slowly. "I'm sorry, boy, but I already have more help than I need. You'll have to go." He did sound honestly regretful.

His sincerity didn't help any. Dumery asked, "Are you sure?"

"I'm quite sure, yes. Asha herself is here more from pity than because I needed another wench."

"Oh," Dumery said. "Ah . . . but couldn't I sleep right here, in this chair? I don't need a bed." His stomach growled, and he added, "And I have a bit, in copper; could that buy me some scraps?"

The innkeeper sighed, looking about the room as if the furnishings might offer advice.

The furnishings remained silent, and Valder asked, "Do you have any family, boy?"

"Yes, sir, back in Ethshar," Dumery replied.

"Then what in the World are you doing *here*?"

"I'm . . . I'm on my way to take up my apprenticeship, sir." That was close enough to the truth, Dumery thought.

"And nobody gave you any money for the road?"

Dumery shrugged and looked woebegone. Given his exhausted condition, that wasn't hard to do.

The innkeeper turned away, throwing up his hands. "*Hai*, what a world!" he said. He turned back.

"All right, boy," he said, "you can sleep in the stable, not in here where you might annoy paying customers. And I'll be bringing scraps out after everyone's eaten. Keep your bit; people farther up the road may not be so generous."

"Thank you, sir," Dumery said, relieved that he wasn't

going to be thrown out entirely, but disappointed that he would have to sleep outside and eat table scraps.

He had never eaten table scraps. He'd heard about poor people doing that; in fact, the scraps from his father's table were regularly left by the street for beggars, which was where he'd gotten the idea of asking.

He looked forward to his dinner with as much trepidation as anticipation.

The innkeeper stood over him for a moment, and Dumery realized that the conversation was at an end and it was time for him to leave. Reluctantly, he got up and left.

The only comfort, he thought as he made his way around the corner of the inn and into the stableyard, was that at least the man in brown hadn't spotted him.

The front of the inn wasn't bad, because of the torch over the door, but the stableyard was almost black with the night. The sun was gone; neither moon was in the sky just now, and the stars were obscured by high, thin clouds. Dumery had to find his way mostly by feel.

One thing he felt was that the ground beneath his feet was muddy and slippery; twice his feet almost went out from under him, but each time he managed to catch himself on something.

The stableyard was roughly square, with stalls around three sides—the fourth side was largely taken up with the gate he had entered through. The stalls were under roof, and awash in gloom, while the yard itself was open to the sky and held what little daylight still lingered.

He heard large animals moving around in the darkness along the sides, and glimpsed shadowy forms in the gloom, and decided against trying to get into a stall with one of them. Yes, the stalls would have straw, which would be relatively warm and dry, but he didn't like the idea of getting stepped on by a horse or ox that failed to notice him in the dark.

Instead he worked his way to a back corner and curled up there, huddling miserably, trying to ignore the mud and the dirt and the heavy animal stink.

Was it really worth it? he asked himself after a few minutes. This seemed like a lot of hardship to put up with just to get an apprenticeship, even in a trade as exciting and exotic as dragon-hunting.

Maybe he should go back home and pack proper supplies and put on proper traveling clothes and borrow a reasonable amount of money, and then set out anew.

Of course, the problem with that was that the man in brown would be long gone by then and picking up his trail might be impossible. Dumery had no idea how often he came to the city, either, so he couldn't rely on finding him at the Dragon's Tail again; if his visits were annual, as many tradesmen's were, then by the time he came back to the city Dumery would be too old to be apprenticed.

His stomach growled loudly. He was not accustomed to going this long without plenty of good food.

Something ran across his foot, and he started, looking about wildly, but unable to make out, in the darkness, just what it was that had startled him.

He settled back again and sat there, waiting.

After a time, he found himself wishing he had some way to send a message home to his family. They were probably worried about him; he had, after all, vanished without warning. His mother was probably sitting up, sewing to keep her fingers busy while she got more and more worried.

Well, it wouldn't kill her, and at least she would catch up on the mending. And his father might not even notice his absence until his mother or one of his siblings pointed it out.

And his siblings probably wouldn't miss him.

Even if they did, they would survive, he was sure. They would all survive, even his mother, and he would get word to them eventually, letting them know he was safe.

He wasn't going to think about that, he decided. Right now he had enough to be miserable about in his own situation without worrying about how miserable he might be making others.

It seemed hours later—and in fact may have *been* hours later—when light came spilling suddenly into the stableyard. A door in the wall of the inn had opened, at the back of a narrow passageway that Dumery had mistaken for just another stall, and a figure was standing in it, lamplight pouring out around him.

"Are you out here, boy?" the innkeeper's voice called.

"Yes, sir," Dumery replied, getting stiffly to his feet.

"I've got the scraps for you. Leave the bowl on the step when you're done. Sleep well."

Before Dumery could say anything, the figure stepped back and closed the doorway.

Dumery hurried to the doorstep and found a large wooden bowl, full of something he couldn't see at all. It smelled of grease.

He dipped in a hand and came up with a crust of bread, soggy with congealing gravy; he ate it eagerly.

It took some chewing, and as he worked on it he ambled back through the short passageway to his corner of the stable-yard, where he settled down, cross-legged, with the bowl in front of him.

He began picking through it, working by smell and touch, dropping back the pieces he considered unfit to eat.

Unfortunately, most of it he considered unfit to eat.

He was pawing through it, trying to find something edible, when his hand hit something unfamiliar. He tried to pick it out, to see what it was, but it pulled away.

He blinked, startled, and peered through the gloom. Was something sitting there on the other side of the bowl?

Yes, something was, something about the size of a kitten, but more or less human in shape, with its hands in the bowl of scraps. He stared.

It was sitting cross-legged, a pot belly slopping across its lap, and it was staring at him with outsize, bulging eyes. Dumery couldn't make out much more than that in the darkness; he had no idea of its color, or what any features except the big white eyes might look like.

"Gack," Dumery said, snatching his hand away.

"Gack?" the thing replied.

Dumery suddenly guessed that this was probably one of those little green things that had been running about Ethshar lately, tripping people and getting in the way.

That didn't tell him what it was, though.

"What are *you*?" he asked.

"Spriggan," the thing said in a squeaky little voice. "Hungry," it added pitifully.

Dumery looked down at the bowl; even in the dark he could

see that the thing had both its arms thrust into the scraps almost to the elbows.

"Oh," Dumery said. He gently pushed the bowl away, toward the spriggan. "Here," he said, "help yourself."

He had lost his appetite.

As if eating garbage weren't bad enough, he was supposed to *share* it with some vile little monster? A monster that had shoved its dirty little paws into the bowl like that?

That was simply too much. He wouldn't stand for it. He turned away, huddled up against the stableyard wall, and tried to go to sleep.

Given his exhausted condition, that didn't take long.

# CHAPTER 8

*F*aléa had begun wondering around midafternoon just what Dumery was doing that was keeping him so long. Was he still at Westgate Market? Had he found something to do, some apprenticeship or other prospect, that appealed to him? Had he, perhaps, wandered off to some other part of the city?

If he'd found an apprenticeship, that was fine—if it was something completely inappropriate Doran could refuse to co-operate, and that would put an end to it, and if it was anything halfway respectable, then the problem of Dumery's future was solved.

If he hadn't found an apprenticeship, that didn't matter; he had plenty of time left before his thirteenth birthday.

She did wonder, though, what was keeping him.

The wondering turned gradually to worry as the sun set, and supper was cooked and served and eaten, and still Dumery didn't return.

This wasn't the first time Dumery had missed a meal, of course, or even the fiftieth, but still, Faléa worried.

Doran, of course, hadn't even noticed the boy's absence. He was involved with the accounts from the *Sea Stallion*'s latest run out to Tintallion of the Isle—Faléa knew that there were apparently some discrepancies and that this was important, so she didn't force her worries about their youngest son on her husband.

Doran the Younger and Derath and Dessa all made the predictable snide adolescent remarks about their brother's absence, naturally, and Faléa hushed them halfheartedly.

Their father paid no attention.

After dinner Faléa and Derath cleaned the table and kitchen, while Dessa swept and Doran the Younger hauled water in from the courtyard well. The elder Doran finally found the flaw in the records about an hour after dinner, as Dessa was settling to bed, and spent the next twenty minutes loudly arguing with himself as to whether he should have his agent whipped for theft, or merely fired, or whether he should forgive her this one last time—a keg of good Morrian brandy was missing and unaccounted for.

"Why not ask her what happened to it?" Faléa suggested. "It might be an honest mistake."

"Ha!" Doran bellowed. *"Honest? Her?"*

"It *might* be." While she had her husband's attention, she added, "By the way, have you seen Dumery? He wasn't at supper."

"I'll ask her, all right," he said. "I'll ask her first thing in the morning, with a guardsman at my side." He snorted.

"Have you seen Dumery?" Faléa insisted.

"What? No, I haven't seen the boy. Ask his brothers."

Faléa did ask them, catching them just before they retired for the night. Both of them insisted that they hadn't seen Dumery since breakfast.

"You're sure?" she asked.

They took offense at that, unsurprisingly, and she could get nothing more out of them. She let them go on to bed.

Ordinarily, she would have gone to bed herself not long after, but this time she didn't. She sat up, waiting, instead.

She got out her sewing basket and did the mending. That kept her hands busy, but didn't really distract her thoughts from all the terrible things that might have happened to her youngest child.

There were slavers over on New Canal Street, and prowling the streets. There were drunken sailors starting brawls all along the waterfront.

Dumery had gone to Westgate Market; that was near Wall Street and the Hundred-Foot Field. There were thieves in the Field, and maybe worse. Slavers never dared enter the Field itself, but they patrolled Wall Street, collecting strays.

There were stories about evil magicians kidnapping people from the Hundred-Foot Field for various nefarious purposes—as sacrifices to demons or rogue gods, as food for monsters, as a source of ingredients for strange and terrible spells. Young innocents were supposed to be especially prized—virgin's blood, hair, and tears were reputed to be necessary ingredients in several spells.

That was usually presumed to mean *female* virgins, but perhaps boys had their own uses.

And there were stories about other people than magicians finding uses for boys. She had never heard such stories about Westgate, but over in Camptown there were rumored to be all-male brothels.

Any number of horrible things could have happened to Dumery. Her needle jerked through the cloth she held as she considered just how dangerous her native city actually could be.

Around midnight Doran put away the account books and looked around for Faléa. He found her waiting in the parlor, staring at the front hallway, her sewing done and heaped on the floor; he remembered suddenly that Dumery was missing.

He snorted under his breath. That damned troublesome boy. The little fool was probably playing some stupid prank, Doran told himself, or else he was staying with friends and had forgotten to tell anyone.

Telling Faléa that wouldn't do any good, though. She knew it as well as he did, but still, she worried.

Nothing wrong with that, Doran thought. A mother had every right to worry about her youngest. And Dumery was a bright lad, a promising lad—Doran was proud of him. He would have been even prouder had the boy not been so pig-headed and prone to wild fancies and foolhardy adventures.

Still, Dumery would turn up, safe and sound, he was sure. He always had.

Doran waved a good night to his wife and went to bed.

Faléa waved back, halfheartedly, and sat.

An hour later, her head still full of thoughts of her Dumery captured by slavers, or set upon by thieves, or run off on reckless adventures, Faléa joined her husband in bed.

# CHAPTER 9

*D*umery *awoke at the sound of a rattling harness; a traveler* was fetching his mount from the inn's stable.

The boy blinked up at the bright blue sky and then panicked. He leaped to his feet, sending the scrap bowl spinning and knocking aside the spriggan that was curled up against him, and he ran for the gate, spooking several horses. The traveler shouted at him angrily, but Dumery paid no attention. He was too worried.

It was morning, and none too early. What if the dragon-hunter had already gone? Dumery didn't even know which fork of the road the man in brown would be taking, north or west.

He paused at the door of the inn to catch his breath. Looking up, he saw that the torch above the door had burned away to a blackened stub. The sun was still low in the east, but it was clear of the horizon.

If the man in brown was gone Dumery would have no way of finding him again. He would be left with little choice but to give up and head home to Ethshar.

That would mean giving up his dream of becoming a dragon-hunter himself, though, and he wasn't going to give in that easily if he could help it. He was *determined* to be a dragon-hunter and rub Thetheran's nose in it.

He opened the door and, suddenly nervous about being spotted, peered carefully in.

The man in brown was there, sitting at one of the tables, eating grapes, carefully plucking out the seeds as he went. He wore a different tunic, this one brown wool rather than brown leather, but Dumery was sure it was he. The man's size and slovenly hair were distinctive enough to make a positive identification.

A sigh of relief escaped the boy. The man was still here. He hadn't left yet. Dumery hadn't lost him.

His ticket to a career in dragon-hunting was still in reach.

Dumery stood in the doorway for a moment, trying to figure out what to do next.

As he stood, it registered with the boy that the man in brown looked clean and well-rested and well-fed and was finishing up a leisurely and generous breakfast. He had undoubtedly slept in a fine bed paid for with Thetheran's gold, while Dumery had spent the night freezing in the stableyard mud, with nothing to eat but a few nauseating scraps. He was filthy and stinking, his feet still ached, his back was stiff, and his stomach was so empty it was trying to tie itself in knots.

This journey was no great hardship for the man in brown, who was well-prepared and well-financed, but it was clearly going to be torture for an ill-equipped boy who didn't even know where he was going.

Dumery turned and looked down the road, back toward Ethshar. He couldn't see any sign of the city, but he knew it was there, and in it his parents' house.

Should he turn back?

He chewed on his lip as he thought it over.

Back in Ethshar, somewhere over the horizon, he had a home and a family and a fine soft bed, regular meals, and a warm fire every night. He had a mother who loved him, a father who treated him fairly well, and three reasonably tolerable siblings who usually left him alone.

He also had no prospects of any interest for the future, however, and the city was home to a dozen wizards and other magicians who had rejected and humiliated him.

That decided him. He would go on.

He would continue on until he reached the dragon-hunter's

home base, and then he would present himself again and *demand* an apprenticeship.

He looked back into the main room of the inn just as the man in brown pushed back his chair and got to his feet.

The serving maid, Asha, hurried up as the man dropped a heavy coin on the table—a silver piece, by the look and sound of it. The two exchanged a few words that Dumery didn't catch.

Worried that he might be missing something important, he slipped in the door as they were talking and crept closer.

"So the boat's there now?" the man asked.

"I think so," the girl replied.

"Well, that's fine, then. I might as well wait there as here. My thanks, to you and to Valder." He reached down and picked up his pack as the girl pocketed the coin—a silver round, all right. That would cover his entire bill, Dumery was sure, and probably leave a bit or two over for the maid.

Well, with a purse full of wizard's gold, the man could afford to be generous.

Dumery realized suddenly, as the man in brown shouldered his pack, that he was about to leave.

Not wanting to be seen, the boy ducked back out the front door as the man in brown turned. He scurried back to the stableyard and through the gate; then he turned and watched, peering around the wall as the dragon-hunter emerged.

The man in brown wasted no time in looking around at the scenery, or admiring the weather; he marched around the far corner of the inn and up the northern fork of the highway, out of sight.

Dumery started to hurry after him, only to trip and fall headlong in the mud.

Blinking, he got to his knees and looked around, trying to figure out what had tripped him.

The little monster that had called itself a spriggan was sitting there, looking as dazed as Dumery felt.

The thing was green, as he had guessed, and would have been about eight inches tall standing upright. It looked like a frog that had started to turn into a man and then changed its mind; it was sitting in a human pose, rather than a batrachian one, its hind legs stretched out before it, its forelegs—arms, really, with hands, fingers, and even thumbs—dangling to either side. It had broad pointed ears, far too large for it, and great protruding eyes.

"Ooooh!" it said, in a piercing, squeaky little voice. "We bump!"

"Yes," Dumery said, "I guess we did."

The creature looked harmless; Dumery decided to ignore it. He got to his feet.

"Oooh, wait!" the spriggan said. "Where we going?"

Dumery looked down at it. "I don't have any idea where *you're* going," he said, "but *I'm* going *that* way!" He pointed to the northern fork, where the man in brown had vanished.

"Come with you, yes! You feed, I come!" the spriggan announced enthusiastically.

"I'm not going to feed you," Dumery said, annoyed. "I don't even have food for myself."

"You feed me last night. I come with you," it insisted, stamping a foot ludicrously.

"Right," Dumery said. "Try it." He turned and marched off briskly, almost running.

The spriggan let out a piercing shriek, hopped up, and ran after him.

Dumery's longer legs made the difference; he easily left the little creature behind as he topped the low ridge that ran behind the inn.

As he did, he suddenly saw why the place was called the Inn at the Bridge.

From the ridgetop the road sloped steeply down toward a river bigger than Dumery had ever imagined rivers could be. He had never seen a real river, of course, just drainage ditches and canals; the broadest canal he had ever seen was the New Canal, between Shiphaven and Spicetown, which was two hundred feet wide for much of its length, big enough for the oceangoing ships to use freely.

The lower part of the Grand Canal, between Spicetown and Fishertown, was about the same.

The two of them could have been put side by side and still not equaled more than a tiny fraction of the river before him now.

And the really amazing part of the view wasn't the river at all; it was the bridge across it. It was stone, soaring arches of stone supporting a roadbed higher and broader than Ethshar's city wall—and built across water, rather than on solid ground!

Dumery stared at it in amazement.

Soldiers, four of them, in the uniform of Ethshar's City Guard, stood at the near end, chatting quietly and watching halfheartedly for approaching traffic. Just now no one was crossing, but on the far side, in the distance, Dumery thought he could see a wagon on the road.

What he did *not* see was the man in brown, and he looked about worriedly as he hurried on down the long slope.

Then Dumery spotted his quarry; he wasn't on the main road at all. Rather than approaching the bridge, he had turned aside onto a smaller and even steeper road that branched off inconspicuously to the left, just where the approaches of the bridge parted company with the natural contour of the land.

This little branch road followed the slope down to the river and a dock.

It wasn't a particularly impressive dock compared with the great trading wharves in Spicetown or the shipping piers in Shiphaven, but it was undeniably a dock. What's more, there were boats tied up there, and the man in brown was heading straight for the biggest one, which waited at the end of the dock, its gangplank out.

Forgetting about any need for secrecy, Dumery broke into a run, chasing after the dragon-hunter, lest the boat leave with the man aboard before Dumery could reach it.

The boat was long and square, without masts or rigging, and with little freeboard. Sweeps were racked on either side of the deck, their blades poking up at a steep angle, giving the whole craft something of the appearance of an overturned beetle with its legs in the air.

Despite its rather ugly shape, the craft was gaily painted; the hull was a deep rich red picked out with gold, the deck and superstructure a gleaming yellow, with predominantly green fancywork around the ports and hatches. Green and gold banners flew at bow and stern. The sweeps were painted green, with gold scrollwork on the shafts.

This was not, Dumery realized, a seagoing ship, nor even a

harbor boat. It bore more of a resemblance to the flat-bottomed barges that were used to haul materials around the waterfront, especially in the shipyard, than to anything else Dumery had often encountered. He thought he might have seen a few such craft here and there along Ethshar's waterfront, but he wasn't really sure; he had certainly not seen many, and never at the deep-water piers.

It had to be a riverboat.

The man in brown marched up the gangplank without slowing and waved a greeting to the handful of brightly dressed people on the boat's deck. Two of them waved back; a third stepped forward and exchanged a few words with the dragon-hunter.

Dumery wished he could hear what was being said, but he was still much too far away.

He was running as fast as he could on the downgrade, but the man in brown's head start and longer legs had given him a sizable lead, and the slope made running difficult. Dumery's feet thumped onto the dock's first plank as the man in brown vanished through a low doorway, his business with the man on deck completed.

Dumery ran out the dock's length and up the gangplank without slowing.

At the sound of his approach—which was easy to hear, thanks to the dock's loose planking—the party on deck turned and looked at him. The man who had spoken with the dragon-hunter, a man in a white tunic and sky-blue kilt, stepped over to the gangplank.

Dumery ran straight into his outstretched arms.

"*Hai*, there," the man said, grabbing Dumery's arms. "What's your hurry?"

Dumery realized he had made it; he was aboard the boat, with the man in brown. "I didn't want to miss the boat," he said, panting.

"No danger of that," the man in the white tunic said. "We won't be leaving until noon."

"Oh," Dumery said, feeling foolish. "I didn't know."

"Ah," the man said, releasing one arm. "Well, now you do." He looked Dumery over, and Dumery stared back defiantly.

He knew he looked terrible, after sleeping in his clothes in the mud and then tripping over that stupid spriggan, but he didn't care, and he waited for the man to criticize him, ready to reply.

"I take it," the man said, "that you'd like to stay aboard for the ride north?"

Dumery blinked and looked around.

No, he wasn't confused; there the sun was on the far side of the bridge, which meant that was east. The other direction on the river was west. Was this boat just a ferry, then?

If so, he could have just walked across the bridge!

"North?" he said.

"Yes, north," the man replied. "Didn't you know, then?" He pointed due west. "We'll be cruising upstream, all the way to Sardiron of the Waters."

"Oh," Dumery said.

Either the entire World was confused somehow and the sun was rising in the south, or else the river to the west turned north somewhere along the way. This was no local ferry—Sardiron of the Waters was hundreds of miles away.

In fact, it wasn't even in the Hegemony of the Three Ethshars. It was the council city of the Baronies of Sardiron, a land Dumery had heard described in countless tales as a barbarous foreign realm of gloomy castles, deep dark forests, icy winters, hungry wolves—and marauding dragons.

Was *that* where the man in brown was going?

It made sense, of course. There were no dragons left in the Hegemony, so far as Dumery knew; certainly not anywhere near Ethshar of the Spices.

He should have thought of that sooner. A dragon-hunter could scarcely ply his trade in such quiet, civilized country.

He might have to pursue the man in brown for sixnights, even months.

He hesitated.

"Were you going to Sardiron, then?" the boatman asked.

Dumery nodded. "Yes," he said.

"Ah," the boatman replied, nodding. "And you have the fare?"

Dumery's heart fell. "Fare?" he asked.

"Of course," the boatman said. "Did you think we man this boat for the sheer delight of it?"

"No, I . . . how much?"

"To Sardiron?"

"Yes."

"The full fare, lad, is five rounds of silver, but for a boy your size—call it three."

"Oh," Dumery said. While that discount meant that the price was actually negotiable, Dumery knew there was no way in the World he could haggle three silver pieces down to a few copper bits.

And all he had was a few copper bits.

"Haven't got it, have you?" the man asked, glaring at him.

"No, I . . ." Dumery began. Then he caught the boatman's gaze and just said, "No."

"Off the boat, then," the boatman ordered, pointing ashore and using the grip on Dumery's arm to turn the boy.

"Could I *work* . . ." Dumery began.

"No," the boatman said, cutting him off. "The *Sunlit Meadows* is no cattle barge, boy, to be hiring anyone who comes aboard with two hands and a strong back—and your back doesn't look that strong, for that matter! This is the finest passenger boat on the Great River, and we've had a full crew of trained professionals working her since before we left Sardiron of the Waters; we've no need for a fumble-fingered farmboy." He put his other hand between Dumery's shoulders and began pushing the boy down the gangplank.

"I'm not a farmboy!" Dumery protested. "My father's a wealthy merchant in the city . . ."

"Then have him buy you passage, boy!" He gave Dumery a final shove, not particularly hard or vicious, that sent the lad staggering onto the dock. Then he stood there, astride the gangplank, hands on hips, and stared.

Dumery stared back for a moment, then turned away.

He was not going to get aboard the *Sunlit Meadows* easily, that was plain.

All the same, he was not about to give up. The man in brown was aboard that boat, and wherever he went, Dumery was determined to follow.

He had no idea *how* he would follow, just now, but he'd find a way.

He had to.

# CHAPTER 10

*"He* still hasn't turned up?" Doran asked, startled.

"No, he hasn't!" Faléa answered. She glared at her husband. He hadn't done anything wrong, but she was furious with Dumery for worrying her this way, and he wasn't there, so she directed her anger at his father.

Doran was used to this; it didn't bother him. "Have you asked the others if they've seen him?" he asked.

"Of course I have!" Faléa snapped. "Dessa saw him yesterday morning at breakfast; Doran and Derath won't even admit that much. All three of them swear they haven't seen him since. I've got them out searching the neighborhood, asking his friends, but so far they haven't found any sign of him."

Doran considered this, and said, "You asked that little ratty one with the long hair, what's his name, Pergren of the Runny Nose, or whatever it is?"

"Pergren of Chandlery Street," Faléa corrected him. "Dessa talked to him an hour ago. From what she said I think she threatened to beat him so hard his nose would stop running . . ."

"From what I've seen of him that would probably kill him," Doran muttered under his breath.

". . . But he still didn't know where Dumery was," Faléa said.

"All right," Doran said, "I can see that you're seriously worried and I suppose it's with good reason. What is it you want me to do? What do you think might have happened to the boy?"

"Oh," Faléa said unhappily, "I don't know. Maybe some slaver took him by mistake. Or maybe he ran away to sea. Or . . ." She took a deep, unsteady breath. "Or maybe he got himself killed, somehow."

Doran sighed. "All right, listen," he said. "I'll send a letter to Lord Talden; he'll alert the City Guard and get a description posted everywhere. And I'll check with the Slavers' Registry; if they *did* pick him up, even if they've already shipped him off to Ethshar of the Sands or something, they'll have reported the capture."

"If it *was* a *registered* slaver . . ." Faléa began.

"Well, damn it, woman," Doran burst out, "if he got captured by an *unregistered* slaver, then he's in the hands of outlaws, and it doesn't much matter whether it's slavers or kidnappers or what, does it? There isn't much we can do!"

"Oh, I know that," Faléa admitted dismally.

Doran grimaced at her despairing tone. "Where was he going when he disappeared, anyway?" he asked.

"Westgate Market," Faléa explained, "to see if he could find an interesting career to apprentice for."

"Well, then, maybe he *found* one!" Doran roared. "Why didn't you tell me that sooner? Maybe the boy signed on as an apprentice somewhere and will send word when he can, in which case we're all getting upset over nothing! Have you sent anyone down to Westgate to ask around?"

"Derath," Faléa said. "He left half an hour ago. But, Dorie, we'd have word by now . . ." She let her voice trail off.

"We *should* anyway," Doran admitted. "But some of these tradesmen are eccentric. Listen, are you sure he went to Westgate? If he was looking for an apprenticeship, maybe he went back down to the Wizards' Quarter again—he might have some new scheme for learning magic. *You* know how stubborn . . . how *determined* he can be!"

Faléa did indeed know how stubborn Dumery could be and she considered this suggestion. It sounded plausible, but there was one problem with it. "Why would that keep him overnight?" she asked. "And . . . but, Dorie, if he *did* go there . . ."

"If he went there," Doran finished for her, "*anything* could have happened, with all those magicians and all their spells running around loose."

"Even if he *didn't* go there, maybe *we* should. We could buy a spell to find him." Faléa's tone and expression shifted from woe to delight with amazing speed. "Oh, that's what we'll do! We'll buy a spell! That wizard you went to, what's his name?"

"Thetheran the Mage," Doran replied. He was less enthusiastic than his wife; magic was expensive. He started to say something to that effect, then took another look at Faléa and swallowed his words.

After all, this was his son they were talking about, not an escaped chicken or strayed cat.

"All right," he said, "we'll go buy a spell."

"Good!" Faléa said, almost grinning. "It's chilly out there; I'll get your coat while you find your purse and some money." She bounced toward the doorway.

"I thought we could go after lunch . . ." Doran began.

The grin vanished. *"Now,"* Faléa said.

Doran sighed. "Now," he agreed.

# CHAPTER 11

*D*umery sat on the slope above the dock, to one side of the road, and stared disconsolately at the river.

The World was going about its business all around him, albeit in a more leisurely fashion than a city boy like himself was accustomed to. Travelers were crossing the bridge in both directions, on foot or horseback, or riding in wagons and ox carts, and the soldiers were collecting tolls from all of them. Boats of various sizes and shapes were moving up and down the river, some powered by sails, some by oars, most by magic. Some had tied up to the dock; some had departed.

Dumery just sat, staring at the *Sunlit Meadows* and plotting out possibilities.

What if he headed to Sardiron of the Waters overland? There must be a land route, after all. Could he meet the boat there, in Sardiron, and pick up the dragon-hunter's trail?

Probably not; he suspected that the boat would get there by

water much more quickly than he could on foot, particularly if it used magical propulsion. The boat didn't look as if it could hold enough men to work all those sweeps *without* magic.

And if Sardiron of the Waters was anything like Ethshar, he might not be able to find the right dock even if he got there in time. Ethshar of the Spices was the largest city in the World, yes, but Sardiron was surely good-sized itself.

Besides, he didn't even know whether the man in brown was really going to Sardiron. It seemed likely, but what if he were planning to disembark somewhere along the way? The boat probably didn't just run from the bridge to Sardiron, but made stops at other places along the river.

For that matter, he wondered if this was as far downstream as it came. It was low enough to fit under the central arch of the bridge, certainly. It might have gone all the way to Ethshar itself.

If so, though, why hadn't the man in brown boarded it there?

Well, maybe this particular vessel didn't go that far. After all, Ethshar wasn't on the river, it was on the south side of the bay, and the river emptied into the northwest corner, if Dumery remembered his lessons correctly, where the water was all shoals and shifting sandbars. Getting across the bay wouldn't be easy sailing.

But even if this *was* as far downstream as the *Sunlit Meadows* went, that still didn't mean that it wouldn't make stops on its way north.

Maybe, Dumery thought, he could ask the boat's crew where the man in brown was going. They might know. They might even be willing to tell him.

Just as that thought occurred to him, he felt something like tiny fingers grabbing at his arm. He turned his head, startled, to look for the cause.

The spriggan grinned up at him. "Found you!" it said. "We have fun, yes?"

"No," Dumery said. "Go away!"

"Aw," the spriggan said, "we have *fun*!"

"No," Dumery repeated. Before the spriggan could reply, he demanded, "What *are* you, anyway? Where did you come from?"

"Me, spriggan!" the creature said. "Came from magic mirror, me and all the others."

"A magic mirror?" Dumery asked, intrigued.

"Yes, yes," the spriggan agreed. "Mirror!" It mimed staring at a glass, its eyes bulging absurdly.

"Where?" Dumery asked. "Where was this magic mirror?" He remembered that the very first place he had glimpsed a spriggan had been in Thetheran's laboratory; had that despicable wizard created these little nuisances?

The thing developed an expression of comical and complete bafflement. "Don't know," it said. "Not good at places."

"In Ethshar?" Dumery persisted.

The spriggan thought about that for a moment, then said, "Don't think so."

"Then how did you get here?" Dumery asked. "I saw a couple of you . . . you spriggans in the city before I left, I think."

"Yes, yes!" it said enthusiastically. "All over now. Go on ships and in wagons and ride everywhere we can!"

"Oh," Dumery said. He considered this for a moment, then asked, "Why?"

"Have *fun*!" the spriggan explained. "'Spriggans have lots of fun! You and me, *we* have fun, now!"

"No," Dumery said, losing interest.

"Fun" the spriggan repeated.

Dumery just stared at it, silently.

It stared back.

After a long moment the spriggan realized that Dumery wasn't going to say anything more.

"Have *fun*!" it repeated.

Dumery just stared.

The spriggan looked up at him for a minute longer, then said, "You no fun." It kicked Dumery's leg and walked away.

The kick didn't hurt; in fact, Dumery hardly felt it. All the same, he was tempted to swat the stupid little creature.

He didn't; he just stared after it as it stamped off.

When he looked back at the dock he saw the tillerman on the *Sunlit Meadows* casting off a final hawser. While Dumery had talked with the spriggan the crew had been readying the boat for departure.

"*Hai!*" he shouted, jumping up and running down the slope, "hey, wait!"

His feet pounded on the planks, and one popped up beneath him and tripped him. He fell sprawling.

When he lifted himself up again the *Sunlit Meadows* was well clear of the dock, the sweeps working steadily, propelling it upstream. Dumery could see no one aboard paying any attention to him, or to anything else the boat was leaving behind.

In fact, he couldn't see much of anyone aboard save for the man at the tiller; the sweeps were working by themselves, by magic—or at least by some completely invisible force—and everyone else seemed to be belowdecks.

Dumery wanted to cry. The man in brown, the dragon-hunter, the key to his future, was aboard that boat.

And he, Dumery, wasn't.

He looked around and saw a few miscellaneous people smirking at the pratfall he had just taken; he didn't cry, but instead climbed solemnly to his feet. He brushed dust from his sleeves and pretended to ignore his surroundings, including the slow, uneven drumming noise that was coming from somewhere.

"*Hai*, boy," someone called, "better look out behind you!"

Startled, Dumery turned and looked back at the land.

A small herd of cattle, perhaps a dozen head, was marching down the road toward the dock—straight toward him.

Dumery blinked and started backing farther onto the dock, but then stopped.

That wasn't going to work if the cattle were really going to charge right out; he would just be crowded off the end of the dock into the river. Since he didn't know how to swim that was not a pleasing prospect—to say the least.

Instead he turned aside and jumped from the edge of the dock onto the deck of a convenient, if small, boat.

He misjudged his landing and sprawled once more. This time, when he lifted his head, he found himself looking at an old woman's grinning face.

"Hello," Dumery said.

"Hello yourself, boy," the old woman replied gleefully.

"I, ah . . . I wanted to get out of the way," Dumery explained as he shifted around into a sitting position.

"I gathered that," the woman said, with a smile that exposed her two remaining teeth. "And you're free to stay until the dock's clear; I'm in no hurry."

A possibility occurred to Dumery. He asked, "Where are you going, then?" Perhaps he could beg a ride, if she were headed upstream, and maybe he could catch up with the *Sunlit Meadows* somewhere.

"Downstream to Ethshar," she said, dashing his hopes. "Got family there I haven't seen since the third moon last rose."

Dumery puzzled for a moment over that expression. He'd heard "when the third moon rises" used to mean "never," but this was different. If there had ever actually been a third moon it had been gone for a thousand years or more, or so Dumery had heard, and this woman didn't look *that* old, so he assumed it was a figure of speech.

It must just mean not for a long time, he eventually decided.

"Oh," he said, disappointment plain in his voice.

"You were looking for a ride upstream?" she asked.

He nodded.

"Can't help you there. You missed the *Sunlit Meadows*, and by the look of you you couldn't have afforded it anyway. Only other boat I know bound for the north is that cattle barge they're loading and I wouldn't expect them to carry passengers."

"Cattle barge?" That reminded him of what the crewman on the *Sunlit Meadows* had said when Dumery had offered to work for his passage. He stood up and peered across the dock.

Sure enough, the cattle were being herded across a heavy gangplank onto a great flat-bottomed barge.

"That's right," the old woman said. "'The lords up in Sardiron like to get their beef from the south. I've heard they think it's better-tasting and more tender than the local meat."

"Oh," Dumery said, reaching a quick decision. "Excuse me, but I think I'll be going. Thank you very much for your help."

"You're welcome, boy," she said, watching with amusement as Dumery clambered back up onto the dock.

He had had a sudden inspiration when she had said the cattle were going north and now he acted on it; he ran forward and slipped between two of the steers as they were herded across the gangplank onto the barge.

The drovers were too busy keeping the cattle headed the right direction to worry about anything else, and the barge crew was crowded to the ends, out of the way of their frightened and rambunctious cargo. If the drovers noticed Dumery at all they didn't mention it, and the barge crew, he was sure, hadn't seen him.

Of course, his chosen method of boarding was not particularly comfortable. The cattle jostled against him from all sides, and several times he narrowly avoided falling and being trampled. Even staying upright, three or four times a heavy hoof landed directly on his toes, making him gasp—but not cry out—with pain.

He'd seen cattle now and then in the markets and had passed a few on the way from Ethshar to the Inn at the Bridge, but up until now he had never come directly into contact with the beasts. They were, he discovered, quite large, completely solid, surprisingly warm to the touch, and not very pleasant company.

He stood there, half smothered by steerhide pressed against his face, for what seemed like half of eternity, getting bumped back and forth and scraped about. Several of the steers were lowing plaintively, their hooves were thumping loudly on the decking, and people were shouting incomprehensible orders, adding up to a real cacophony. The stink of unwashed, frightened cattle was thick and foul in his nostrils. He could see nothing but brown hides.

Then the barge began moving, and though the shouting died away, the cattle made more noise than ever, stamping about and bellowing. Dumery waited, concentrating on continuing to breathe.

He was considering several interesting questions, such as whether it was time to reveal his presence to the crew, whether he wanted to reveal his presence at all, how he could attract their attention in the first place, and whether he was going to survive this little escapade, when he raised his head to take a breath and found himself looking up directly into a man's face.

"Just what the hell are you doing there, boy?" the man demanded, in oddly accented Ethsharitic.

"Mmmph," Dumery said.

*"Hai!"* the man called; he slapped the steers surrounding Dumery, and they parted, as if by magic.

Relieved, Dumery obeyed the man's order to march up to the little deck at the bow of the barge. The man followed close behind.

Dumery found himself the center of attention for the five-man crew as he clambered up onto the narrow deck; all eyes were on him.

"Who are *you*?" one man demanded.

"Dumery of Shiphaven," Dumery replied. There wasn't any point in lying.

"And what are you doing *here*?" asked another.

"I needed a ride north," Dumery explained.

The five just stared at him for a long moment, and he added, "I can work for my passage. I have no money, but I really want to go up north . . ."

The five men exchanged glances with one another.

"You'll work?" one of them asked.

Dumery nodded. "Whatever's needed," he said, "if I can do it, I will."

Another man grinned. "Kid," he said, "I think you've got a deal."

"Hey, Kelder," another called, "where's the shovel? We've got someone here who's really going to need it!"

# CHAPTER 12

"Well, now," Thetheran said, "It's not really my specialty, finding things . . ."

"Dumery is not a *thing*," Faléa said. "He's our son."

"Oh, I know, I know," Thetheran assured her. "I merely meant that locative magic is outside my usual practice."

"Your sign says you're a mage," Doran pointed out, "and when I brought my boy here I was told you were one of the best wizards in the Quarter. Are you telling me you can't even find my son?"

"Oh, no, no, nothing like that," Thetheran said hurriedly. "Merely that it's not a spell I commonly use, so that I may not have the ingredients readily available! I'll need to check. And I'm not sure just which spell would be best. Do you merely wish to know *where* he is, or do you want to know his state of health? Do you want a message conveyed? Would you . . ." He stopped, catching himself. He didn't want to promise anything he couldn't deliver. The truth was that he had no idea what spells he had that might apply in this case, or which spells he could buy from the neighbors without his customers finding out about it.

"Well, we certainly want to know if he's still alive and well!" Doran snapped. "It isn't going to do us any good to locate a . . ." Suddenly realizing that completing the sentence with the word "corpse," as he had intended to do, might upset his wife, he let it drop and instead said, "I mean, yes, we want to know the state of his health!"

"And if there's some way we could talk to him . . ." Faléa added, ignoring her husband's blunder.

"Ah," Thetheran said, stroking his beard. "Well, if you actually want to *talk* to him, that will call for a little research.

Tell me, do you have any idea at all where he is? Is he still inside the city walls?"

"We don't know," Doran said, annoyed. "All we know is he's gone."

"Well, then," Thetheran said, "I suggest that the two of you go keep yourselves busy for an hour or two while I investigate the matter, and when you come back I hope to have a spell ready for you."

He *hoped* he would, but he admitted to himself that it wasn't very likely.

The merchant and his wife hesitated, and whispered to each other for a moment, but then they rose from the velvet chairs and made a polite departure.

The moment they were outside Thetheran slammed the door and ran for his laboratory. He snatched his personal book of spells from the shelf and began flipping through the pages, encountering one useless or inappropriate spell after another.

"Eknerwal's Lesser Invisibility," he muttered to himself, "Felojun's First Hypnotic, the Polychrome Smoke, the Dismal Itch. Damn. Love spells, curses, invisibility, levitations, nothing about finding anything. The Iridescent Amusement. Fendel's Aphrodisiac Philtre. The Lesser Spell of Invaded . . ."

He stopped and turned back.

"The Lesser Spell of Invaded Dreams," he read, "requires fine gray dust, incense tainted with morning mist . . ." He nodded to himself as he read over the instructions and the lessons of his own long-ago apprenticeship came back to him.

Then he got to the detailed description of the spell's effects and stopped, cursing.

"*That* won't do," he said. He stood staring at the page for a moment, then looked up at the ceiling, thinking. "There's something, though. This isn't quite what I remember."

Then it struck him. "The *Lesser* Spell," he said, and he began hurriedly flipping pages again.

He found what he wanted and stopped. "Ah!" he said, tapping the page with his finger. "Here we go!" He began reading avidly.

An hour later he was waiting in his cozy front room when Faléa and Doran knocked on the door. Thetheran sent the sylph to let them in, while he stood and adjusted his robe to make the most imposing figure possible.

"I believe, Doran of Shiphaven, Faléa the Slender," the mage declaimed as the pair entered, "that I have just the spell you need."

Doran was suitably impressed. Having spent the intervening time buying and eating a more-than-adequate luncheon, Doran was in a much better mood than before. "Oh?" he said politely.

Faléa had spent the entire meal worrying about whether Dumery had found anything to eat in the past day or so and was too upset to say anything.

"Yes," Thetheran said. "It's known as the Greater Spell of Invaded Dreams. It will permit me to speak to your son in his dreams and to question him regarding his present circumstances. By performing the spell in a certain way, I believe that I can put one of you—not both, however—into the dream as well, so that you, too, will be able to speak to him. That *is* what you wanted, I believe?"

Both of Dumery's parents nodded, Faléa with rather more enthusiasm than her spouse.

"I cannot perform the spell with any chance of success until the boy is asleep, however," Thetheran explained. "That means that I had best wait until well after dark tonight. I will also need to know the boy's true name, if it is not Dumery of Shiphaven . . ."

"That's the only name he's got," Doran interrupted. "Only one he ever had."

"Then it is his true name," Thetheran said, unperturbed. "Now, which of you will speak to him?"

Doran glanced at his wife, who immediately volunteered.

"I will need your true name, as well, then," Thetheran said. "And it would be easiest if you were to remain here, with me, throughout, though in fact it should be possible to conduct the entire affair successfully if you are at home and asleep in your own bed."

"I'll stay here," Faléa unhesitatingly replied.

Doran eyed her briefly, then looked over the mage, and decided that the risk of being cuckolded was minimal. "All right," he said. "Is there anything else you need, wizard?"

"Not for the spell itself," Thetheran replied, "but there is the matter of my fee . . ."

# CHAPTER 13

*There may, Dumery reflected, be worse ways of paying for* one's passage than by shoveling manure, but offhand he couldn't think of any.

Seeing the five crewmen lolling about doing nothing much most of the time didn't make the work any easier or more enjoyable, either. Oh, they fed the cattle four times a day and directed the gaseous spirit that was pulling the barge along at an impressive speed, but that was about the extent of it. Dumery wondered why all five of them were along, since it seemed that three would have been plenty, even if he hadn't been there himself to help.

It wasn't any of his business, though. He stuck to his shovel—sometimes literally, when the sweat from his hands mixed with the accumulated crud on the handle—and didn't ask questions.

An hour or two after leaving what the crewmen called Azrad's Bridge came the first really enjoyable part of the journey, when the bargemen hauled out provisions and ate lunch. Dumery was included and stuffed himself with cold smoked ham, creamy cheese, hard brown bread, and a thin, watery ale.

It was simple food, but after the near starvation of the last day or two it was absolutely delicious and wonderfully filling.

The break didn't last long, though.

Dumery was pleased to see, when he looked up from his shovel and considered the sun's position an hour or so after that excellent repast, that the river had indeed turned north rather than continuing to the west. Sardiron of the Waters, everyone agreed, lay to the north, and the dragon-hunter was on board a boat bound for Sardiron of the Waters.

Not that Dumery had seen any branches where the *Sunlit Meadows* could have turned aside, or that he thought the crew of the barge had lied to him about where they were going; it was just reassuring to know that the World around him was behaving in a consistent and rational manner and that they hadn't all gone mad or wandered into some demonic netherworld. Being outside the familiar walls of Ethshar was not good for Dumery's peace of mind; he didn't entirely trust the exterior World to stay solid and consistent. The whole experience of gliding along a river had a feeling of unreality to it.

The sun grew steadily less visible as the day wore on; clouds gathered and thickened, but no rain fell that afternoon.

As soon as the barge had pulled over to the side and tied up to a tree for the first night, Dumery and the five crewmen ate a simple, hearty dinner, very similar to their lunch. It wasn't until after they had all finished eating and were settling in for the evening that Dumery got up the courage to ask how long the journey to Sardiron would take.

"Oh, a sixnight or so," the first mate, Kelder the Unpleasant, told him. "Depends on the weather and how well the sylph does. Those things are pretty unpredictable."

"Short of hiring a seer, anyway," Naral Rander's son remarked.

Dumery guessed that the sylph was the almost invisible thing that pulled the barge—all he could see of it by day was an occasional flicker, like the distortion in the air over a hot stove, and now that night had fallen it appeared as a faint filminess, like a wisp of steam. Emboldened, he asked, "Where'd you get the sylph, anyway?"

"Oh, it's not ours," Kelder explained. "The baron who bought this load of cattle has a wizard working for him who sent it along. It's fast. We need to be quick so we can fit enough feed on board; wouldn't want the cattle to starve. The baron likes his meat fat and tender, I guess. Anyway, getting pulled by the sylph is a lot faster than poling upstream, or hiring some sort of tug, or rigging a treadmill and paddle-wheel.''

Naral snorted. "I'd like to see anyone *pole* a loaded cattle barge upstream!'' he said.

Kelder whacked the back of Naral's head, and the conversation degenerated into general insults.

Not long after the crew bedded down for the night, four of the five crawling into the tiny, cramped space under the foredeck—too small to be called a cabin, really—where four narrow berths took up virtually the entire space.

The fifth, Kelder the Unpleasant, took the first watch, sitting quietly on the foredeck.

Dumery was tossed a decaying brown blanket and told he could sleep on the afterdeck, a space about two feet fore and aft and fifteen feet across.

Dumery eyed his assigned bed nervously. There was no railing across the back, only a low coaming, and the prospect of rolling off the barge into the river was unappealing.

His only other option was to bed down under the hooves of the cattle, however, and getting stepped on seemed rather more likely than rolling into the river, and almost equally undesirable. There were other unpleasant aspects to sleeping in the bottom of the barge, too, since Dumery hadn't done any shoveling since just before supper. The planks of the afterdeck were blackened by several years' accumulation of grease and grime, but the bottom of the barge was far worse.

Reluctantly, Dumery climbed up, dismayed by the slimy feel of the planking, and lay down. He pulled the ragged blanket over himself, curled up, and tried to sleep.

Cramped and uncomfortable as he was, dismayed by the hard planking and the smell of cattle, it took time, time he would have spent counting stars had any been visible through the overcast. The outside world seemed all too real, now.

Eventually he dozed off.

His last waking thought was that that was the end of the day's adventures, but he was wrong. He had been asleep no more than half an hour when he began dreaming.

The dream began in an ordinary enough way; he was on Wizard Street, wandering from door to door, looking for someone—but he didn't know who.

At first none of the doors were open, and no one answered his knocking and calling, but then he saw that all the rest of the shop doors *were* open, and he had somehow failed to notice before. He ran up to one and found himself facing Thetheran the Mage.

He didn't want to talk to Thetheran; he turned away and ran to the next door.

Thetheran was there, too.

Again Dumery turned away, and this time Thetheran was there behind him, looming over him. He looked taller and more gaunt than ever.

"Hello, Dumery," the wizard said.

Dumery turned away, and found himself facing another Thetheran.

"Sorry to bother you, lad," this one said, "but your parents are quite worried about you. You went off without a word of warning, and they were concerned for your safety. They hired me to contact you and make sure you're all right."

Dumery turned, and turned, and turned, and Thetheran was always there in front of him.

"I'm fine!" Dumery said angrily. "Go away and leave me alone!"

"Don't worry," Thetheran told him, "your parents only paid me to talk to you, in your dreams, not to bring you home. They just want to know what's become of you. Your mother's very worried."

"I'm fine!" Dumery repeated.

"Well, I'll let you tell her that, then." Thetheran stepped aside, and Dumery saw that the door of the shop on Wizard Street led into the front hall of his home in Shiphaven. "Go on in, she's waiting," Thetheran urged him.

Reluctantly, Dumery obeyed; he stepped into the corridor, and Faléa emerged from the parlor to greet him.

"Dumery!" she said. "Is it really you?"

"It's *me*," Dumery said a little doubtfully, "but is that *you*?"

"Of course it is!" Faléa replied. "Or at least . . . I don't know. I don't understand all this magic. It doesn't matter. All that matters—Dumery, where *are* you?"

"I'm on a cattle barge," Dumery said.

"A what?"

"A cattle barge," he explained. "You know, a big flat-bottomed boat with a lot of cows and steers on it."

"What are you doing *there*?" Faléa demanded.

"Well . . ." Dumery wasn't sure what he wanted to say. For one thing, he wasn't entirely certain whether he was talking to his mother, or Thetheran, or himself. He knew he was dreaming, but he didn't know any way to be sure that it was a magical dream sent by the wizard and not just his own imagination running amok.

And if it was really a magical sending, did that he mean that he was talking to his mother, or to Thetheran? He had no idea how such things worked.

"I'm going to be an apprentice," he said.

His mother blinked at him, startled.

"On a cattle barge?" she asked.

"Well, that's how I'm getting there. I met a man in West-gate Market and arranged to meet him in Sardiron, and I didn't have time to tell you before I had to leave."

The possibility that Thetheran had some mystical means of telling truth from falsehood in this dream occurred to him, a trifle belatedly. If the wizard *did* have such a spell . . .

Well, he wouldn't worry about that.

"What kind of an apprenticeship?" Faléa asked.

Dumery hesitated. "Well, dealing in exotic goods, mostly," he said.

"You need to go to *Sardiron* for that? Couldn't your father have found you something here in Ethshar?"

"I wanted to do it on my own!" Dumery burst out.

"Oh," his mother said. "Oh, well, I suppose . . ." Her voice trailed off, but then she gathered her wits and said, "You be careful! Are you safe? Is everything all right? You tell me about this man!"

Dumery sighed. "I'm fine, Mother," he said. "Really, I am. I'm perfectly safe. I didn't have the fare for the fancy riverboat, so I'm working my way north on a cattle barge, and the crewmen are treating me well, and I have plenty to eat and a good place to sleep." This was not, perhaps, the exact and literal truth, but it was close enough. "I'm going to meet this man in Sardiron and sign on as his apprentice

and I'll send you a letter telling you all about it as soon as
I can.''

"*What* man?" Faléa demanded. "Who is he? What's his
name? Where did you meet him?"

"He didn't tell me his name—he said he wanted to keep
it a secret until I'd earned it." Dumery had considered making up a name, but had caught himself at the last moment; if
and when he really *did* sign up as the dragon-hunter's apprentice, he didn't want to have an awkward lie to explain.
He continued, "I met him at the Dragon's Tail, and he offered me an apprenticeship if I could prove myself by meeting him on . . . on the Blue Docks in Sardiron of the Waters
in a sixnight.''

Dumery hoped that this impromptu lie would hold up—he
had no idea if there *were* any "Blue Docks" in Sardiron, or
whether his mother would know one way or the other. As far
as he knew, she had never been to Sardiron—but he was a bit
startled to realize that he didn't really know much of anything
about her past, even though she was his own mother. *Had* she
ever been to Sardiron?

Either she hadn't, or there really was such a place as the
Blue Docks, because she was somewhat mollified by his tale.

"All right," she said, "but you be careful, and take care of
yourself!"

She turned and was gone; her abrupt disappearance reminded
Dumery that this was all a dream.

He looked about, wondering what would happen next, and
as he did Thetheran stepped out of nowhere.

The mage told Dumery, "Well, lad, I've done what your
parents paid me to do, so I'll let you get on with your regular
night's sleep now. In case you aren't sure this dream is really
a wizard's sending—well, I can't give you any proof, but I
think you'll find you'll remember it more easily and more
clearly than a natural dream. I hope that you'll send a letter if
and when you can and save your parents the expense of doing
this again—I don't particularly enjoy staying up this late working complicated spells just to talk to an inconsiderate young
man who runs off without any warning. Good night, Dumery
of Shiphaven, and I hope your other dreams will be pleasant.''

Then the mage's image popped like a soap bubble and vanished, taking with it the corridor and everything else, and Dumery woke up, to find himself staring stupidly at the hind end of a steer, faintly visible in the diffuse light from the watch-lantern on the foredeck.

# CHAPTER 14

*F*aléa stared at the packed dirt of the street as she walked, shading her eyes from the morning sun. "I don't like it," she said.

"Don't like what?" Doran asked. "Arena Street?"

"No," Faléa replied, without rancor. "I don't like it that Dumery's on that barge—if that's really where he is."

"That's where he *said* he was," Doran pointed out. "Why would he lie?"

"That was where the *dream* said he was, anyway."

Doran looked at his wife, puzzled. "Do you think the wizard was trying to trick you? That there was something wrong with the dream?"

"No," Faléa said, "or maybe. Or . . . I don't know. I just don't like it."

"Well," Doran said, trying to sound determined and cheerful, as if everything were satisfactorily settled, "I can't say I do, either, but if that's what Dumery wants to do . . ."

"But *is* it?" Faléa asked. "There's something wrong here. That man he says he met—who *was* that? Why would he arrange to meet Dumery in Sardiron, instead of accompanying him along the way?"

"I don't know," Doran said. "I suppose to see if the boy can follow instructions and handle himself alone."

"But it's dangerous," Faléa said. "And making the boy do something like that before even starting an apprenticeship, isn't that awfully severe?"

"Well, yes," Doran admitted. "I'd have to say it is."

"And this place he's meeting him in Sardiron, what's it like? Is it safe? Maybe if we knew more about it . . ."

"Well, then, what did the boy *say* about it? You didn't mention that. I've been to Sardiron—remember, when you were pregnant with Derath, and I didn't want to be away too long, so instead of the regular run to Tintallion I went up the river to Sardiron, and it took just as long as Tintallion would have, and I didn't get back until two days before he was born?"

"I remember that," Faléa agreed. "Was that Sardiron? I thought it was Shan."

"No, it was Sardiron. Strange place. Cold. Very damp."

"Oh. Do you know the Blue Docks, then?"

"Blue Docks?" Doran puzzled for a moment, then abruptly stopped walking.

Startled, Faléa stopped, as well.

"There aren't any 'Blue Docks' in Sardiron of the Waters," Doran told her. "The riverfront's not . . . everything's named for the person who owns it, usually Baron somebody-or-other. Are you sure Dumery said 'Blue'?"

"Yes, I'm sure," Faléa said. "Are *you* sure about the names? Or is there a Baron Blue, perhaps? Or a baron who uses blue as his colors?"

"I never heard of any. And you said Dumery was supposed to meet this man there in a sixnight?"

Faléa nodded.

"A sixnight isn't much time to get to Sardiron, either," Doran pointed out. "It took me eleven days; you'd almost need magic to get there from here in a sixnight. Or did he mean a sixnight from where he is now?"

"I don't know," Faléa said, worried.

"There's something wrong here," Doran said.

"Do you think Dumery lied to us?"

"Maybe," Doran said. "Or maybe Thetheran did." He turned and said, "Come on, we're going back."

Together they marched back to Wizard Street.

Thetheran listened to their worries in polite silence. When at last both of them had said all they wished, the mage said, "I assure you, to the best of my knowledge the spell worked perfectly, and if it did, then I did in fact speak to your son

Dumery. If he did lie about where he is and what he's doing, I have no way of knowing—the spell does not force the truth. At least you know that he is alive and well and that he is not in any immediate danger. Had he wanted help, he would have said so; one hardly need worry about being overheard in a dream!"

Doran grumbled an uneasy wordless agreement.

Faléa was not so easily swayed. "I want him back," she said. "*Something* is wrong!"

Thetheran sighed. "Lady," he said, "nothing was wrong with my spell. If you wish to pay an additional fee and stay here again tonight, I can perform the spell again, and you will be free to argue with your son all you like—or at any rate, up to half an hour or so; I doubt I can sustain the contact much longer than that."

"I don't want to just *talk* to him" Faléa snapped. "I want him brought back here!"

"And what does that have to do with me?" Thetheran asked.

"I want you to fetch him!"

Thetheran blinked at her. "Lady," he said, "while I may be able to find a spell that would transport your son back here, consider carefully. It would be very costly, I make no pretenses about that. Furthermore, if your son does indeed have a legitimate appointment in Sardiron of the Waters a few nights from now, fetching him back here would almost certainly cost him the apprenticeship he has gone to so much trouble to arrange. I doubt he would thank you for that."

"Then you can go and find him and see if his story is true and bring him back if it's not!" Faléa shouted.

Thetheran stared at her in astonishment. "Lady," he said, "I sincerely doubt that your husband has enough gold to pay me to do that. If he does have that much, I'm sure he has more sense than to waste it so. I am not interesting in leaving the city. If you're determined to send someone after your son, find someone else."

"You won't do it?"

"Not willingly."

"Why not?"

Exasperated, Thetheran looked at Doran, who merely

shrugged. The mage turned back to Faléa and explained, "I, Lady, am a wizard. I make my living from wizardry, not by traveling hither and yon about the countryside. I have a shop here; if I were to go gallivanting off after your son I would need to close it down for a few days, which would undoubtedly hurt my regular business. Furthermore, there is no telling what sort of hazards I might encounter out there, and I would be hard-pressed to know which spells I would need to prepare and which ingredients I would want to take with me. Wizards do not travel well; we are too dependent upon our books and supplies. Or at least, *I* am. I am not desperate for work; I make a comfortable living here in Ethshar and see no reason to face hardship and danger elsewhere."

Faléa glared at him for a long moment.

"Then you won't go after him and you won't send a spell to fetch him back?"

"Lady, I will do either one if you pay me enough," Thetheran said mildly. "I merely state that I think it would be a very, very bad investment to hire me, in this case. Why don't you go after your boy yourself, or hire someone else to do it? I'm not the only one who has magic for sale that can locate him."

Faléa started to say something, but Doran cut her off.

"The wizard has a point," he said. "If he's not interested, we'll find someone who is. Thetheran, is there anyone you'd recommend?"

Thetheran frowned, considering. "Not offhand," he said. "There are wizards who specialize in information and who could find out exactly what the boy is doing and where he is, but they can be very expensive and they wouldn't be interested in fetching him back if you did decide on that. You might try another school of magic—they aren't *all* charlatans."

Doran nodded. "Is there a theurgist around here?" he asked.

"Dozens of them," Thetheran replied. "And you might also consider a witch—some of them have a knack for finding lost things, I understand. Or a warlock. I'd stay away from sorcerers, though—they make big claims, but half the time their spells don't work. And of course demonology is dangerous, but it might serve, if you want to risk it. I can't see much use for most of the lesser varieties of magic in a case like this . . ."

"We'll try a theurgist," Doran said.

They tried a theurgist. In fact, they tried three theurgists.

Two of them said they could find Dumery; one of them even did so, for a fairly modest fee, and reported that the boy was on a cattle barge on the Great River, a good many leagues northwest of the city.

None of the three, however, was willing to go after the boy, nor to fetch him home by magic.

They tried a warlock next.

She claimed she had no way of finding the boy except to go out looking for him. She was perfectly willing to do that, if they could give her rough directions and would pay her rather exorbitant fee.

Or at least she said she was perfectly willing, right up until they told her about the barge.

"North?" she said. "How far north?"

Faléa and Doran looked at each other.

"We don't know," Doran said. "The theurgist just said it was a long way to the northwest, he didn't say exactly how far."

She looked uneasily about, then down at the ornate carpet that covered most of the floor of her shop.

"I'm sorry," she said, "but I can't go far to the north. It's too . . . well, it's risky, for a warlock."

"Why?" Faléa demanded. "I never heard of anything that made the north any more dangerous than any other direction!"

"You aren't a warlock," the warlock told her. "I don't dare go too near to Aldagmor."

"Why not?" Doran asked. "What's in Aldagmor?"

"I don't know," she said, "but I won't go near it."

Dumery's parents argued for another twenty minutes before they gave up and went elsewhere.

The next shop they tried bore a sign reading "Sella the Witch, Diviner & Seer."

Sella was a smiling, rosy-cheeked woman of fifty or so; Faléa found herself rather resenting the existence of so much bounce and cheerfulness in a woman older than she was. The moment the two of them stepped into the shop, Sella was there, bustling them to a pair of overstuffed chairs and fetching them oversweetened herb tea. They were so caught up in this whirlwind of domesticity that neither of them had time to spare a thought for the thin, sad-looking girl standing in a shadowy corner of the room.

Once Faléa and Doran were seated, and before either of them could get out a word, the witch said, "You're worried about your son? Well, I'm afraid that I can't tell you very much; he's too far away. He's alive, though, and tired, but healthy."

Doran's eyes narrowed with suspicion.

"No, sir, I'm not a fraud," Sella told him. "Your son's name is . . . Dumery, I think? And he ran off to find an apprenticeship, though I can't see the details. You want someone to find out the exact truth of his situation and to bring him safely home if possible. I can't tell you the exact truth; no witch could, at this distance. Nor am I willing to leave the city myself and fetch him home. However, for the appropriate fee, I would be willing to send my apprentice, Teneria of Fishertown, after your boy." She gestured toward the girl in the corner, who managed a weak smile.

Doran hesitated. This was all going too quickly; he had expected to have to explain the situation, negotiate details, and wait while the witch worked her spells—and instead, they had been in the shop scarcely two minutes, and everything seemed to be all but settled.

He didn't like that. It might be witchcraft—or it might be fraud. Sella might have had informants, or as scrying spell, and been watching while Doran and Faléa talked to the other magicians.

Faléa wasn't worried about authenticity; she had another concern.

"An apprentice?" she asked. "A mere apprentice?"

"Almost a journeyman," Sella said, dismissing that worry with a wave of her hand. "She's ready for journeyman status; in fact, she's as good as some master witches. We're merely waiting for her eighteenth birthday, which is still three sixnights off."

"But if she's . . ." Doran began.

"Yes," Sella said wearily, "she's over fifteen, but she

wasn't *ready* at fifteen. We witches make our journeymen at eighteen—or at least, *I* do. I want them to reflect well on me, not just to know a few tricks and fidgets, so I don't let them go until they know all I can teach. And, sir, I see you suspect me of some sort of trickery and I assure you there is none. I worked a spell this morning to see who would come to me and what they would want—it saves a great deal of time and trouble. And a witch, a good one, can read a man's thoughts before they reach his lips.'' She smiled wryly. ''I'm afraid I'm too impatient to wait for your words to work their way from your tongue to my ears.''

Doran considered that, brows lowered. Faléa turned to stare at Teneria.

''He's a little above average in height, for his age,'' Teneria said in a low, soft voice. ''But thin. His hair is black and his eyes brown, like most Ethsharites; when last you saw him his hair was still fairly short, having been cut for his apprenticeship trial with Thetheran, but had gotten a little ragged. He was wearing a green cotton tunic and an expensive pair of boots, boots meant for looks rather than hard wear. He left Westgate Market through the gate around midmorning of the day before yesterday, passing near the south gate tower. I can follow him from there, I think.''

''And the sooner she does, the better,'' Sella said. ''The trail isn't getting any fresher. I have a pack prepared, since I knew you were coming, and Teneria can leave as soon as you pay our fee.''

Doran started to speak, but Sella cut him off. ''One round of gold—yes, it's a lot, but we will refund all but our expenses should Teneria lose his trail or should Dumery be harmed while in her company, and will swear to that before the overlord's officers, if you insist, or register it as a geas with any competent magician. She will leave immediately, if you consent.''

Faléa and Doran looked at each other. Doran saw the look in his wife's eyes and reached for his purse.

Teneria bent down and picked up her pack from the corner. Without a word, she left the shop and headed for Westgate.

# CHAPTER 15

*T*eneria was understandably nervous as she walked out the city gate, her pack on her shoulder. This expedition was, she knew, the final trial of her apprenticeship. If she succeeded, if she found the boy and either brought him home safely or saw that he reached his destination and was safe there, then she would be a real witch, entitled to call himself Teneria the Witch if she chose, free to travel when and where she pleased, no longer at Sella's beck and call—not that Sella was a harsh mistress, or unpleasant to work for, but any sort of servitude chafed.

If she failed she would need to prove herself all over again. She would still be a mere apprentice.

And as if that wasn't enough to worry about, this was very nearly the first time she had ever left the city alone. Oh, once before she had been sent to fetch herbs from outside the walls, alone, at night—but she had always stayed in sight of the gate, Southgate it was that time, and she had known that Sella was watching over her from afar.

This time, Sella would not be watching—at least, not once she had gone a few leagues. Her range was limited.

Teneria's own range was even more limited, of course; she could barely make out a person's aura just a few blocks away, let alone all the way across the city. The Wizards' Quarter— which really *ought* to be called the Magicians' Quarter, she thought for the thousandth time, and probably would have been if not for the political power of the Wizards' Guild—was in the southeastern part of Ethshar of the Spices, a long way from Westgate.

Her native Fishertown was on the waterfront to the north, just to the east of the Grand Canal, and as a child she had roamed through Hempfield and Allston and Newmarket, but she had never been in Westgate before. Even so, she was too concerned with the task before her to pay much attention as she passed through the district and out the gate.

She did spare a glance around at the farmers' wagons along the roadside and the fields beyond, before she turned her attention inward, looking for the psychic trace her quarry must surely have left.

It wasn't easy. There were so *many* traces here! A young woman, a farm girl about Teneria's own age, had passed by here recently in a turmoil about an unwanted and unexpected pregnancy. An older farmer had been worried about his debts, hoping he could hold out until the harvest—and that the harvest wouldn't fail this year, as it had last. Thoughts of money, loneliness, worry, love, greed, excitement, anticipation, despair—this was such a *busy* stretch of highway!

She couldn't find Dumery's.

She wasn't really very surprised; after all, it had been more than two days since he had passed this way, and she had never even met the boy. She doubted even Sella could have tracked Dumery from his traces alone.

Fortunately, that wasn't necessary. Sella had read everything she needed from the minds of Dumery's parents or from Thetheran, or had heard it, and had passed it on to Teneria. All of them had been thinking about nothing else, which made it easy enough to see the needed information.

Teneria smiled to himself. Witchcraft had its advantages. It didn't have the raw power that *any* of the other major magicks had, only the strength of the witch's own body, but she had never heard of any wizard or warlock who could do to people's minds what witches could. And it was so easy, really, once one knew how.

She still remembered how, when she was thirteen and still just beginning her apprenticeship, she had first used the witch's trick of convincing someone to do what she wanted without him even knowing that magic was in use. She had gotten credit from a notoriously stingy candy butcher on Games Street.

She had also overdone it, not realizing how easy it was. She had exhausted herself, pushing at his mind, and had almost collapsed right there on the street. When she had finally made it back to Sella's shop she had fallen into bed and slept for a day and a half—and only found out later that the candy-seller had been so affected that he was giving credit and free samples to every kid in sight for the next sixnight.

And when it wore off, it gradually sank in that he had been the victim of a witch's spell, and Sella had had to use her *own* persuasive magic on him to prevent retaliation.

Teneria had watched and had seen how subtly it was done.

She had also, even at that age, seen the hurt and confusion in the candy-seller's mind and had felt horribly guilty for the next four months. She saved up what she could and finally paid the man back for his losses—but that still didn't entirely re- move the pain.

When people wondered why some witches were so adamant in their refusal to work harmful magic, no matter how much they were paid, Teneria always remembered the empty candy basket and the baffled expression of the man holding it, the puzzled discomfort of his aura. It wasn't worth it. Better to just persuade people to go elsewhere for their curses and assassinations—or better still, to persuade them to give them up entirely.

Some witches weren't so sensitive; some had even gotten involved in some of the petty wars that were a permanent feature of the Small Kingdoms. There were even stories about witches helping the Great Warlock establish the Empire of Vond, a few years back.

Teneria didn't understand how they could do that.

Finding a runaway, though—that should be no problem. And once found, it would be easy enough to learn his true situation; no one could lie successfully to a witch.

It was unfortunate, though, that he had a two-day head start. She picked up her pace a little.

She could levitate, she thought, but there wasn't any point in it. She would just wear herself out. Levitating would be like carrying her ninety-four pounds over her head; walking was far easier, and almost as fast.

And she didn't need to worry about following his trail, not

yet; Sella had seen in Faléa's mind that Sander the Theurgist had located Dumery of Shiphaven somewhere on the Great River, and a check of Sander's mind had confirmed as much, so Teneria knew she had to get to the river. There was only one road from Ethshar to the river.

She could have gone by sea, of course, and would have preferred to, but Faléa and Doran expected her to follow their son's path exactly, so that was what she was attempting to do.

It was well after dark, and she was nearing exhaustion, when she knocked on the door of the Inn at the Bridge.

The man who opened the door, Teneria knew immediately, was the innkeeper, Valder himself—she could sense in him the presence of someone far, far older than he looked, and she knew that Valder the Innkeeper, also known as Valder of the Magic Sword, had been enchanted long ago.

He helped her to a table and had food and drink fetched.

She didn't need to say a word, nor to even begin to frame a spell; Valder was well versed in handling weary travelers.

He did pause, though, just before putting her dinner on the table.

"You do have money, don't you?" he asked.

She nodded; he smiled and placed the platter before her.

She slept that night in a warm feather bed, too tired to worry about where Dumery might be, or for that matter much of anything else.

At breakfast, however, she pursued her mission and asked Valder if he remembered seeing a boy of Dumery's description.

He cocked his head and gazed at her warily, and she began to prepare a small coercion spell.

"Why do you ask?" he said.

"His parents hired me to find him," she said.

Valder looked at her for another moment, then shrugged.

"He was here," he said. "The night before last. He looked pretty bad, dirty and frazzled. He didn't have any money, but I let him sleep in the stable and gave him a bowl of scraps. He looked harmless enough."

"So he stayed here all night? In the stable?"

"As far as I know, he did," Valder said. "I didn't see him

in the morning. And I'm not sure how much he ate; there were spriggan tracks all over the bowl I'd left him.''

"Spriggan tracks?"

"That's right."

"Excuse me, but what's a spriggan?"

Valder looked startled. "You haven't met them yet? Well, maybe you haven't. We've had them here for months now; they hide in people's baggage, and on wagons.''

"But what *are* they?" Teneria asked.

"Little creatures about so high," Valder said, holding his hands out to demonstrate. "They look like frogs trying to be human, sort of, with big pointed ears, and they talk, after a fashion. And they get into everything and make real nuisances of themselves. They come from somewhere in the mountains in the Small Kingdoms, I'm told, and the rumor is that they came about from some wizard's spell gone wrong, four or five years ago. No one knows how many there are, or how long they live, or how they breed—*if* they breed. They like to play games, though, and they're always hungry—when one turns up I need to warn the guests and keep a careful eye out, or it'll be stealing food right off customers' plates.''

Teneria was fascinated. "I never heard of anything like that," she said. "How do you get rid of them?"

Valder frowned. "Well, you can kill them, of course—they aren't *that* magical. Run one through with a steel blade and it'll die, just like anything else. I hate to do that, though—the creatures don't really mean any harm. When I can, I just catch them and throw them outside and tell them not to come back, and usually they don't. Most of the time they'll wander off down the road somewhere. Sometimes if there's a whole gang of them—we had six at a time, once—they'll work up their courage and try to slip back in, and I'll have to get more drastic.''

"More drastic?" Teneria asked. "How? Magic?"

"No, they're not worth wasting magic on."

"What, then?"

Valder looked around as if slightly embarrassed, then leaned forward and whispered, "I get them drunk."

Teneria smiled. "You do?"

"I do. It was my wife's idea. I put out a bowl of brandy or

*oushka* with cherry syrup in it—they love cherry syrup—and wait. Sooner or later they'll drink it, and when they do they pass out drunk on the floor—can't hold their liquor at all, not even as well as a Tintallionese. And they wake up with hangovers. All I need to do is pick them up while they're unconscious and dump them out by the highway, and when they wake up they're too sick to *want* to come back."

"Always? None of them develop a taste for the stuff?"

"Well," Valder said, "none have so far, anyway."

"Are there any around now?" Teneria asked, looking about at the inn's main room. "I'd like to see one."

"I haven't seen any lately, but as I said, there were spriggan tracks in the boy's bowl."

Teneria nodded. "Thank you," she said. "You've been very helpful."

She settled her bill, picked up her pack, and left the inn.

Outside she paused and looked about. From this point on, Dumery had had a choice of ways. He could have crossed the bridge to the east bank, or headed up the highway on the west bank, or gone down to the dock and boarded a boat right there.

If he was on a cattle barge by his second night away from home, boarding right there seemed most likely. It also *felt* right. She wasn't sure if it was witchcraft causing her hunch, or common sense, or nothing at all, but she decided to trust it. She headed for the dock.

As she walked, she thought about spriggans. She hadn't heard of them before, at least not by that name.

One of them had gotten at Dumery's food; did that mean anything?

Maybe it did—and if that spriggan was still around maybe she could learn something from it.

That was an idea. She stepped off the path onto the green, lush grass of early spring, and settled down, cross-legged, her skirt spread around her. She rested her hands on her knees and filled her mind with thoughts of warmth and affection, good food and soft fur and friendly smiles; she held those thoughts while she watched the sunlight dancing on the river, projecting them in all directions at once.

A fieldmouse wandered up, walked onto her skirt, curled up,

and fell asleep. A rat eyed her warily but didn't approach—which was just as well, as she didn't like rats.

Some of the people down on the dock were starting to glance in her direction; she realized she was radiating a little *too* much warmth.

Then the grass rustled behind her, and she turned to see a peculiar little figure, seven or eight inches tall, standing there. It was green and had spindly little legs and an immense belly, which did give it a froglike appearance, but its feet and hands were not webbed, and its oversize head was fairly human in appearance, if one ignored the big pointed ears and complete lack of hair.

"Hello," she said quietly, trying not to startle it.

"Hello, hello!" it said back, in a squeaky, rather irritating voice that was not quiet at all. "You like spriggans?"

"Yes, I do," she said.

"We have fun?"

"If you like."

"We have *fun*!" it replied emphatically.

"All right," Teneria agreed, "we'll have fun. But I'm looking for a friend of mine first. We could have more fun if we found him. Maybe you can help."

"Friend?" The spriggan looked puzzled.

"Yes, a friend. His name is Dumery of Shiphaven. He slept in the stable up at the inn there the night before last—a half-grown boy with black hair and brown eyes. Did you see him?"

"Saw him, saw him," the spriggan said, bouncing up and down as it spoke. "No fun. No fun at all. Went on boat, went away."

"On a boat?"

"Cow boat, went that way." The spriggan pointed at the river, then waved a hand in a vaguely upstream direction.

"I see," Teneria said. "Then I'm afraid I'll have to go after him."

The spriggan looked suddenly crestfallen, and Teneria had to smother a laugh even as she wanted to cry at the thing's misery. "You go, too?" it asked.

"Yes," Teneria said. "But we can have fun when I get back." She smiled.

The spriggan didn't care. "You go?" it asked, its voice cracking. "Got to? Can't stay?"

Teneria couldn't stand it; the thing was *so* woebegone that her witchcraft-heightened senses could not face it. Besides, she realized that she had a use for the little creature, a very important use. It had seen Dumery and had probably talked to him. Stupid as it appeared to be, it might provide a psychic link that she could use.

"Listen," she said, "I could take you with me."

"Go with you?" The spriggan's woe vanished. "Ooooooh, fun!" it burbled. "Go, go! Yes, yes, go!" The change was overwhelming; black despair had transformed instantly into golden delight. Teneria burst out giggling.

"Yes, go," she said. "Come on; we'll hire a boat."

# CHAPTER 16

*B*y his third day on the barge Dumery no longer noticed the smell as he worked, nor the stickiness. His feet still hurt, and his back ached, but he was able to do his work without giving it much of his attention, which left him free to admire the scenery—what he could see of it. Most of the time the grassy banks were too high for him to see much of anything from his place down in the bottom of the barge.

Sometimes, though, the river spread out a little, or the land flattened, and he could see farms and fields, pleasant little villages, and, on the western bank, traffic along the highway that paralleled the river. People on foot, ox carts, even full-size caravans passed along that road, bound upstream and down.

Since the barge stayed mostly toward the eastern shore Dumery could make out none of the details of these fascinating figures; the wagons were squares of bright color and the people like walking twigs.

Docks were a frequent sight along the river, even where the

banks were high. Some were no more than rotting remnants, while others were large and clean and relatively fresh. Some, Dumery could see, were there to service villages, and those might be individual docks or entire rows of them; others seemed to be alone, out in the middle of nowhere, perhaps serving local farmers or fishermen.

Trails down to the riverbank, where livestock could come and drink, were also commonplace, and every so often one of these would be in use by cattle. The herd on the barge and the herd on the shore were likely to start lowing on such occasions, calling to one another, and Dumery would have to watch carefully for the stamping hooves of the disturbed animals.

There was traffic on the river, as well, of course—boats and barges of every description, from flat-bottomed fishing skiffs that drifted idly by the banks to sharp-prowed express boats that plowed past Dumery's barge as if it were motionless, leaving behind a wake that thumped rhythmically across the barge's underside.

And as if these sights weren't enough, every so often, starting late on the third day, the barge passed a castle, the stone towers and walls brooding heavily over the countryside. Dumery assumed, when he saw the first castle and finally figured out what it was, that the barge must have left the Hegemony of the Three Ethshars, where by the unanimous decree of the ruling triumvirate no castles or other fortifications were permitted outside the walls of the three capital cities.

Dumery decided, however, when he had had a bit more time and had thought the matter over a little more, that although they were at least very near the border, they might not have actually crossed it. He noticed that the castles were always on the east bank of the river, and always set well back from the water. Perhaps the west bank and the river itself were still in the Hegemony.

This came to seem more likely not long after, when the river's curves found them traveling west again, rather than north. The "east bank" was now on the north, the "west" on the south—that meant the occasional castle was to the north.

Sardiron lay to the north of the Hegemony, as everyone knew. This stretch of river, Dumery thought, made a perfectly reasonable border.

He was encouraged by this. He was eager to get to Sardiron and catch up with the man in brown, but on the other hand there was something rather frightening about leaving the Hegemony, and he preferred to put it off as long as possible.

And the third day passed.

That evening, when the sun was down, the barge was tied up to a tree. Each evening it had been tied up to a tree or a rock. Even when two of the crewmen had waded ashore to buy more provisions, a mere hundred yards from a village pier, the barge's tow-line was secured not to the pier or a dock but to a great oak. It was on the third night that Dumery finally got up the nerve to ask why they never used the docks.

"Trees don't charge fees," Kelder told him.

It was around midmorning of the fourth day that the barge passed under a bridge, the first bridge they had encountered since Dumery came aboard. The whole structure was built of wood, raised into a great arch above elaborate framework, and the central opening was easily wide enough for two barges to pass—though in fact there didn't happen to be another in sight just then.

The roadbed across the bridge, Dumery judged, was wide enough for a wagon—but just barely. He wondered what happened if wagons arrived from both ends at once; how did they decide who would wait while the other crossed?

He was so interested in the bridge that they were well out into the lake beyond before he realized there *was* a lake.

Dumery had never seen a lake before and he stared. It was so *flat*! Large bodies of water didn't bother him, but he was used to Ethshar's harbor, where the water was in constant motion, waves rippling in from the Gulf and breaking against the piers and quays. Even the river, while it had no waves, had a visible current.

The lake, though, appeared as calm and still as a puddle.

The barge was hugging the right-hand shore—what Dumery thought of as the eastern bank, though in fact at the moment it was still to the north. After a few moments of staring out at the open expanse of water, Dumery turned and saw that they were passing a dozen yards or so from a stone tower.

He blinked in surprise and looked more closely.

They were passing a castle, a castle built right on the shore of the lake!

*Hai*,'' Dumery called, ''where are we?''

Naral Rander's son looked up.

''Take a good look, boy,'' he replied. ''We've just crossed the border. Welcomer to the Baronies of Sardiron!''

''We have?'' Dumery asked.

''That's right; the boundary runs across the middle of this lake—Boundary Lake—from that tower, which is Sardironese, to one on the other side, which is Ethsharitic. From here on we'll be on Sardironese waters—up until now the river was Ethsharitic.''

''Oh,'' Dumery said, looking about uneasily, half expecting to see some difference in the water itself.

There was none; it was still clear and blue.

''There's a third tower over on the western shore,'' Naral remarked, ''between the two rivers that flow into the lake— that's Sardironese, too. The Baronies claim both the rivers going in, the Hegemony has the one going out.''

''*Two* rivers coming in?'' Dumery asked, suddenly seriously worried.

''Certainly,'' Naral said, startled by the question. ''The Great River and the Shanna River.''

''Which one are we taking?'' Dumery asked.

''The Great River, of course,'' the crewman said. ''We told you when you came aboard, we're bound for Sardiron of the Waters.''

''And the Shanna River doesn't go there?''

''No, of course not—it goes to Shanna.'' Naral considered for a moment, then continued. ''Or really, it comes *from* Shanna, since we're downstream here. Not much business out that way, and the river's not easy to navigate, either—it's wider and slower and shallower, and you can run a boat aground if you aren't careful. Even a barge.''

Dumery had stopped listening. He had panicked at the thought that maybe the boat he was on was going to take one route, while the *Sunlit Meadows* took the other, and he would *never* have a chance of catching up with the man in brown.

He was calming down now, though. The *Sunlit Meadows*

was bound for Sardiron of the Waters; the crewman who chased him off had stated that quite definitely. The barge, too, was bound for Sardiron of the Waters. Neither one had any business in Shanna. There was nothing to worry about.

He looked around and realized that they were already approaching the western end of the lake—he could see trees and something that might have been the roof of the other Sardironese tower, beyond the water in that direction.

An hour later they had left the lake behind and were into the Upper Reach of the Great River, inside the borders of the Baronies of Sardiron.

Not long after that they passed under another high-arched wooden bridge; this one was guarded by a castle on the western shore, just in case anyone had had any lingering doubts as to whether this land was truly a part of the Baronies.

The change of government made little difference; the barge still passed farms and fields, trees and villages, and docks new and used. The river was still blue, the sky was still blue, and Dumery still had shoveling to do.

It was late in the afternoon of the fifth day when he glanced up from his shovel, to the east, and saw a familiar boat, tied up at a dock that the barge was passing.

It was the *Sunlit Meadows*, gleaming bright in the sun. He had finally caught up to it.

He looked around, but saw only the cattle and the river and the blue sky above. He wished he could swim; the shore wasn't so very far away.

Unfortunately, he couldn't, and trying to get ashore wasn't worth the risk of drowning.

He waited, biding his time, growing steadily more frantic with the thought that even now, the man in brown might be getting farther away—and even if the man was still on that boat, Dumery himself was now moving steadily farther away from it.

The possibility that the dragon-hunter had gotten off the *Sunlit Meadows* days ago hadn't escaped him, but he tried not to think about that. At least, if he could catch up to the crew of the passenger boat, he could *ask*.

For a moment he considered simply asking the crew of the

barge to put him ashore somewhere along the eastern bank, but he couldn't bring himself to do it. He had signed on for the journey to Sardiron of the Waters and he knew that the men were glad to have him there to man the shovel; they weren't likely to let him off that easily.

Particularly not Kelder the Unpleasant, whose goal in life seemed to be to make everyone else miserable. So far he hadn't bothered Dumery much, since the job Dumery had was already about the worst thing that could be inflicted aboard the barge without interfering with business, but the boy didn't doubt for a moment that if Kelder knew Dumery wanted off, he'd make absolutely certain that Dumery stayed on the barge.

So Dumery waited, not saying anything about his plans.

Finally, as the sun dropped below the western horizon, the crew called to the sylph. That seemingly tireless creature obeyed, looping the tow-line around a stump on the steep eastern bank.

Dumery breathed a little easier upon seeing that; he had worried about what he would do if they had tied up on the *western* shore.

Not that they ever had yet.

The remainder of the day was torture. He didn't dare try to slip away until most of the barge's crew was asleep and until the man on watch was someone he wasn't scared of.

The evening repast and the subsequent chatter seemed interminable, but eventually the men were yawning and stretching and climbing into their narrow little bunks below the foredeck.

Kelder took the first watch, unfortunately, and Dumery lay on his own rough perch at the stern, wrapped in his borrowed blanket, trying to stay awake without letting Kelder know it.

He had dozed off, but started awake at the sound of voices. Kelder was rousing Naral for his shift.

Dumery tensed, but lay still.

He heard Naral complaining about having a particularly pleasant dream interrupted, and Kelder snarling that he was too tired to care, and then, over the steady breathing of the sleeping cattle, he heard scuffling and scraping as Kelder climbed into a berth.

Naral's footsteps sounded as he climbed up to the foredeck and settled onto the stool there. Dumery lifted his head and peered across the length of the barge, over the cargo.

Naral was sitting on the foredeck, yawning and rubbing his eyes.

Dumery slipped out from under his blanket and crept over toward shore.

The barge was tied at the bow, and the stern had been left to drift until it bumped gently against the bank. Dumery knew that in the morning, if the sylph could not tug the barge away because it had snagged or run aground, the cattle would all be herded over to the left—rather, portside, though in fact the barge usually tied up along the starboard—and the barge would be rocked free.

He reached the starboard corner of the stern and got to his feet, casting a cautious glance toward Naral.

The man hadn't noticed anything. If he did happen to look, he would probably just assume Dumery was answering nature's call.

Dumery looked down; the barge was not hard up against the bank. A couple of feet of dark water, catching occasional flecks of light from the greater moon that rode high overhead, swirled along between the hull and the grass.

He reached out, but he couldn't touch the bank.

It had looked vertical, but it wasn't. Really, it sloped away. Dumery glared at it.

He took three steps back, then ran and jumped.

His hands and knees hit the bank, and he discovered that it isn't easy to grab hold of a steep, grassy, dew-covered slope; he slid down until his feet and legs were in the chill water of the river, almost up to his knees.

Naral, Dumery was sure, must have heard the noise. He lay there on the bank, his feet in the water, waiting to see what Naral would do, whether he would come to investigate.

No one came, and after what seemed like hours Dumery turned his attention to climbing.

It could be done, by digging his toes into the sod with each step and wrapping his fingers tightly around the strongest tufts of grass, sometimes inadvertently pulling them out and jamming his fingers into the holes they left.

He began to worry about whether he would reach the top before dawn, but the night seemed to go on forever, and by the time he was finally able to stretch his arms out full-length onto nearly level ground and pull himself up onto his feet he was more concerned with whether the dawn would ever come at all. Had the sun burned out, was it gone forever? Surely it had taken him *years* to climb that slope!

Everything looked normal enough, though. He was at the edge of a farmer's field and had to climb over a split-rail fence.

Once inside the field he looked up at the stars and moons, then back at the still-dark eastern horizon, and decided the sun was just late. The lesser moon had just risen in the east, almost full, while off to the west the greater moon was still in the sky, a broad crescent, horns upward, like the smile of a small god looking down at him.

Something looked odd about the east, though, and Dumery looked again.

The horizon was in the wrong place. It was too high. The lesser moon's light gleamed pinkly on hilltops that seemed to be halfway up the sky.

The hilltops looked awfully steep and pointed, too.

Mountains, Dumery realized suddenly. Those were mountains. He was looking at mountains.

There were no mountains anywhere in the Hegemony of Ethshar, any more than there were castles. A shudder ran through Dumery at the thought that he had, beyond all doubt, left behind the only civilized land in the World.

He was truly in the Baronies of Sardiron, the cold, wild northern land, where the evil taint of the ancient Empire still lingered, where the people had deliberately turned their backs on Ethsharitic civilization, choosing chaos and brutality over order and sanity. Castles and sorcerers, stone and snow and fire—that's what those mountains promised.

He shuddered.

Then he grimaced wryly. The mountains might be alien and frightening, but they weren't the real problem. The real problem was mostly that his feet were wet. *That*, he told himself, was why he was shuddering. He needed to get warm and dry.

A glance at the dark farmhouse in the distance was not

encouraging. Visitors arriving in the middle of the night were not likely to be made welcome there.

Walking would dry his feet and warm him. He stepped up onto the bottom rail of the fence and peered back over the bank he had just climbed, back down at the river.

The barge was still there, and Naral was still perched on his stool on the foredeck. He appeared to be asleep.

Sleeping on watch, if discovered—well, Dumery didn't know just what that would entail, since he had never been trusted enough to be put on watch, but he was sure it wouldn't be pleasant.

Maybe Naral would replace Dumery in wielding the shovel. Somebody would have to, certainly.

Well, whatever happened to him, it wasn't Dumery's problem. He hopped down, turned left, and began walking downstream, toward the dock where the *Sunlit Meadows* had tied up.

# CHAPTER 17

*R*iverbanks, *Dumery discovered, are not highways.*

Riverbanks, he found, can be slippery, boggy, overgrown, leech-infested, mosquito-infested, strewn with sharp rocks and day-old manure, and generally hard to traverse. They can have fences blocking access to them. They can even have rabbit snares on them that wrap around your ankle and feel as if they're going to rip your foot right off, which you have to remove slowly and carefully, in the dark, while sitting on cold, wet mud.

All the same, the sun still hadn't cleared the mountaintops when Dumery, filthy and exhausted but still determined, finally reached the inn and dock where the *Sunlit Meadows* had tied up for the night.

He identified it as the right dock by the simplest possible method: The *Sunlit Meadows* was still there, its distinctive outline recognizable even in the faint light of approaching dawn, augmented by the lesser moon, which had crossed the sky, set, and was now rising again, a thin bow this time.

In the dimness the upraised sweeps looked more like an insect's legs than ever.

This stretch of waterfront was clear and level and easy to walk. A set of wooden steps led down to the dock; at the top of the steps a plank walk led to the verandah of a good-size inn. Beyond the inn was a small village, a handful of houses and shops along either side of a single street leading up the slope, away from the water.

Dumery knew the big building by the river was an inn because a signboard hung over the verandah showing a brown pig on a black spit, with a jagged orange border below that was clearly intended to represent a cooking fire. He could see the colors because lanterns hung to either side of the sign, both of them burning.

He found himself faced with a difficult decision. Should be approach the inn, where the man in brown might be staying, or should he go down to the boat?

After some thought, he chose the boat.

He tripped and very nearly fell on the top step, which would have made for a noisy and painful tumble, but he caught himself at the last minute and made his way gingerly down to the dock.

When he stepped off the last step and could spare attention to look at something other than his own feet, he looked up and found he was being watched.

A guard had been posted on the *Sunlit Meadows*, just as on the cattle barge—a man was sitting on a stool on the foredeck, a sword across his lap. He was staring at Dumery.

"Uh . . . hello," Dumery said. He spoke loudly enough to be heard over the chirping crickets and the gentle splashing of the river going about its business. He was horrified at how loud his voice sounded. The crickets and water weren't making anywhere near as much noise as he had thought; his normal tone sounded like shouting.

"Hello," the watchman answered warily.

Dumery strolled down the dock, trying to look casual. "I was looking for someone," he said. "I saw him on that boat of yours a few days ago."

"Oh?" the watchman asked.

"Yes," Dumery said. "Big man, dark brown hair, wore brown leather, came aboard at Azrad's Bridge."

"I might know who you mean." For the first time, Dumery noticed that the guard spoke Ethsharitic with an accent.

"Yes, well," Dumery said, "I'm looking for him. I need to talk to him."

The watchman's hand had crept to the hilt of the sword; now he lifted it and gestured at the eastern sky. "Odd hour to go visiting, isn't it?" he asked.

"Oh, well," Dumery said, "I didn't want him to slip away before I had a chance to talk to him, you know."

"Ah. In a hurry, were you?"

Dumery nodded. "Yes, I was," he said.

"In too much of a hurry to clean up?"

Dumery looked down at himself.

His tunic was muddy rags. His breeches were split at the crotch and frayed to threads for much of their length, and his skin was covered with scrapes, scratches, and dirt. His boots were badly scuffed, but still, thank all the gods, sound.

"I missed the road in the dark," he explained. "Fell down a couple of times."

"Well, boy," the guard told him, "I'm sorry, but you're not coming aboard the *Meadows* like that and I don't care if you're a boy baron in disguise or one of the gods themselves."

"He's on board, then?" Dumery asked excitedly. "The man in brown leather? The dragon-hunter?"

The watchman squinted at Dumery. The eastern sky had started to pale; the greater moon had set, but the lesser moon was climbing rapidly, filling out as it rose. A ship's lantern hung at each end of the *Sunlit Meadows*, shining brightly. In short, there was light, but not enough to read faces easily.

The watchman decided it wasn't his problem. "The man's name is Kensher Kinner's son, boy—that the one you're looking for? Anyway no, he's not aboard. He's probably at the Roasting Pig. This is his stop, where we pick him up twice a year and drop him off on the way back."

A great weight he hadn't known was there seemed to vanish from Dumery's chest, and his breath rushed in, then out, in a great sigh of relief. "*Thank* you!" he said. "Then I *haven't* missed him!" He whirled and charged back up the steps, ignoring the watchman's shouted admonitions to watch his step and not to say who'd told him.

He even knew the man in brown's name now—Kensher Kinner's son. Not exactly an ordinary name, by Ethsharitic standards, but not particularly exotic. Dumery had a vague impression that Northerners used patronymic names like that more than city dwellers did.

He dashed headlong up the boardwalk and onto the verandah and smacked his hands against the door of the inn, expecting it to open.

It didn't. His damp feet slipped on the oiled wood of the verandah, and his nose and chin slammed up against solid oak hard enough to bruise, but not to break anything.

He caught himself and stepped back, rubbing his injured nose, then reached forward and tried the latch.

The door still wouldn't open.

Dumery frowned. Who ever heard of an inn where the door wouldn't open? What good was *that* to anyone?

Well, maybe the owners were worried about bandits wandering in. After all, this wasn't Ethshar. Dumery looked about for a knocker or bellpull.

A black metal rod hung down just behind the signboard; he hadn't noticed it before, taking it for a shadow or part of the bracket holding the sign. The upper end vanished into a boxy structure protruding from the wall.

He reached up and gave it a tug.

It moved freely, and when he released it it swung back up into place—obviously counterweighted somewhere. He wasn't sure whether he heard a clunk somewhere when he let it go, or not.

An unfamiliar voice, oddly hollow, called, "*Ie'kh gamakh.*"

Dumery blinked. That wasn't Ethsharitic.

It was probably, he realized suddenly, Sardironese. He was presumably somewhere in the Baronies of Sardiron, so that would make sense.

Unfortunately, Dumery didn't know a word of Sardironese and couldn't begin to guess whether the phrase he had just heard meant, "Welcome," or "Go away," or "Give the password," or "The key's on the windowsill," or something else entirely.

"I don't speak Sardironese," he called—not too loudly, as he didn't want to annoy anyone.

Nobody answered.

He stood there, looking about and trying to think what he should do, until he was startled by a scraping sound.

He spun back toward the door, and there, an inch or two above the top of his head, a panel the size of a man's hand had slid open. Bleary green eyes beneath bushy white eyebrows were looking out, and from what he could see of them, Dumery thought they looked puzzled.

"Hello," Dumery said.

The eyes blinked and looked down, suddenly discovering Dumery.

"Hello?" a voice answered, the voice of an old man.

"May I come in?" Dumery asked.

The voice replied, "*H'kai debrou . . . ie'tshei*, yes, one moment." The panel slid shut, metal rattled against metal, and the door swung open.

Dumery stepped in and looked around, to see what he could see, and discovered that mostly he could see the starched white apron and voluminous red nightshirt of the man who had admitted him. That worthy was standing in Dumery's way, looking down at him with an unreadable expression on his face.

"By all the gods, boy, you are a . . . a *mess*!" the man exclaimed.

Dumery was relieved to hear the man deliver a complete, coherent sentence in Ethsharitic, even if it *was* accented.

But then, an innkeeper would naturally want to speak several languages.

"I'm looking for a man dressed in brown leather, going by the name Kensher Kinner's son," Dumery said.

"He is—*ie'tshei*, is he expecting you?"

"He's yetchy?"

"No, no. Is he expecting you?"

"Is he here?"

"I am . . . *ie'tshei*, why should I tell you?"

Dumery was tired. He was, in fact, exhausted, and as a result he was in no mood to deal with obstructions when he was so close to his goal. "Just tell me, all right?" he said. "And what's that 'yetchy' mean, anyway?"

The man glared down at him fiercely, and Dumery realized he'd said the wrong thing.

"*Ie'tshei* is Sardironese for 'I meant to say,' boy," the man said. "You don't make fun of my Ethsharitic, all right? You want to hear me use all the right words, you talk to me in Sardironese. We aren't in the Hegemony here. Since I was your age, I could speak four languages enough to run this inn. I don't hear you saying anything in anything but Ethsharitic. You don't sound so smart to me, boy, so watch your manners."

"I'm sorry," Dumery said, not really meaning it.

The innkeeper ignored the interruption. "You come in here an hour before dawn, when I need my sleep, you drip mud on my floors and look like the worst garbage, like someone who takes what the dogs won't eat, you don't say who you are, you make fun of how I talk in a foreign language when I'm half asleep, you want to talk to one of my guests who is *also* still asleep, assuming he's here, which I haven't said . . . boy, you better have the money to pay for a room and a bath and a meal and new clothes, because if you don't you go right back out that door. I don't want you in here like this. You make me look bad."

"I'm sorry," Dumery said again, a little more sincerely.

"Sorry, nothing. You have money?"

Dumery looked down at the purse on his belt. Six bits, he knew, wasn't going to buy him much here. It certainly wasn't going to buy him any sympathy, let alone new clothes and all the rest of it.

The innkeeper saw Dumery's look and interpreted it readily enough.

"No money," he said. "Out, boy. Out." The man put a hand on Dumery's chest and pushed gently.

Until he felt that hand it hadn't really registered with the lad just how big the innkeeper was, which was very big indeed. Dumery doubted very much that this particular innkeeper had ever had to hire anyone else as his bouncer; he was clearly capable of handling the job himself.

Unwillingly, Dumery stepped back out onto the verandah, and the heavy door slammed shut an inch from his face.

# CHAPTER 18

*D*espite the discomforts of his hiding place in the bushes along the river bank, Dumery kept dozing off, waking only when he started to fall forward, branches scraping his face.

Each time he would jerk himself back up to a sitting position and stare wildly about before settling back down to watch the door of the inn.

Finally, about midmorning, the man in brown, the dragon-hunter, emerged. He was wearing his brown leather outfit again, not the more ordinary clothes he had on when he had left the Inn at the Bridge and boarded the *Sunlit Meadows*.

He stepped out, turned to his right, and marched across the verandah to the steps at the north end. He trotted down the steps without any hesitation, turned again, and strode off to the east, down the main road of the tiny riverside village, away from the inn and toward the mountains.

Dumery scrambled from concealment and followed.

He had had enough of secrecy. He had every intention of running right up to this Kensher person and announcing himself, then demanding an apprenticeship. After all, Dumery had followed the man all the way from safe, familiar Ethshar out into the wilds of Sardiron—didn't that prove his resolution? Didn't that show how determined he was? Wouldn't that be enough to impress *anyone*?

Dumery tripped over a branch and fell sprawling. He picked himself up quickly and looked ahead.

Kensher was already well down the road, almost out the far end of the village—if the tiny collection of buildings qualified as a village; being a city boy, Dumery was not sure just how small a village could get and still deserve the name.

The dragon-hunter was walking along quickly, in the brisk, determined stride of a man who knows exactly where he's going and who wants to get there. Dumery broke into a run.

Tired as he was, he couldn't sustain it, and after a hundred feet, when he was scarcely past the inn's stables, he slowed to a stumbling trot. Halfway through the village, as he passed through the rush of warm air from the smithy, that became a walk.

Well, Dumery told himself, he'd catch up eventually. The man would have to stop and rest sometime.

Stopping to rest sounded like an absolutely wonderful idea, but he knew he didn't dare to do that.

But maybe just a *minute* wouldn't hurt.

But he didn't dare lose sight of Kensher!

He trudged on and on, out of the village, out of sight of the village, past the farms that lined the river, up into the hills and forests where the road narrowed to a trail, and when at last, despite the best his tired legs could do, he *did* lose sight of Kensher, he collapsed in a heap by the side of the road. Promising himself he would only rest for a moment, the better to run on and catch up to the dragon-hunter, he immediately fell asleep.

When he awoke, he sat up and looked around, puzzled.

Where *was* he, anyway?

He was sitting in a pile of dead leaves in the midst of a forest, beside a trail that seemed to wander aimlessly through the trees. The ground was uneven; it sloped in various directions. The air seemed unseasonably cool. The sun was sending slanting light down through the leaves, leaves that spattered the ground with shadow, and Dumery, upon consideration, decided that the sun must be in the west.

That gave him a sense of direction. The road ran east and west; to the east it sloped up and over the crest of a hill, while to the west it sloped gently downward and, by the look of it, into a valley.

Dumery's mind gradually cleared, and he remembered the little village by the river, the desperate chase after Kensher Kinner's son, through the village and into the forest and all along that valley and on up here, to where the road had wound up and over the hill and out of sight and he, Dumery, had finally collapsed.

There was no sign of Kensher, of course.

Frustration and lingering fatigue caught up with him, and Dumery burst out crying.

When that was over, he stood up, brushed himself off as best he could, and thought about what he should do.

Back down the valley lay the village and the river, and somewhere downstream—a hundred leagues? More?—lay Azrad's Bridge, and the road back to Ethshar and home.

Up the slope lay—what?

Kensher's home camp might be just across the hill; why not? After all, this was a Sardironese forest; wouldn't there be dragons around?

That was a disturbing thought, and Dumery immediately reconsidered.

No, there wouldn't be. He was still too close to the river, the village, and civilization in general.

All the same, he owed it to himself to go on. Surely, it couldn't be much farther! And to come all this way and then give up—that would be ridiculous. His brothers would never let him live it down.

At the very least he should take a look over the summit, he told himself.

He wiped his eyes, looked around, and, seeing nothing dangerous, he marched on, up the hill.

At the crest he stopped and looked. There was the road, winding down the other slope—to a fork. Dumery stared at it in dismay.

Which way had Kensher gone? Which fork had he taken? Was there any way to tell?

These questions got Dumery thinking, and he realized that he didn't know whether Kensher was still on the road at all. The man was a dragon-hunter, and therefore he was surely an expert woodsman and dweller in wilderness. He wouldn't need roads. He might have gone off the road anywhere.

Dumery would probably *never* find him then.

But if one dragon-hunter worked in this area, maybe others did as well. At the next village he came to he could ask, or if he found no villages, then a house or even a camp—*somebody* lived out here, or there wouldn't be a road, let alone a fork. The locals would know about dragon-hunters in the area.

He didn't need to apprentice himself specifically to Kensher; *any* dragon-hunter would do, really.

And he might yet catch up to Kensher. If he *had* stayed on the road, maybe there would be some way to tell which fork he had taken. The ground around the fork in the road looked soft; there might be footprints, and Dumery hadn't seen any sign of anyone else on the trail.

He made his way down to the fork, where the earth was, to Dumery's delight, damp. Then he knelt down and studied the ground.

The left fork, which led eastward, showed fresh footprints in the soft, moist earth; the right fork, which veered off to the south, did not.

Dumery took the left fork and marched on, over the next hill.

And the next hill.

And the next.

And there, at last, he came across a house.

It was a rather peculiar house, by Dumery's standards, being built entirely of heavy, tarred timbers, with no plaster, no stonework, and no fancywork of any kind. The hinges on doors and shutters were simple iron straps. It was set back from the road, among the trees; behind it Dumery could see a few small outbuildings built of gray, weathered planks, and a gigantic woodpile. There were no signs of life.

Still, it was a house, and Dumery was delighted to see it. He quickened his pace—not to a run, he couldn't manage that, but to a brisk walk—and hurried up to the door.

He knocked and waited.

No one answered, and he knocked again.

"*Setsh tukul?*" a voice called from inside—a woman's voice.

"Hello!" Dumery called. "Is anyone home?"

The door opened, and a woman looked out—not an old woman, by any means, but one past the full flower of her youth. Her hair was light brown, with no trace of gray, and her skin was still smooth, but there were lines at the corners of her eyes and a certain hardness to her face. She wore a plain brown skirt and a tan tunic and held a heavy iron fireplace poker.

"*Kha bakul t'dnai shin?*" the woman demanded.

"Do you speak Ethsharitic?" Dumery asked.

Her eyes narrowed. "*Ethsharit?*" she said. "*Ie den norakh Ethsharit. Ha d'noresh Sardironis?*"

Dumery could make nothing of that, but he correctly concluded that in fact the woman did *not* speak Ethsharitic.

Surely, though, she might know a few words.

"Dragon-hunters?" Dumery asked. "I'm looking for dragon-hunters."

She glared at him. "*Ie den norakh Ethsharit,*" she said. "*D'gash, d'gash!*" She gestured for him to leave.

"Dragon-hunters!" Dumery repeated. "Please!"

"*D'gash!*" She pointed angrily at the road.

Desperately Dumery tried, "Kensher Kinner's son?"

She paused and peered down at him. "Kensher?" she asked. "Kensher *fin Kinner*?"

Dumery nodded, hoping that she meant the man he was looking for and that he hadn't accidentally spoken some inappropriate Sardironese phrase.

She shook her head. "*Da khor,*" she said. "*Pa-khorú.*" She pointed down the road in the direction Dumery had been traveling.

Dumery had no idea what the words meant, but the gesture was clear. "That way?" he said. "Thank you, lady! Thank you!" He bowed and backed away.

She stood and watched until he was back on the highway and heading east again. Then she stepped inside and slammed the door.

Dumery trudged onward, wondering how far back into these wild hills Kensher was going to go.

Surely, if the woman knew the name, Kensher's home couldn't be *too* much farther.

Dumery passed five more houses before night fell and knocked at each one; three were apparently unoccupied, but at the other two a scene similar to his first attempt was repeated— Dumery would ask questions in Ethsharitic and receive uncomprehending and incomprehensible replies in Sardironese. At one house even the name Kensher evoked no response, and he gave up and went on; at the other, the name elicited immediate recognition and careful directions, using gestures. Dumery took a moment to grasp that when the man there held out his first two fingers, spread wide apart, while pointing with his other hand, that it represented a fork in the road ahead.

Once he had that, though, the crossed index fingers for a crossroads seemed obvious, and running another finger along to show which fork to take, or drawing an imaginary left turn in the air, was clear enough.

The man gave Dumery a list of four forks and two crossroads, which Dumery carefully memorized.

Surely, he thought, it wouldn't be long now! He marched on almost merrily, and even whistled for a moment or two.

He stopped, however, because it made him notice the cold more when he blew all that air out. The weather had very definitely turned colder—or perhaps it was because he was far to the north, and spring came later here.

Cold or not, though, he expected to find Kensher's home shortly.

By sunset he hadn't even reached the first fork.

Not long after he stopped at a marker stone, bearing an inscription he couldn't make out in the failing light, and decided that he needed to rest. He couldn't go on in the dark; he might wander off the road or get himself eaten by wolves. Besides, he was exhausted.

He was hungry, too, but there was nothing he could do about that.

He would go on in the morning, he decided.

He spent the night curled up by the road, shivering with the cold and listening to his stomach growl. In the stories he'd heard when he was younger the heroes had wandered about in forests for years, living off nuts and berries and roots, picking fruit from the trees—but he could see no nuts or berries or fruits and the roots were mostly well-hidden, while those that weren't looked quite surprisingly unappetizing.

Water was no problem; there were streams and pools all through the hills, especially along the valleys between ridges. It was often dirty, stagnant, and foul-tasting, but it was water.

Food, though, he could not find.

He had chewed a few stalks of grass as he walked, but that

was not really satisfying. He had eaten reasonably well on the barge, but he hadn't eaten *at all* since coming ashore, except for the grass, and he was beginning to wonder how long it took to starve to death.

Some of the houses he had passed had had gardens, and he wondered if he might do well to backtrack until he found one and pick a few things, but it was too early in the year for much of anything to be ripe yet, and he didn't like the idea of stealing.

Besides, it was getting dark very rapidly, and he was afraid he'd lose the trail if he tried to go anywhere.

When he awoke the sun was already high up the eastern sky; his discomfort had kept him awake well after he should have slept, but once asleep his exhaustion had taken over. He rose quickly and started on toward the east once again, but almost immediately began to think about turning back and searching for food, maybe going back to the house where he had gotten directions and begging. That man had seemed kind; surely, he would feed a hungry stranger!

This idea grew steadily more appealing for almost half an hour. Then he topped the next ridge and reconsidered.

Ahead of him, at a fork in the road that was surely the first of the four he had been told about, stood an inn.

It had to be an inn. It was much larger than any of the houses he had seen out here in the wilderness, with a large, cleared yard, and a stable attached at one end. The main building was all wood, but decorated with carvings and paint in a way that none of the houses had been. A large herb and vegetable garden spread across the hillside to the rear, with a wellhouse at one back corner and what appeared to be the roof of an icehouse at the other. A signboard hung over the door.

If he had only gone on a little farther in the darkness—but that didn't matter now. Dumery staggered happily down the slope; surely his six bits would buy *something* edible here!

When he got closer he saw that the signboard showed a pine tree splitting in half from the top down, with a jagged yellow line in the center of the split that extended up to the top of the wooden panel—lightning, Dumery guessed.

That hardly seemed like a favorable omen, but Dumery didn't really believe in omens in everyday life.

The front door was open, and Dumery tottered in without hesitation. He found a chair and fell into it and hauled his few pitiful coins out of his purse.

*"Ukhur ie t'yelakh?"*

Dumery looked up at the serving maid who stood over him; he had been too busy with his money to notice her approach.

"Do you speak Ethsharitic?" he asked, depressingly certain that she would not.

*"Ethsharit?"* she asked. *"D'losh. Shenda!"* This last word was shouted in the direction of the kitchens.

Another, older serving maid appeared in reply. *"Uhu?"* she asked.

*"Da burei gorn Ethsharit."* With that, the younger woman turned and headed for the kitchen, while the older one emerged to take her place.

"Yes, sir?" the new arrival asked.

"You speak Ethsharitic?" Dumery asked, amazed and pleased.

"Yes, sir. What would you like?" Although she spoke politely, Dumery saw her looking askance at the rags he wore.

"I haven't eaten in two days," Dumery said. "This is all the money I have left. May I have something to eat? Anything?"

She looked at the coins and considered. "I think we can manage something," she said. Dumery noticed she had only a very slight Sardironese accent.

She turned and headed for the kitchen, and Dumery sat, waiting nervously.

She emerged a few moments later with a platter and set it before him.

He stared, mouth watering.

There were soft brown rolls and two green apples and white-streaked orange cheese and the remains of a chicken—the legs were gone, and the breast meat stripped away, but one wing was still there, and Dumery could see a fair bit of meat still on the bones.

"Leftovers from breakfast," the serving maid explained. "Four bits."

Hand shaking with anticipation, Dumery pushed over four of his six coins and began eating. The thought of haggling didn't even occur to him.

The rolls were still good, only slightly stale, but the apples weren't anywhere near ripe, the white streaks on the cheese were an unpleasant mold, and the chicken was cold and greasy.

All the same, to Dumery it was all ineffably delicious. When he was done nothing remained on the platter but chicken bones and the stems and seeds of the apples.

He sat back, hands on his stomach, enjoying the sensation of repletion.

The serving maid reappeared at his side.

"Are you a warlock?" she asked. "You look so young!"

"No, I'm not a warlock," Dumery replied, mystified. He stared up at her for a moment, then asked, "Should I be?"

"Oh," she said. "Oh, well, most of the people who come here who have forgotten to eat for long periods are warlocks."

"I didn't *forget*," Dumery said, flabbergasted by the very concept of forgetting to eat. "I just didn't have any food!" He continued to stare up at her.

She stared back. Dumery grew uncomfortable.

"Why would . . . I mean, do a lot of warlocks come here?" he asked. He couldn't see any reason they would; while the inn was pleasant enough, he saw nothing magical about it.

"Sometimes," she replied.

"Why?" Dumery asked, puzzled.

She shrugged. "I don't know," she said. "They don't talk much. They're always headed southeast, down the main highway. Usually they fly."

This news did not set very well with Dumery. "Southeast, down the main highway" described his own intended route. The idea of encountering several warlocks along the way wasn't appealing. If he couldn't be a magician himself, he preferred not to deal with them at all until he could somehow hold his own.

"Just warlocks?" he asked. "What about wizards, or sorcerers?"

"No, just warlocks," the woman said. "I've never even met a sorcerer, and it's been years since a wizard's stopped here." She paused, then added, "I met a demonologist once when I was a little girl, but that wasn't anywhere near here."

"Oh," Dumery said. He thought for a moment.

He couldn't think of any reason that warlocks would want to

travel the area, but then, he didn't know much about war-lockry.

It didn't really concern him, he decided.

He would want to stay out of the way of any warlocks he encountered, of course—not just now, but always. Warlocks had a nasty reputation. Being a dragon-hunter and demanding piles of gold for dragon's blood would give him a way to get back at wizards, but warlocks used no potions or spells; even a dragon-hunter wouldn't impress them.

But on the other hand, they would have no reason to bother him. He was harmless enough, and his business wouldn't interfere with theirs.

And now that he thought about his business, he had another question for the serving maid.

"Um . . ." Dumery said, "I'm looking for an apprentice-ship to a dragon-hunter. Would you know of any around here who might be interested?"

The woman blinked and thought for a moment.

"I don't think I do," she said. "Of course, there aren't very many dragons right around here; they're mostly to the east, up in the mountains. Or north. Or south. There are certainly dragon-hunters in Aldagmor, but I don't know where."

"Where's Aldagmor?" Dumery asked.

She stared. "*Here*, of course!"

"I thought this was Sardiron," Dumery said, puzzled.

"It is."

"But you said . . ."

"The gods help you, boy, Aldagmor is *part* of Sardiron! Or at least, it's part of the Baronies of Sardiron."

"Oh," said Dumery. "It's one of the Baronies?"

"The largest of them," the woman replied.

"How many are there?" Dumery asked. "I mean, there are three Ethshars, and everyone knows that because it's called the Hegemony of the Three Ethshars, but how many Baronies are there?"

"I have no idea," she replied. "I think it varies—barons can divide their lands up between heirs, and sometimes a marriage will merge two of them. Right now, well, there's Sardiron of the Waters, of course, where the Council meets, and there's Tazmor, which is east of the mountains and the richest of them all, and Srigmor, in the north, except much of it's abandoned, and The Passes, where the highways cross the mountains into Tazmor, and then there are all the Lesser Baronies along the river, Hakhai and Tselmin and Takranna and the rest . . . *I* don't know."

"Oh," Dumery said again.

"We're in the North Riding of Aldagmor here," she volunteered after a moment of awkward silence. "Though I think it's actually more to the west than to the north of the others. You crossed the boundary about a mile back, if you came down the highway from the river—didn't you see the marker stone?"

Dumery remembered where he had slept the night before. "I didn't read it," he admitted.

This was all very interesting, he thought, but they were getting farther and farther from what he really wanted to know.

"So you don't know where I can find a dragon-hunter who needs an apprentice?" he asked.

"No," she said, "I'm afraid not."

Dumery sighed, then asked his next question. "Do you know a man named Kensher Kinner's son?"

She stared at him. "Why, yes," she said. "He stayed here last night."

"He *did*?" Dumery yelped.

"Yes, he did," she confirmed. "He comes by about four times a year, and he has for as long as I can remember. Everyone along the road knows him; he always has a good word for everyone he sees. You're not from around here, though; do you know him?"

"Sort of," Dumery said, while cursing himself for not pressing on the night before. He had been so close!

"Well, he just left, oh, half an hour before you got here, at most. Maybe if you hurry, you can catch him on the road."

"Maybe," Dumery said, looking at the platter of chicken bones and wishing he'd stuffed the food in his pocket to eat on the road instead of wasting time at the inn. "I'd better get going." He rose, put his last two bits in his purse, and headed for the door.

"Good luck!" the maid called after him as he rushed out. He didn't take time to answer.

A moment later, though, Dumery's head reappeared in the doorway. "Which road did he take?" he called.

The servant pointed. "That one," she said, indicating the right fork.

That was in agreement with the gestured directions Dumery had gotten the night before. The boy nodded, turned, and ran.

# CHAPTER 19

*Teneria turned and studied the bank again. "Do you think* we're getting close?" she asked.

"Don't know," the spriggan said. "Don't care. Like you better."

"To Sardiron of the Waters, or to the barge?" the boat's owner asked.

"The barge," Teneria replied.

"I doubt it," the boatman said. "Those cattle barges are usually sylph-propelled; they can really move along."

Teneria glanced at him, worried. "They can?"

"Oh, yes. I told you when I picked you up that we weren't likely to catch him this side of Sardiron—the city, not the country. We're *in* the Baronies, but it's still a good long way to the city, and we probably won't catch up, not unless you use magic."

"And *I* told *you* that I don't *have* any magic that can move a boat any faster than you can row it or pole it."

The boatman shrugged. "Well, then," he said, "I'd say you aren't going to catch this fellow, not so long as he's on that barge."

"I wonder," Teneria said, "if he *is* still on the barge." An odd uneasiness touched her as she thought about it, and she had learned early in her apprenticeship to pay attention to such things.

She stared at the spriggan for a moment, soaking in its

memories of Dumery—such as they were; spriggans, she had discovered, weren't much on remembering things. Then she turned to the bank, raised her spread fingers to her forehead, closed her eyes, and worked a locating spell Sella had taught her years ago, using the spriggan as her familiar.

Her eyes flew open.

"He's there!" she shouted. "He went ashore at the inn! Take us back, to that inn we just passed, quickly!" She pointed desperately, jabbing at the air in her excitement.

How perverse of the boy, she thought, to go ashore without warning, instead of continuing on to Sardiron of the Waters as he had said he would! Teneria was beginning to dislike Dumery without ever having met him.

"What?" The boatman stared at her as if she had gone mad, but already he was backing water with one oar. "How do you know?"

"I just know," Teneria said.

"Magic? Is it magic? You're a wizard?" His voice was both eager and apprehensive.

"I'm a witch," Teneria corrected him. Then she corrected herself. "An apprentice, anyway. If I find the boy I'll make journeyman."

"But you said you didn't have any magic . . ."

"I said I didn't have any magic that could move the boat faster than you can. I don't. Witchcraft doesn't work that way."

"But you say you know . . . I mean, if you can do one kind of magic . . ."

Teneria decided to just ignore the boatman's questions, and after a moment they trailed away into silence as he concentrated on bringing the boat safely up to the dock.

Teneria fished in her purse and found the silver bits she had promised. She handed them over, tossed the spriggan gently up onto the dock, then climbed up after it.

"Thank you," she called back.

The boatman just nodded as he pushed off. "Crazy witch," he muttered a moment later, clearly unaware that witches were known for their remarkable hearing.

Teneria heard the remark, but paid no attention. She was scanning the area, looking for psychic traces.

There, behind the bush—someone had crouched there for at

least an hour, probably much more, yesterday morning. It was a boy, about twelve.

It was Dumery. No doubt at all, it was Dumery. She had found his trail.

From here, it would be easy. The traces weren't as fresh as they might be, but there were no crowds and no conflicting signals up here in the wilds of Sardiron. The traces were there; all she had to do was follow them.

How difficult could it be?

With a smile on her lips and the spriggan perched unsteadily on her shoulder, she marched up the trail into the forest.

By nightfall it had begun to sink in that Dumery still had a good, solid lead on her, and she wasn't gaining much on him. Oh, she was gaining, but only very slowly; she estimated the traces to be only a day or so old, where she had started a good two days behind.

But she still had a lot of catching up to do.

She passed the spot where Dumery had slept, curled up beside the path, and noted it, even it the darkness. She wasn't about to stop there herself; this was her chance to gain a little ground.

Besides, there was an inn ahead, she could sense it, no more than a mile away. She forged on, finding her way by moonlight and witch-sight. The spriggan, half asleep, tottered and almost fell from her shoulder; she put a hand up to steady it.

Her legs dragged with weariness, but she kept moving.

After a time she paused to catch her breath. The inn was just over the ridge, she knew that; she was almost there.

Then the night was torn open by a blaze of orange light from above, light that spilled in sharp-edged blades through the dark trees, turning the forest into a jagged maze of bright color and black shadow. She heard the sound of a man's scream, thin with distance, and she looked up, seeking the source of the light.

A man was hanging unsupported in the night sky, perhaps a hundred yards up and two hundred yards to the north, and the light came from his body, burning like a miniature sun.

He was screaming and appeared to be struggling with the empty air, as if something were pulling at him, dragging him somewhere he didn't want to go.

Then his head jerked, the light went out, the screaming stopped, and he fell.

Teneria stood frozen in astonishment for a moment, listening to the sound of branches snapping beneath the fallen magician's weight—for anyone who flew about glowing like that was clearly a magician.

Then she heard the dull thud of the body hitting the ground and she came to her senses.

The spriggan, wide awake now, whimpered. She petted it once, quickly, then turned her attention back to the fallen man.

Witchlight was tiring, and she was already very tired indeed, but she managed a small, pale glow from one palm, enough to find an old tree limb; setting it afire at one end also used up more energy than she could really afford, but was not as taxing as maintaining a witchlight would have been.

Once the wood was burning steadily she picked it up and began to pick her way through the forest underbrush by the light of this impromptu torch.

At first she almost walked right past the man because she was expecting to see an orange cloak. Without the magical glow, though, his cloak was black, and she took it for a shadow until the torch's illumination failed to dispel it.

He was lying facedown atop a pile of dead leaves and broken branches, and she was unsure whether he was alive or dead until she heard his breath rustling the leaves. She stooped and pushed at his shoulder, as the spriggan clung precariously.

There was no response; he was at least dazed, more likely unconscious.

In fact, he *was* unconscious, she realized; had she not been so weary she would have seen it immediately. His aura was dim but steady, and she could not sense any thought at all.

He was hurt, as well; she worked a quick diagnostic spell and discovered that the fall had broken two of his ribs and cracked the bone in his left wrist.

It was a very good thing, she thought, that he was unconscious, because if she had looked as a witch upon anyone that badly injured while the person was awake, *both* of them would probably have passed out from the pain. This man was seriously damaged.

He needed attention and slow healing, and she was in no

condition to provide it here in the middle of the forest, alone in the dark.

Just a quarter of a mile away, however, was an inn. The fallen man was tall and broad, but he had clearly not eaten well lately, and his skin was stretched tight on his bones, with little muscle left—she could move him.

Carrying him a quarter mile, though, through the woods in the dark, without even the trail for much of the way . . .

Well, did she really have any choice? She couldn't *leave* him here!

She plucked the spriggan from her shoulder and placed it gently on the ground; the little creature started to protest, but she hushed it. Then she bent down and picked the unconscious magician up, using a levitation spell to help when her grip was not strong enough or the man's body started to flop in the wrong direction, and got him hoisted up across her shoulders.

She got a look at his face as she lifted him; he was in his thirties, she judged, but his features were lined and troubled, even in his unconscious state.

When he was secure, she started walking—or rather, staggering—toward the inn, the spriggan following in her footsteps, making unhappy little worried noises.

As she walked, she used little pushes of witchcraft to steady her, and a lifting spell whenever her burden started to shift or slide, but she fought the temptation to just levitate him entirely. That was too risky. She could kill herself that way—or so Sella had always warned her.

"Levitation drains just as much from you as lifting with your hands and legs," Sella had insisted. "It's just that when you use your muscles, they'll protest when they're overworked, they'll tell you when you're tired, when you're doing too much. They'll ache and twinge and not hold. It's your body's natural warning system. But witchcraft isn't natural, and your body isn't made for it—there *are* no warnings. In trance, you can keep up a spell until your body has no life left in it at all, hasn't got the energy remaining to keep your heart pumping. A witch can keel over and die, just like that, if she tries to do too much."

Teneria had taken Sella's word for it; she had seen how she could feel fine and alert during a spell, and exhausted the moment she released her concentration, and had never cared to test the theory any further.

But now, after a long and strenuous day, instead of eating her supper and getting a good night's rest she had worked a whole series of little spells, and in addition she was carrying a weight of at least a hundred and fifty pounds. She could hardly have much of an energy reserve left; if she tried any more spells she *might* keel over and die.

She stumbled at the very thought and almost went headlong, catching herself at the last instant.

When she saw the lights of the inn through the trees she let out her breath in a great sigh of relief—but she wasn't there yet, and she didn't have the energy to shout. She staggered on.

After what seemed like days she dropped her torch, lowered the inert man to the ground, fell heavily against the door of the inn, and managed a weak pounding with one fist.

Someone answered her knock, and she actually got herself inside and into a chair before, amid mutters and exclamations in Sardironese, she passed out.

# CHAPTER 20

*T*eneria came to with a spluttering; someone was holding a glass of *oushka* to her mouth, and she felt as if the fiery liquor were burning her lips, its fumes scouring out her nose.

She sneezed and went into a fit of coughing, then gasped for breath, and when she was finally able to pay attention to something other than her own distress she realized that a woman was talking to her, in a language that she was not quite able to make out—probably Sardironese.

"What?" she said, in Ethsharitic. She didn't have the energy to use an interpretive spell.

"She was asking," another woman's voice said, in Ethsharitic, "whether you are a warlock."

"No," Teneria said, puzzled. "I'm a witch." She wondered why anyone would ask such a question. It seemed an odd thing to ask, under the circumstances. She blinked at the two women, both wearing aprons over simple dresses, who were looking worriedly at one another and muttering in Sardironese.

The one who spoke Ethsharitic turned back to Teneria and asked, "Then the man you brought—is *he* a warlock?"

"I don't know," Teneria answered. "He might be."

"Where did you find him?"

"He fell out of the sky near me, in the forest. He was screaming, and glowing orange." She remembered something else, and added, "He has two broken ribs and a cracked wrist; handle him carefully!"

The women looked at one another.

"Listen," the one who spoke Ethsharitic said, "he *is* a warlock, from what you describe. We have seen this before. We will handle him *very* carefully—but we will not let him under this roof. He must stay outside."

Teneria's head was swimming with fatigue, and she had very little idea of what was going on, but she asked, baffled, "Why?"

"Because he is a warlock."

The Sardironese women seemed to think this was a completely adequate explanation, and Teneria was too tired to argue. She let her head fall back against the back of the tall chair she sat in.

Her stomach growled.

The two women glanced at each other, and one studied the purse on Teneria's belt for a moment. It looked reasonably plump.

"Would you like some food?" the older woman asked.

Teneria managed a nod.

A moment later a thick slab of fresh bread, smeared with yellow butter, was in her hand; a moment after that it was in her mouth.

And not long after that she began to feel considerably better. All she had needed was food and rest to replenish her depleted reserves; she knew that, and had known it all along—or would have if she had had the energy to think about it. She sat up straighter and looked around.

The two women were going about the inn's business; there were half a dozen customers—rather unsavory looking, all of them, Teneria thought—and a fire, so there were trays and mugs to be carried, logs to be shifted, and ashes to be poked. The young witch watched for a few minutes, but when one of the serving women glanced her way she caught her eye and gestured.

The woman put down the poker she had been wielding and came over to where Teneria sat.

This was the older of the two, the one who spoke Eth-sharitic. "Can I help you?" she asked.

Teneria had any number of questions she wanted to ask, but before she could think of any of them she heard herself saying "More food, please. Meat, and fruit, and wine. I can pay."

"Yes, lady."

While the servant was fetching food, Teneria considered and decided that questions could wait until after she had eaten.

It was half an hour later and the other customers had all drifted away when Teneria paid for her meal. As she counted out the coins she asked the older serving woman, whose name she had learned was Shenda, "Why won't you let warlocks inside?"

"We will sometimes," Shenda replied. "It depends on the circumstances. But they seem to be prone to a sort of madness, and when we have any doubts about whether the madness is upon them, we keep them out. If we don't, they're likely to damage the place."

"Damage it?" Teneria looked about. The inn did not appear damaged.

Shenda nodded. "The madness," she said, "it . . . well, there's a compulsion involved, a geas or something. They all want to go *that* way." She pointed to the southeast. "And they don't care what's in the way. And with their magic, if the madness is on them, they can go right through the wall, or the roof—or if they aren't *that* far gone, they may still smash furniture and set fires on the way out." She made an uncomfortable little gesture. "That one you brought—from your description, flying and glowing, the madness was prob-ably very strong in him. He may have been fighting it—that would be why he fell. But when he wakes up, he may not be ready, and the madness may carry him away." She grimaced. "The south wall has been rebuilt twice in the past twenty years; I don't want to make it three times. And the roof went once."

"They go . . . warlocks go right *through* the wall?" Teneria stared at the plastered stone and timber in disbelief.

Shenda shrugged. "Magic. You're a witch, you said?"

Teneria nodded.

"Couldn't a witch's magic take you through a wall like that?" Shenda asked.

"I don't know," Teneria admitted. "I suppose I could— yes, I think I could break through a wall. But it might kill me, and I certainly wouldn't be going anywhere right afterward."

Shenda had no answer to that.

"Different magicks," Teneria said with a shrug. "There's no connection between witchcraft and warlockry. We have no madness that comes on us." Her eyes narrowed. "In fact, I hadn't heard that warlocks did, either. I wonder about wizards, and sorcerers, and the others?"

Shenda shook her head. "Not around here, anyway. We never see anyone but warlocks. But there are a lot of warlocks around here. I've heard that they're more common in Aldagmor than anywhere else, that it's easier to become one here than elsewhere."

"I wouldn't know," Teneria said.

She was considering what to say next when the screaming started outside.

She leapt to her feet without thinking and was surprised to find Shenda grabbing her arm, trying to hold her back.

"I've got to go," she said, trying to shake the older woman off.

"No, you don't," Shenda said. "It's dangerous."

"Maybe I can help," Teneria insisted. "I'm a witch, I can heal and calm."

Shenda hesitated, but did not let go; Teneria used a subtle spell, loosening the other's finger muscles and making her own sleeve smoother and more slippery, and pulled free. She hurried to the door.

It slammed open before she could reach it, and brilliant

golden light poured in, blinding her momentarily. Artificially speeding the contraction of her pupils, Teneria shaded her eyes and peered out.

The warlock was hanging in the air above the crossroads, eight or nine feet up, spinning like a top and shrieking in agony, light pouring from him as if he were a living flame or a piece of the sun itself. A whirlwind surrounded him, carrying twigs and rotting leaves in circles about him; it was the wind that had flung open the door. The inn's signboard was flapping wildly.

As Teneria watched, the warlock began to drift southward.

Wanting to help, or at least to understand, Teneria reached out with her witchcraft and touched his mind, as delicately as she could, and found a roiling mass of terror and confusion. Something was compelling him, something irresistible that whispered obscenely and unintelligibly directly into his mind; it was dragging him south, pulling at him, and he was fighting against it, hopelessly.

Part of him didn't even *want* to resist, and that part was growing stronger—and he knew it.

That was why he was screaming. It wasn't pain; it was terror and despair.

Teneria stepped forward and reached up with her own thoughts, calming him, pushing his fear back, trying to block off that overpowering lure, whatever it was.

It wasn't easy. In fact, it wasn't possible to close it off completely.

She was able to muffle it slightly, though, and the warlock's own resistance strengthened. His spinning slowed, and he began to look down.

He spotted her, his eyes locked with hers, and then his head snapped away as he continued to rotate.

His gaze met hers again on the next rotation, though, and held for half a second.

His spin slowed further, and three turns later he had stopped.

He sank slowly to the ground, staring fixedly at her, trying to think of nothing else, trying not to think of the *thing* that had been calling him, had been drawing him to it. He tried to think only of this mysterious girl who was somehow help-

ing him fight back. Teneria sensed all this through her tele-
pathic spells, though communication was made difficult by
the fact that the warlock was doing all his thinking in his
native Sardironese.

She could get the basics, though, and in fact was absorbing
the language quickly.

As the warlock's attention became unfocused from his in-
ternal conflicts, he became aware of the pain from his ribs and
his wrist. Without really thinking about it he repaired the damage to the bones, reshaping the material with his magic as
easily and casually as a potter works clay.

Teneria gasped, and her hold on the compulsion slipped for
an instant; terror swept across the warlock's face and through
his mind, but then she recovered herself.

She had not known that warlocks could heal, and certainly
not that they could do so nearly instantaneously. The bone-
knitting he had done in seconds would have taken her three or
four hours of careful concentration.

The warlock was as surprised at the situation as she was, but
for an entirely different reason.

"I didn't think the Calling could be fought," he said in
Sardironese. "My master never taught me that. How do you do
it?"

Teneria struggled with the unfamiliar words for a moment,
then replied in the same language, "Witchcraft." She concentrated for a moment, trying to find the right words in the
unfamiliar tongue, and then asked, "How did you heal your
wrist?"

He glanced down at his hand, startled. "Warlockry," he
said. He looked up again. "Aren't you a warlock?"

"No," Teneria said. "I'm a witch."

The two of them stared at each other for a long moment.

"I'm afraid I don't know very much about warlocks," Teneria said at last.

"And I don't know much about witches," the warlock replied. "I don't think any warlock does. We keep to ourselves
and avoid the other magicians—ever since the Night of Madness, I'm told."

Teneria cocked her head to one side. "I'd heard that," she

said. "I wonder whether it might be a mistake, this avoidance?"

"If you can help us fight the Calling," the warlock said, "then I think it *is* a mistake."

Teneria nodded. "And if you can heal like that, I'd say we have a lot to talk about."

The warlock nodded. "I think you're right," he said. He looked around.

He was standing at the crossroads, Teneria on the threshold of the inn; behind her, Shenda and the other serving woman were watching cautiously.

"May I come inside to talk?" the warlock asked.

"No!" Shenda shouted immediately.

Startled, the warlock started to say something, but Teneria held up a hand. "I'll come out," she said. "These people have had bad experiences with warlocks."

The other serving woman called, "There are benches in the garden, out back."

"Thank you," Teneria replied. She looked around for the spriggan, but didn't see it anywhere—the noise must have frightened it away, she decided.

That was just as well. She held a hand out to the warlock. "Shall we head for the garden, then?"

The warlock nodded, and his tortured face managed a weak smile as he took her hand in his.

# CHAPTER 21

*The first crossroads had almost fooled him; one branch* was so small, nothing more than a trail, really, that at first Dumery thought there were only three roads at the intersection.

The man had been quite definite about the order, though— fork, fork, crossroads, crossroads, fork, fork.

There was an inn at the second crossroads, but Dumery didn't stop; it was hardly past midday.

He also ignored various markers along the way; they were all written in Sardironese, which used runes similar to Ethsharitic, but which Dumery could not otherwise read. He recognized the name "Aldagmor" on most of them, now that the tavern girl had alerted him to where he was, but the rest was just gibberish as far as he was concerned.

He passed houses, as well, but didn't stop to investigate any of them.

Since leaving the inn where he had breakfasted, the road he followed had run more or less parallel to the ridges, rather than across them; that made traveling significantly easier.

The slopes were getting steeper, though—much steeper.

And the weather was growing steadily colder, which seemed almost unnatural. It was spring, after all—the weather was supposed to be warming up.

The hills undoubtedly had something to do with it, as well as the fact that he was well north of Ethshar.

At sunset he still hadn't found the last two forks, nor an inn. His generous breakfast was long past, and his gnawing hunger had returned. All the same, he had little choice but to curl up by the roadside and try to sleep.

He tried to think of somewhere, anywhere, that he could find food, but nothing came to mind. It had been hours since he had has passed a house with a garden, and when he had he hadn't seen anything that was even close to ripe yet. He still hadn't found any of the nuts or berries that always seemed to be at hand in the stories, either.

Well, he had always thought most of those stories were lies. He lay there listening to his stomach growl.

Eventually, exhaustion overcame hunger.

He was awakened well before dawn by a thin, cold drizzle. He sat there, huddled and soaking, until there was enough light to see, and then began stumbling slowly onward, always watching carefully for even the faintest paths.

The rain had ended, the clouds had dispersed, and the sun was finally peering over the mountains when he passed a rather decrepit inn; he was tempted to stop, but remembering that his total fortune was down to a mere two bits, and that Kensher Kinner's son might be just a few steps ahead of him, he reluctantly forged onward.

He found the third fork around midday and turned left, up into the mountains.

After that the journey got worse. The road ran up and down slopes steeper than Dumery had ever imagined climbing, and often wiggled so much on the way up or down that he felt as if he were constantly doubling back on himself. On occasion he found himself looking straight ahead at the tops of mature pine trees, trees rooted at the base of a cliff or drop-off, sixty or seventy feet down.

The mountains he had seen in the distance back by the river were no longer distant at all; in fact, he wasn't sure whether the hills around him were merely hills, or whether he was actually among the mountains now.

He certainly wasn't up among the highest peaks, which still towered to the east, but the slopes he was climbing were long and steep enough to qualify as mountains by most definitions. Small mountains, perhaps, but mountains.

He passed very few houses along this stretch, and those few were all set well back among the trees, doors closed and windows shuttered. He didn't inquire at any of them.

He might have tried robbing a garden or orchard if he had

seen any, no matter how unripe the fruits might be, but he saw none.

His boots, which were soft-soled city boots that had lasted longer than he had really had any right to expect, finally began to give out around midafternoon—the shredded left sole pulled loose from the stitches that had held it, so that it hung down and flapped awkwardly with each step he took. After tolerating this for the better part of a mile he gave up, took the boots off, and tucked them in his belt as best he could. Then he trudged on, barefoot.

The sun was behind the treetops in the west when he reached the fourth and final fork.

Another of the stone markers was set up at this fork, the first one he had seen in hours, but as it was entirely in Sardironese he couldn't make out any of what it said. He ignored it, and took the right fork.

The left fork was plainly the main trail—it could no longer honestly be called a road, even in comparison to the paths he had followed thus far. The right fork was little more than a trace.

It led almost directly up a mountainside—unquestionably a mountainside, this one, and not a hillside—and Dumery followed it as best he could, but he had not yet reached the peak when the fading sunlight made it impossible to proceed. He was certain he was nearing his goal, the lodge or cabin whence Kensher based his dragon hunts, but stumbling on in the dark would be too dangerous. He could fall over a cliff all too easily.

Reluctantly he settled in for the night, curling up on a pile of fallen pine branches, all too aware that he hadn't eaten in almost two days. He could hardly hope for an inn up here in the wilderness, of course, and in fact he had seen no human habitations of any kind since a few miles before the final fork. His city-bred eyes had not spotted anything he knew to be edible and reasonably nontoxic anywhere along the way—no apples nor pears nor anything else he recognized as food. The few berries he had seen had been unfamiliar, unripe, and not very appetizing.

He would need to find food very soon. If he didn't catch up

to Kensher by midday, or find some place he could beg a meal, he would have to turn back.

Even now, he wasn't entirely sure he could retrace his steps far enough to find food before he collapsed.

With that depressing thought, and the gnawing in his gut, it took him a long time to get to sleep.

When he awoke the sun was already high in the east. He stood, and stretched, and took a moment to orient himself, ignoring the pain in his stomach.

The path led upward, over a rocky outcropping and through a line of pine trees on a shoulder of the mountain; beyond that he couldn't see where it went, but at least it would have to be going down, rather than climbing any farther.

He stretched again, took a deep breath, and marched on.

He only took about fifteen minutes to top the shoulder and look down through the pines, and when he did he stopped dead in his tracks and stared.

The path led down from the rocky shoulder onto a broad, flat plateau, through a large herb-and-vegetable garden, between two small, well-tended flower beds, and up to the front door of a large, comfortable-looking farmhouse built of square-cut timbers, topped by a red tile roof. To the left of the house was a cliff, the edge of the plateau; to the right was a sizable fenced-in pasture extending across the plateau and up the slope toward the mountain's peak, where a few dozen head of cattle were going about their bovine business.

Dumery didn't notice any of this until later; he was too busy staring at what lay *behind* the house.

There, in huge pens made out of massive black metal beams, were dozens of dragons, ranging from little ones not very much bigger than a housecat, up to monsters perhaps twenty feet in length.

Dumery stared, flabbergasted.

One of the larger dragons, a green one, raised its head and looked at him, and Dumery swallowed.

The dragon roared and was answered by a cacophony of shrieks and bellows from its companions.

Dumery blinked and felt tears welling up, tears of exhaustion, frustration, and despair.

This was no hunting lodge, no trapper's cabin. Kensher

Kinner's son was quite obviously not a dragon-hunter at all.

He was a dragon-*farmer*.

Dumery let out a sob.

This possibility had never occurred to him, never would have occurred to him. A dragon *farm?* It went against everything he had ever heard. All the stories were about wild, treacherous beasts living free in the forests and mountains. Oh, there were people who had brought home dragon eggs, hatched them, and kept the dragons as pets until they reached an unmanageable size and had to be butchered—the Arena had had a dragon on display once when he was very young—but he had never dreamed of anything like this.

No wonder Kensher hadn't wanted an apprentice *hunter!*

Dumery wiped away tears with the back of his hand and tried to get himself under control. Crying wasn't going to do him any good, no good at all.

And besides, wouldn't a dragon-farmer need apprentices? There were a lot of dragons in those pens; it must take several hands to do all the chores for an operation this size. There must be special skills involved in running it.

Farming was not an occupation that Dumery had ever taken an interest in; farmers, as he understood it, were generally people too poor or stupid or unambitious to find any better trade. Dragon-farming, though, dragon-farming would have to different.

Dumery began to feel a little better. Dragon-farming might not be so bad.

And hunting or farming, if he had a supply of dragon's blood, it didn't matter how he got it; he could still lord it over Thetheran and the other wizards who had rejected him.

And most important of all, if he didn't get something to eat soon he would never make it back down out of these mountains, he'd die up here, of cold or hunger or something.

Still shocked, he forced himself to march onward, over the rocky shoulder and down toward the farmhouse.

Dumery was in worse shape than he realized; he had barely managed to knock on the door before his legs gave out and he collapsed heavily on the doorstep.

His cheek was pressed against the cold stone of the threshold, one hand underneath, the other out to the side, his feet off in some other direction, and he didn't care about any of it any-more. He didn't want to move, and in fact he didn't think he *could* move any more. His determination had finally run out. He just lay there, dazed and unable to move, and even when the door swung open he didn't react. It took too much effort.

In fact, everything took too much effort. Even staying conscious took too much effort.

So he didn't.

# CHAPTER 22

*T*he warlock's name was Adar Dagon's son, he told Tene-ria, and he had grown up a farmer's son in the Passes. On the Night of Madness, in 5202, as a boy of ten, he had woken up with screaming nightmares, and afterward he had found that he could move things without touching them, could sense what lay beneath the surfaces of things, could create heat and light from nothing—had, in short, become one of the original war-locks.

He had had no idea what to do and had at first treated his new gifts as a toy.

At age twelve an older warlock had taken charge of him and seen to his training and upbringing. This older warlock, Gen-nar of Tazmor, had told him about the Calling, which had taken hundreds of people on the Night of Madness, and more since.

As Adar explained to Teneria, the Calling was something that came from the same source as a warlock's power. The more magic a warlock used, the more powerful he became—warlocks improved with practice, like anyone else, only more so—and the more powerful a warlock became, the stronger the Call was for him.

The Calling and the warlock's power came from somewhere in southeastern Aldagmor, and when the Calling became too strong to resist warlocks were drawn to the Source, whatever and wherever it was.

Some people referred to the Source as the Warlock Stone, but Adar didn't know why; no one really knew what it was, because nobody who saw it ever came back. Warlocks who were drawn to it, who gave in to the Calling, were never heard from again.

*No one* came back. Even nonwarlocks didn't come back. People who got too close to the Source *became* warlocks—and most were quickly overpowered by the Calling. The closer to the Source a warlock got, the more powerful he became—and the stronger the Calling became for him.

Adar had known all this for years and had taken precautions. He had been careful, or at least he thought he had. He had thought he still had a respectable margin of safety, at least in his native village.

Then he had ventured south from the Passes on an errand for a friend. He had known he shouldn't go south, of course, but it wasn't really that far, and Aldagmor and the Warlock Stone were a long way off, so he had thought it was safe. Oh, he expected a nightmare or two, perhaps, but nothing more than that.

But as he went about his business he felt something slip, and before he knew what was happening he had found himself flying off, destination unknown, out of control of his own mind and powers.

When he realized what was happening he tried to resist, he struggled, and although it had seemed hopeless, he had fought the Calling to a momentary standstill, there over the forest.

Then he had passed out from the strain, and when he had come to and resumed the struggle, there Teneria was, helping him.

And here he was beside her, astonished and relieved, even though he knew the reprieve might be only temporary.

Temporary or not, it was quite a surprise. "We didn't know witches could help," he said.

"Neither did we witches," Teneria replied, smiling. "I'm as surprised as you are."

He nodded, and then asked jokingly, "If you didn't come just to save me, then what are you doing in Aldagmor?"

"Oh, I came to save somebody else entirely," Teneria said.
He raised an eyebrow in inquiry.

She told him about Dumery; he listened, but quickly lost
interest.

Teneria, herself, was not really terribly concerned about the
boy at this point. She realized that his trail was growing cold
and that she could be in serious trouble with her mistress if she
lost him, but somehow she couldn't bring herself to worry too
much about that when she had something as mysterious and
important as the warlock's problem to worry about. Dumery
surely knew where he was going; he couldn't have wandered
this far into the wilds of Aldagmor just by chance. After all, if
he had been seeking his fortune, with nothing in particular in
mind, wouldn't he have gone to Sardiron of the Waters, rather
than Aldagmor?

And thanks to the psychic traces she had been following, she
knew he was traveling alone, so he wasn't being kidnapped.
What she could sense of his state of mind didn't seem to
indicate any particular distress; he was all right, at least so far,
even if she didn't know what he was doing.

Whatever he was up to, it could wait. All this new information about warlockry and the Calling was much more in-
triguing. For one thing, the possibilities of an alliance
between witches and warlocks were obvious to both Teneria
and Adar.

The two schools of magic used roughly similar magical
skills—the sensing from afar, the levitation, and the rest—but
in radically different ways. Witches, with the limits imposed
by the finite energy of their bodies, had devoted themselves to
subtlety, to the crucial fine adjustment, the touch in the right
spot. Warlocks, with seemingly infinite power not just available, but pressing upon them and *asking* to be used, while at
the same time they knew that to use too much power could
mean the unknown doom of the Calling, had developed a different style—avoiding the actual use of magic much of the
time, but then turning raw brute force onto the matter at hand
when called for.

As an example, had Teneria healed Adar's wrist, she would
have encouraged the bone to grow back together cell by cell
and fiber by fiber. Adar had simply forced the pieces back

together and fused them in a single operation. That would have exhausted a witch for hours, but was nothing at all for a warlock.

And another difference was that warlocks lacked the ability to sense, interpret, and manipulate the minds and emotions of others—the talent that was the very heart of witchcraft.

It was those skills at mental manipulation that had made it possible for Teneria to partially block the Calling, and that block was what let Adar resist it.

Teneria's account of her pursuit of Dumery was cut short when Adar asked impatiently, "So which way did this kid go?"

"South," Teneria answered, pointing.

She sensed the worm of fear that stirred in his mind as Adar asked, "Are you going to follow him?"

She hesitated, remembering that south was where the Source was, and then said, "No. At least, not right away."

Adar sighed with relief.

"What, then?" he asked. "What *are* you going to do?"

Teneria blinked and looked around at the night-shrouded garden. Torches burned at the rear door of the inn, and the greater moon was in the sky. For a moment she thought she might have seen the spriggan peeping around a rock, but then it was gone, and she was too busy with Adar's mind to probe for the little creature.

"I don't know," she said. "What are *you* going to do?"

"I should head back north," Adar said uneasily, "as soon as possible. I need to get farther from the Source."

The witch nodded. "I'll come with you and help," she said. "At least until you're safe again."

Adar smiled. "Good," he said. "Now?"

Teneria hesitated again, and a yawn caught her. "In the morning," she said. "Right now I need some rest."

Adar's smile vanished.

"But, Teneria," he said, "you can't sleep."

"Huh?" She blinked, smothering another yawn. "Why not?"

"Because if you sleep . . ." he began. Then he stopped and demanded, "Can you work witchcraft in your sleep?"

"No, of course not," she replied, baffled.

"Then if you sleep . . ." He took a deep breath, then said, "If you sleep, it'll get me."

A sudden coldness clamped down on Teneria's heart.

"Oh," she said. "Oh."

# CHAPTER 23

*W*hen Dumery woke he found himself lying on something warm and soft, surrounded by the scents of soap and lavender. He heard gentle creakings and rustlings and thumps, the sounds of a household going about its ordinary business.

It took a moment before he had the nerve to open his eyes, but when he did he was looking up at an undistinguished plank ceiling.

His eyes worked their way down from there.

He was in a small bedroom, lying in a well-fluffed feather-bed, under a fine warm blanket. Blue sky was visible through the one window. A washstand stood at the bedside, and two plain wooden chairs were nearby. A boy perhaps half his own age was standing at the window, looking out at the World.

Dumery coughed.

The boy turned, looked at him, then ran to the door of the room and shouted something in some language other than Ethsharitic—Sardironese, presumably.

Then the boy turned back and stared at Dumery.

"Hello," Dumery said. His voice didn't sound very good.

The boy just stared.

Footsteps sounded, and people began pouring into the room.

The first was an old man, surely at least sixty years old, Dumery thought. He had been a big man once, and was still tall, but he was bent now, and his muscles sagged rather than bulged. His left arm was gone from the elbow down, the long-healed stump projecting from the shortened sleeve of his tunic.

Behind this rather frightening figure came a swarm of small children—Dumery thought there were four of them, but they moved about so much he wasn't entirely sure he hadn't missed one.

And finally, a black-haired woman, small and pretty, appeared and stood in the doorway.

The one-armed old man said something in Sardironese.

Dumery blinked up at him and tried to sit up, but wound up leaning on one elbow instead.

"Does anyone here . . .'' he began, before being interrupted by a cough. He cleared his throat and tried again.

"Does anyone here speak Ethsharitic?'' he asked.

"Yes,'' the old man said, "of course I do. Could never have done much business without it. Is it your only language? You don't know any Sardironese?''

Dumery nodded.

"That's too bad,' the old man said. "The little ones won't be able to follow what we're saying, then.'' He smiled. "Well, when I tell them all about it later I can dress it up a little, make it sound better, right?''

As he spoke, the woman in the doorway slipped away.

A girl, perhaps four years old, tugged at the old man's tunic and asked him a question in Sardironese.

The old man answered, and Dumery caught a word that sounded like "Ethsharit'' in his reply.

The girl asked another question, and the old man shook his head. *"Ku den nor Sardironis,''* he said.

The child started to ask again, but the man held up a hand and said something. Dumery could only guess what all this was about and he was still too battered and worn to give it much thought, but he supposed the girl had wanted to know why he and the old man were talking funny.

In any case, the girl stopped asking questions after that, and the old man turned his attention back to Dumery.

"Now, boy,'' he said, "who are you and just what were you doing turning up on my doorstep? You looked half starved, and half frozen, and you weren't wearing anything but some rags that look like they used to be fancy city street clothes—how in the World did you get way up here in the mountains?''

This mention of his clothes brought to Dumery's attention that he was wearing an unfamiliar, but very comfortable, flannel nightshirt. He wondered what had become of his own attire, but he didn't ask; instead he answered, "I'm Dumery of Shiphaven. From Ethshar."

"Which Ethshar?" the old man asked, before Dumery could say anything else.

"Ethshar of the Spices," Dumery replied, startled. It wasn't a question he had ever been asked before.

But then, he had never left the city until this trip.

The old man nodded. "Go on," he said. "How did you get way up here?"

Dumery hesitated, unsure what to say.

If he told the truth, that he had followed Kensher Kinner's son into the mountains, what would happen?

Where was he, anyway? Was this the house at the dragon farm? If so, where was Kensher? Wasn't it his farm?

"I was lost," he said.

The old man frowned.

"Where am I, anyway?" Dumery asked, a trifle belatedly. "And who are all you people?"

"My name's Kinner," the old man said, and Dumery's heart jumped at the name. "That's Talger, Kalthen, Kirsha, Shatha, and Tarissa, some of my grandchildren," the old man went on, pointing first to the boy who had been in the room when Dumery awoke, then to another boy, then to three girls. Kirsha had been the one asking questions.

Just then the black-haired woman reappeared in the doorway, holding a tray, and the old man added, "And that's Pancha, my son's wife."

"I brought soup," the woman said in heavily accented Ethsharitic, raising the tray.

Dumery groped for words as he sat up, and couldn't find them; he settled for looking as grateful as he could as the tray was set down atop the washstand.

Then he didn't worry about words or appearances as he began slurping up the soup. It was a thick beef broth with carrots and peas and other vegetables in it, and Dumery considered it the most wonderful thing he had ever eaten in his entire life. It was warm and filling and savory and settled very nicely in his empty gut.

When he had to stop eating to catch his breath he managed to say "Thank you." Then he picked up the spoon again and continued.

When the last trace was gone and the bowl almost dry, he looked up and realized that the old man, the woman, and the five children were all staring at him. They had apparently been whispering among themselves, but that stopped when they saw his eyes upon them.

"Thank you, lady," he said. "That was delicious."

She shrugged, but a pleased smile lit her face.

"Now," old Kinner said, "you were explaining how you got here."

That wasn't quite how Dumery remembered the conversation, but he had learned long ago that arguing with adults was usually a mistake. "I walked," he said.

Kinner looked exasperated. "But why *here?*" he demanded.

Dumery hesitated. These people seemed friendly enough, and he was grateful that they had taken him in and fed him— but on the other hand, it seemed very likely that the existence of this farm was supposed to be a secret, and he had stumbled upon it. Admitting that he was interested in a career involving dragons would draw attention to that fact.

But then, they must know he'd seen what was going on, and it really didn't matter how or why he had come here—he still knew the secret.

Besides, he couldn't think of a good lie.

"I was following someone," he said. "A man named Kensher Kinner's son."

Talger glanced up, startled, at the sound of the familiar name. Kinner eyed Dumery with interest. "Were you, indeed," he said.

Dumery nodded.

"And why were you following my son?" Kinner asked.

That confirmed Dumery's suspicion. "I thought he was a dragon-hunter," he admitted.

"Oh? And why were you interested in following a dragon-hunter?"

"I was seeking an apprenticeship."

Kinner stared at him silently for a moment, and Dumery stared back defiantly. The children, puzzled, looked from one to the other and back again.

"You want to be a dragon-hunter?" Kinner asked.

Dumery nodded.

Kinner said, "What made you think that Kensher was a dragon-hunter?"

"I saw him selling dragon's blood to the wizard back in Ethshar," Dumery explained.

"Ah," Kinner said, a satisfied smile of comprehension spreading across his face. He rocked back on his heels. "And you assumed he'd gotten it by hunting dragons."

Dumery nodded again.

"I supposed you saw this place clearly before you passed out," Kinner remarked.

Once more Dumery nodded.

"Then you now know that Kensher isn't primarily a dragon-hunter," Kinner said.

"He's a dragon-farmer," Dumery agreed. "That's all right. I still want an apprenticeship."

Kinner sighed. "Boy," he said, "you may have the most wonderful reasons in the World for wanting to be Kensher's apprentice, but I'm afraid it doesn't matter. It will never happen."

"Why *not?*" Dumery demanded.

The old man stared at him, considering, for a moment. Then, holding up an admonitory finger, Kinner said, "Wait." He stepped out the door of the room and called something in Sardironese.

Dumery had little choice; he waited.

A moment later footsteps sounded, and faces appeared in the doorway—young faces, varying from a little younger than Dumery to several years older.

"That's Seldis," Kinner said, "and Wuller, and Kinthera, and Shanra, and Kashen, and Korun, and Kinner the Younger. You already met Talger, Kalthen, Tarissa, Kirsha, and Shatha. They're all my grandchildren except Wuller, who's married to

Seldis—and more important, they're all Kensher's children. And Pancha's, of course," he said, with a slight bow to the woman.

Dumery stared. Eleven children, ranging in age from a young woman down to a boy of two or three—not to mention the young man Wuller, who had married into the family.

"And every one of them has a prior claim to an apprenticeship here on this farm," Kinner pointed out.

"But . . ." Dumery began.

"Boy," Kinner said, cutting him off, "it doesn't take eleven people to run this farm. It doesn't take more than, oh, two or three, really, though more hands mean less work for each. And this is the only dragon farm left in all the World, so far as we know, so there's no point in training you with the idea you'll find work elsewhere once you make journeyman."

Dumery hesitated. "The only one in the World?" he asked.

Kinner nodded. "So we're told."

"But how . . . if it's the only one . . ." Dumery puzzled over this for a moment, and then asked, "How did it *get* here?"

Kinner sighed. As he did, the girl—young woman, really—he had called Seldis whispered something in his ear. Kinner nodded and muttered something in reply.

Seldis and Wuller vanished from the doorway, and as Kinner told his tale most of the others gradually drifted away, as well.

"You know about the Great War," Kinner said.

Dumery nodded. "When Ethshar destroyed the Northerners," he said.

"Yes, exactly," Kinner agreed. "It was a long, long war—nobody knows anything about what the World was like before it began, not really. So we don't know where dragons came from originally, because they were around from the earliest days of the war. Personally, I suspect some wizard invented them, maybe by accident—why else would they have so much magic in their blood? And they aren't like any other animals I ever heard of, the way they grow and behave . . ." He blinked, stared silently and thoughtfully at nothing for a moment, and then recovered himself.

"Well, anyway," he continued, "wherever dragons came

from, originally they were all raised by people, there weren't any wild ones at all, anywhere. They were used as weapons in the war—if they weren't just an accident, that must be what they were invented for. They were fighting animals. One big dragon can tear up a whole town pretty quickly, after all, and that's without even mentioning that some can breathe fire, and some can fly, and most of them have hide like armor, and if you let them grow big enough they get smart enough to talk—I mean, how does that fit in with the rest of the World, animals that can learn to talk *as adults*, when it's too late to civilize them? It just doesn't make any sense unless somebody invented them for the war.''

Dumery stared. This was beyond him; the idea that somebody might have *invented* dragons was all new to him. After all, did squid fit in with the rest of the World? Had someone invented those, too? What about camels, or nightwalkers? Did they make any sense?

Kinner noticed the dazed expression on the boy's face and realized he was losing his audience. He hurried to get on with his tale.

''So,'' he said, ''during the war the army kept dragons around as fighting animals and bred them as part of the war effort. Some were trained to fight; others were just turned loose behind enemy lines, where they grew up in the woods and ate up all the game, and when that was gone and they got hungry they turned on the livestock and the civilians, and they just generally made life more difficult for the Northerners.

''And of course, Ethshar's military wizards needed a steady supply of dragon's blood for their spells—the war was fought as much with magic as with swords, Southern wizards and theurgists against Northern sorcerers and demonologists. So the army ran its own dragon-breeding operations—I don't know how many, but several of them. And toward the end of the war one of them, right up near the front but hidden in the mountains, was run by a man named Thar, who was a sergeant in General Anaran's elite Forward Command.'' Kinner smiled. ''Sergeant Thar was my . . . let's see . . . my great-great-great-great-great-great-grandfather. Six greats—that sounds right.''

Dumery blinked. "Oh," he said. "But the war . . . I mean, that was hundreds of years ago . . ."

"That's right," Kinner agreed. "It was. And when the war ended, about two hundred and thirty years ago, Sergeant Thar simply kept on raising dragons. The government didn't care. Or maybe they didn't even know. The way I heard it from my grandfather, orders came down saying the dragons were surplus, that the army didn't need them any more and they should all either be killed, or set free up north, to help polish off any survivors after the Northern Empire fell. Well, Sergeant Thar thought that was stupid and wasteful, so he kept the dragons and the breeding camp for himself and passed them down to his son, and so on, and so on, until I inherited them from my father. And when I die, my son Kensher will inherit the dragons and the farm from me."

"And you sell their blood?" Dumery asked, mildly revolted by the idea of raising the animals just for that. It seemed awfully wasteful.

"That's right," Kinner said, nodding. "We kill them and sell the blood. It's a fine business, too. There are plenty of wizards out there who need the stuff, and there isn't a lot of dragon's blood around. It seems, from all we've heard, that the other old dragon-breeding operations, the other ones that the army ran during the war, all *did* shut down. At least, we've never heard of any others and we don't seem to have much competition out there selling blood. I guess the other breeders didn't see that wizards would still need dragons even in peacetime—or maybe they just didn't want to disobey orders. So they must have all killed their stock, or set it free. So we're the only dragon farm left."

He smiled and added, "At least, as far as we know."

"So you . . ." Dumery began, then stopped and tried again. "So this one farm is where all the wizards in the World get the dragon's blood for their spells?"

"Well," Kinner said judiciously, "maybe not all the wizards in the World. We have a good-size operation here, though. We can satisfy most of the demand from wizards in the Hegemony of the Three Ethshars and throughout the Baronies of Sardiron, and that's where we sell. The wizards in the Small Kingdoms—what few there are, magic isn't very popular there—well, anyway, in the Small Kingdoms, or in the Tintallions, or in any of the other Northern lands, the wizards have to get their dragon's blood elsewhere. They can buy it from middlemen in Ethshar, where there's always some trader who'll get it from us and double the price, or they can try to obtain it magically, which is *extremely* difficult—I mean, it involves things like demons—or else they can buy it from *real* dragon-hunters.''

He laughed, and Dumery didn't like the sound of it. "If you think we dragon-*farmers* charge a lot, boy," Kinner said, "you should try buying from a dragon-*hunter*!" He sobered. "There's a good reason for it, too—a beginning dragon-hunter is lucky to live more than a few months. Or maybe days.'' He shrugged. "We know dragons here, since we grew up with them and work with them every day; they're dangerous creatures, no doubt about it. And the wild ones can grow bigger than we ever let them get here. There are ways to deal with them, but it's risky. Dragons are *mean*, sometimes. It was a dragon that did this.'' He gestured with the stump of his left arm. "Not a wild one, either—one here on the farm. After that happened I decided I was getting old and I let my son Kensher make the sales trips down to Ethshar and run things around here, instead of doing them myself. And my granddaughter Seldis does the run to Sardiron of the Waters.'' He smiled reminiscently. "Seldis killed a wild dragon once—that was how she met her husband, Wuller. This dragon was preying on his village, and they sent him for help, and he saw Seldis in Sardiron of the Waters selling dragon's blood and talked her into getting rid of it for them. But we know dragons, as I said—she did that with a trick, she didn't hunt the thing down out in the open, with a sword or a crossbow or something. And my other sons, besides Kensher—two of them took up dragon-hunting, and last I heard, one of them was still alive. We've lived with dragons all our lives and we don't do anything stupid. Most dragon-hunters don't live long enough to learn what's stupid.''

Dumery struggled to take all this in.

It was too much. He fell back on the bed, trying to think.

Kinner realized he'd been rambling, taxing his guest's strength. He called quietly, "You rest, boy." Then he herded the remaining children out of the room and stepped out himself, closing the door quietly.

Dumery looked at the closed door for a moment, then lay back, decided it wasn't worth the effort to think about it all just now, and fell asleep.

# CHAPTER 24

*T*he witch and warlock had left hastily, *without even a word* to the innkeepers at the Blasted Pine—Adar's only hope of escaping the Calling was to get far enough from the Source to resist it before Teneria passed out from exhaustion, so there was no time to spare. Teneria quietly rebuked herself for wasting time in explanations and histories, while Adar cursed his own stupidity and his insensitivity in not seeing how tired Teneria was. He levitated both of them effortlessly and began flying north.

He found that he could not move quickly, though; the Calling was fighting him every inch of the way, slowing him, trying to pull him back south. If he sped up he found himself turning, his path curving back toward the southeast; if he kept himself firmly on course it was like fighting a strong headwind, forcing himself northward yard by yard.

And Teneria was fading; she had put in a long day walking, had carried Adar a quarter-mile on her back, and now she was maintaining a tricky and unfamiliar spell constantly. The meal and brief rest at the inn had helped, but weariness was closing up around her.

If Adar had been a witch, Teneria thought, he could have passed her some of his own energy—but of course, if he had been a witch, she wouldn't have needed to stay awake. And warlocks did not seem to be able to transfer energy as witches could; Adar was completely unfamiliar with the concept. After all, why should warlocks need to share energy? They all shared the same inexhaustible Source.

All the same, despite the differences, Teneria thought that she might have been able to tap Adar's energy if she wasn't so tired and if she wasn't doing anything else.

She couldn't possibly do it in her current state, though. And she certainly couldn't do it without dropping her defenses against the Calling.

If they had met elsewhere, under other circumstances, Teneria was sure that they could have done much more, could have shielded Adar against the Calling with his own energies—but that wasn't what the gods had wanted.

So they flew unsteadily northward, Teneria in Adar's arms like a bride being carried across the threshold, and she might have enjoyed the sensations and the novelty had she not been so desperately trying to stay awake.

Perhaps half an hour after their departure from the inn she dozed off for an instant, only to be awakened by a shriek from Adar.

Quickly, she restored her dropped spell, but both were shaken by the incident.

They survived that one.

They had survived that one, but it wasn't the last.

Teneria never did know exactly what had happened; the events blurred in her memory, lost in a fog of fatigue. She knew that she had finally lost consciousness somewhere over the forested hills, in the black depths of the night—that much she remembered.

But that was all she knew until she awoke atop a bed of pine needles, lying on her back with dawn's golden light in her face.

She lay on a hillside, surrounded by trees, their shadows black on the ground around her, the sun bright in the east. Her cloak was draped over her.

There was no sign of Adar.

She guessed that when she had passed out he had been unable to wake her, and had had enough control to put her down gently before being carried off to the southeast.

She *hoped* that they had gotten far enough north to be safe and that he had put her down and gone on home by himself—but she didn't believe it, no matter how hard she tried.

And when she used her magic to locate herself and realized that she wasn't north of the inn at all, but east, she knew that she would never see Adar again.

Maybe he had headed back and had been able to stop partway and put her down. Maybe, in the darkness and fighting against the compulsion, they had drifted off course or unwittingly circled back even before she passed out.

Whatever had happened, here she was, alone and lost in the forests of Aldagmor, and Adar was gone. She had only herself to depend on.

Despite her night's rest she was still worn and weak from witchcraft overuse. She needed food and drink. She pushed herself up on one elbow.

A squirrel chittered overhead; startled, she looked up. The animal was sitting on a branch above her. Desperate, she managed to summon the strength to catch its attention, to work a quick little spell.

The strain was more than she had expected for so small a piece of witchcraft; she lay back and shut her eyes, recuperating, unsure whether the magic had worked.

It had; a moment later she was showered with carefully hoarded nuts. Relieved, she rolled over, gathered a handful, then cracked a walnut on an exposed root and ate the meat.

Even that tiny morsel helped; she ate another, and another, as the squirrel above her realized it had been tricked and protested loudly.

Within an hour she had found a small brook and was no longer worried about whether she would survive, but only about how long it would take to return to inhabited lands.

With her witchcraft to guide her she reached the Blasted Pine by noon the next day. The innkeepers—the two women and an old man whom she hadn't met before—were startled to see her again and greeted her enthusiastically.

They didn't inquire after Adar, and she didn't volunteer any explanation.

She ate a proper meal and as she ate she spotted the spriggan peeking out from behind a nearby table, watching her anxiously.

She smiled at it.

The little creature grinned back, then ran out and leaped up on her lap. She petted it, soothing its nerves, as she ate. Although it babbled incoherently, she could see that it had been terrified and had had no idea what was going on. It was very relieved to have her back; it had more or less adopted her as its protector.

She grimaced slightly at that. She hadn't been much of a protector for poor Adar.

When she felt sufficiently fed and rested she gathered up her pack, put the spriggan up on her shoulder, then picked up Dumery's trail and headed off along the south highway.

She wasn't really very interested in Dumery any more, but what else could she do? Adar was gone; there was nothing she could do about that. She was still supposed to be fetching Dumery safely home for his parents—it would complete her apprenticeship and make her a full-fledged journeyman witch. She would follow the little nuisance and find out what he was up to, and then she would go home and figure out what to do about what she had learned about warlocks.

It did not escape her attention that Dumery appeared to be heading directly for the Warlock Stone.

Nor that she was heading toward it herself.

# CHAPTER 25

*S*omeone *cleared his throat, and Dumery turned away from* the window to see Kensher standing in the doorway. He was wearing green wool instead of brown leather, but it was unmistakably him.

"It really is you," Kensher said. "The kid from Ethshar."

Dumery blinked, but didn't answer.

"You have got to be the stubbornest little idiot I ever saw in my life, following me all the way up here from Ethshar!" Kensher said, marveling. "I *told* you I didn't need an apprentice, didn't I?"

"Yes," Dumery admitted, "but I thought that if I showed you how determined I was you'd change your mind."

Kensher snorted. "Not likely! With eleven kids of my own? You'd need magic to change my mind."

"Well, I didn't *know* you had eleven kids—you never mentioned that when you turned me down! And if I had magic, I wouldn't *want* to change your mind!" Dumery replied hotly.

"Exactly my point," Kensher said. "Following me here was *stupid*. Do your parents know you're all right? Do they have any idea where you are?"

"Yes, they know I'm all right," Dumery said. "They bought a spell and checked. A sixnight ago, I think it was—the second night after we left."

"Well, that's good, then," Kensher said. "That's one less thing we have to worry about. Now all we have to do is get you safely back home."

Dumery shook his head. "I'm not going home," he said. "Not until I've served an apprenticeship."

Kensher glared. "I just *told* you, boy, I'm not taking you on! No apprenticeship! No way! You're going home!"

"And if I go home, do you know what I'll do?" Dumery shouted. "I'll tell everyone on Wizard Street that Kensher the dragon-hunter isn't a hunter at all, that you raise dragons, and you have all the blood they'll ever need right here for the taking, and *then* what's going to happen to your precious family farm?"

Dumery caught himself, horrified. He hadn't meant to make the threat so bluntly. He'd been thinking exactly that, that he could force Kensher to keep him on here by threatening to expose the secret, but he'd meant to do it subtly, gradually, not in a single angry outburst.

Kensher stared at him coldly. "Not much," he said. "For all I know, half the wizards in Ethshar already know we run a farm and not a hunt—maybe they *all* know. Haven't you ever heard of divination spells? You can't keep secrets from wizards, boy, not unless you're a magician yourself."

"But why would they have looked?" Dumery asked. "It probably never occurred to them to check!"

"Oh," Kensher said, "I suppose nobody would ever have noticed that three-fourths of the dragon's blood in the Hegemony all seems to come from one hunter. Nobody would ever have gotten curious about that. Nobody would ever have noticed how steady our supply is. No, in two hundred years, no wizard would ever think of that!"

"Oh," Dumery said.

Kensher glowered at him. "If I were you, Dumery of Shiphaven," he said, "I'd be a little more careful about what I said and I wouldn't argue this. We don't need any blackmailers around here, nor anyone who makes threats to the people who took him in and sheltered and fed him, instead of leaving him to die. For all anyone back in Ethshar knows, if your parents haven't checked in a sixnight, you might already have died lost in the mountains somewhere—and if you want to exchange threats, well, you might yet die lost in the mountains somewhere if you aren't careful!"

"I'm sorry," Dumery said contritely, and he was partly sincere. He hadn't wanted to anger anyone.

He just wanted an apprenticeship.

"You should be," Kensher answered, calming somewhat. "Besides," he added, "I thought you want to apprentice to a hunter, not a farmer."

"Oh, I don't care which," Dumery said, "just so long as it's dragons."

"You like dragons, then?"

Dumery hesitated. That hadn't really been what he meant; he was far more concerned with the value of dragon blood than anything about the beasts themselves.

On the other hand, they were pretty interesting.

"Yes," he said, "very much."

"You were watching them out the window just now, weren't you?"

Dumery nodded.

"Do you think you're fit enough to go outside? We could go take a closer look at them, if you like."

"I'd like that," Dumery said.

After all, if he was going to work with dragons—and he

would find a way, somehow—it was never too soon to start learning more about them. Besides, he wanted to ingratiate himself with Kensher. He'd gotten off to a bad start, offending the man with his silly threats, and this might be a chance to get back on better terms.

Five minutes later, wrapped in a fur cape Korun Kensher's son had loaned him, Dumery followed Kensher out the back door of the farmhouse onto the stony ground of the little plateau.

The icy wind hit him like a hard slap across the face, leaving his right cheek red and stinging. He blinked hard, trying to keep his vision clear; it felt as if teardrops were freezing in the corners of his eyes.

"Cold," he remarked, trying to keep his teeth from chattering.

Kensher looked at him, startled. "A little," he said. "For this time of year, especially, I guess. But it's not that bad, really; you've just been curled up indoors for too long."

Dumery gritted his teeth and didn't answer.

"Of course," Kensher went on, as they strolled across the yard to the first of the pens, "you're from Ethshar, aren't you? It doesn't get very cold there, does it? Not like up here in Aldagmor."

"No," Dumery said, "I guess not." He had always thought that Ethshar of the Spices got quite cold enough in the winter, when the snows came, but by the middle of spring—which it now was—the snows were long gone, and the spring rains getting progressively warmer. Warm, damp breezes would be blowing in from the Gulf of the East, nothing like the cold, cutting blast that swept across these northern mountains.

He shuddered, literally, at the thought of what this place must be like in the winter.

It occurred to him that maybe he didn't want to stay here after all.

He thrust that thought aside and looked around.

He and Kensher were standing at the first pen, where wrought-iron tracery connected black iron beams as big around as a man's thigh. The pen was perhaps thirty feet long and fifteen feet front to back, and the iron barrier was at least ten feet high. The ironwork continued across the top in a graceful arch. The ground behind the metal was bare stone.

Inside the pen, a dozen tiny dragons were staring up at them. Dumery stared back.

"Hatchlings," Kensher said. "Broke the shells a sixnight ago, while I was on the way back from Ethshar—I'd wanted to be here to help, but I didn't make it. Just two clutches this year; we usually do better."

The largest baby dragon, which was also the closest, was black, with golden eyes and gleaming white talons. From the nose to the tip of its tail it was four or five feet long, Dumery estimated, but most of that length was in the long, curling tail. It had four legs, thin and bony, each one ending in five long, curling claws; its head was long and narrow, with long, upright, pointed, set-back ears. The gleaming yellow eyes had black slit pupils, like a cat's.

When the dragon realized Dumery was staring at it it opened its mouth and hissed, and Dumery glimpsed a pointed, yellowish-red tongue surrounded by hundreds of tiny white teeth.

They looked very sharp.

It had wings on its back, great black wings, shaped like the wings of a bat, rather than any sort of bird, with thin, leathery skin stretched over a bony frame—except that the wings hung down limply.

"The wings . . ." Dumery said, pointing.

Kensher snatched the boy's finger back away from the bars. "They bite," he said.

Dumery gulped and looked at his finger, making sure it was still there.

"Broken," Kensher said.

Dumery looked up at him. "What?"

"The wings are broken," Kensher explained. "We have to do that to make sure they don't fly away. We don't want a bunch of wild dragons running around loose in the woods down there."

"Oh," Dumery said, looking back at the little black dragon. "But you have a roof on the cage."

"Yes, of course we do, but . . ." Kensher stopped, groping for the best way to explain. After a moment's thought he continued. "Look, when they fly, they're a lot harder to handle. If you go in the cage they can knock you down and slip out the door and get away, and there's no way to catch them if they can fly. That black one there must weight thirty or forty pounds, and it's still a hatchling. In a month it could be fifty or sixty pounds; in three months it could top a hundred. You do not want to argue with a hundred-pound flying dragon. It's bad enough when they *can't* fly, believe me.''

"Oh," Dumery said, looking through the bars.

Behind the big black hatchling were about half a dozen green ones, smaller, but still big enough to be frightening. A reddish-gold one was pacing about in a far corner of the cage; two blue-green ones and a red one were curled up together asleep.

All of them, Dumery noticed, had broken wings.

"So dragons really can fly," he said.

"Oh, yes," Kensher said. "Most of them, anyway. Some don't have the wingspan, or the muscles don't develop right, but most of them can fly. At least when they're young."

"Do any of them really breathe fire?"

Kensher grimaced. "Not around here," he said. "There are fire-breathing dragons, all right, and back during the war they raised them here, but it doesn't make any difference in the blood, and that's the only market we have left, so my great-great-great grandfather culled them all. They're just too damned dangerous to have around. My ancestors used to have to wear armor just to go near them, and even so, a couple of several-times-great uncles got fried. Sometimes we get a throwback—the trait's not completely weeded out of their bloodlines yet—but when that happens, we kill it was soon as we find out about it."

"Oh," Dumery said, looking at the hatchlings. "So none of these can breathe fire?"

"Not that we know of, anyway, and usually they start to at least spit sparks by now."

"Oh," Dumery said, stepping back.

"Come on, let's look at the yearlings," Kensher said, beckoning.

Dumery followed him around to the right, past the hatchlings' cage.

The next cage was several times the size of the hatchlings'; Dumery didn't care to guess its exact dimensions. The wrought-iron tracery was much simpler, but much heavier, with larger openings. Four dragons, each ten or twelve feet long, occupied it; two were green, two golden yellow. There was a strong and unpleasant odor to the place—Dumery wrinkled his nose at it. He noticed the pile in a corner that was presumably the source for most of the stench.

All four dragons were clustered around the remains of a steer, eating noisily. One gave the two humans a red-eyed glance, then turned back to its meal.

All four had wings, and again, all the wings were broken and hanging limp.

"*Those* are just a year old?" Dumery said, looking at the curving talons, claws bigger than his fingers.

"That's right," Kensher said.

Dumery noticed a golden wing flopping. "Don't the wings heal up?" he asked.

"Of course they do," Kensher replied. "That's why we have to break them again every year."

"You do?"

"Of course. Look at those things—four hundred pounds each. And we can't remove the claws or fangs, because then they can't feed themselves. We can't let them fly."

Dumery looked, just as a green dragon lifted its head with a bloody mouthful of beef. He shuddered. "No," he said, "I guess you can't."

The tour continued, past two more cages of yearlings, and then a dozen huge pens for older, more mature beasts. These ranged from about twelve feet long up to twenty or more, and glared fiercely at the two humans. Every so often one would roar, and Dumery would cover his ears against the sound.

A heavy outer fence ran around the entire group of pens, enclosing much of the plateau. Kensher noticed Dumery looking at it as the pair walked on.

"Sometimes they get out of their cages," he said. "We don't know how they do it, sometimes, but they do—dragons are tricky. When that happens, the fence there stops them from going any farther."

"Do any ever get away completely?" Dumery asked.

Kensher admitted reluctantly, "Sometimes, yes."

Dumery looked down across the edge of the plateau toward the forests below. "So there are wild dragons out there?"

"Maybe. I don't know if they survive—after all, they've never learned to hunt for their food, and there isn't much game around here, and they can't fly. Most of them probably don't last long."

Dumery didn't find that very comforting. He remembered that he had come up the path through those woods alone and unprotected, without ever giving the possibility of being eaten by a wild dragon any serious thought.

Then, finally, they came to the slaughterhouse, where Dumery gawked at the tangle of huge iron chains and heavy beams, used to restrain and support dragons while their throats were cut and their blood drained.

"We cull most of them when they're six or seven months old," Kensher explained. "That's where we get most of the blood. By then we know which ones we want for breeding stock, so we dispose of the rest here. If there's any sign of illness or anemia, or if they're unusually vicious, or if we just don't like their looks, we weed them out then. The others we keep until they're about four or five years old, and then they have to go, too." He gestured at the restraints. "A healthy dragon's about eighteen or twenty feet long by then, weighs maybe a ton, but the growth is slowing down, so it's not worth keeping them any longer. Besides, any bigger and they get *really* dangerous, and we can't handle them any more. They aren't just bigger and stronger, either, they're smarter. A hatchling's no smarter than a kitten, and a yearling maybe as bright as a wolf, but by the time a dragon's five or six years old it's smarter than any other animal except people. A really smart one might start learning to talk when it's seven or eight, and we can't have that."

"Why not?" Dumery asked, puzzled.

Kensher blinked. "Ah . . . because if . . . if it can *talk,* then it's not just an animal any more, boy, and it wouldn't be right to kill it." He frowned. "It's bad enough killing the breeding stock as it is."

Dumery considered that for a moment.

How did learning to talk make a dragon a person? It was still a *dragon,* after all.

But he could sort of see Kensher's point. If you could hold a conversation with something, it wasn't just an animal any more.

But if a talking dragon shouldn't be killed, then was it really all right to kill the immature ones? Did that mean that it would be all right to kill a human baby that hadn't yet learned to talk? Maybe it did mean that; he had heard that sometimes girls did exactly that when they had babies they didn't want.

Dumery decided he didn't want to think about that just now.

But if the dragons were killed when they were still babies, too young to talk . . .

"How old do they have to be to lay eggs?" he asked.

"Oh, they'll start breeding as yearlings, if we let them," Kensher said. "We don't, though; that's why there are three separate cages for yearlings instead of one big one."

"Three?"

"Well, we don't usually get nice even numbers of male and female," Kensher explained. "We usually have more males than females. And we don't want them to breed until they're about three; the young are healthier that way. So we have two cages for males and one for females."

Dumery nodded, staring at the ironmongery.

The killing knife hung by the door, a huge saw-toothed blade the size of a broadsword, its metal polished and gleaming. The bottles used for the blood stood ranged on shelves against one wall, all of them empty and sparkling clean.

He hadn't thought about the actual killing when he asked for an apprenticeship. He hadn't thought about feeding almost a hundred hungry dragons every day, about raising the cattle to feed them. He hadn't thought about breaking wings every year, or watching for fire-breathers and killing them young, or losing fingers or hands or arms in a moment's carelessness around the livestock. There was far more to raising dragons than he had considered.

It look like a dull, dirty, difficult, and dangerous business. It meant cruelty and killing.

Dumery didn't like any of that.

All the same, Dumery thought, what else could he do? He had come this far; he was reluctant to throw that away. Besides, for as long as he could remember, all he had wanted out of life was magic, and he had been denied that. There was nothing else he wanted to do. Dragon-farming might not be magic, but it was *something,* anyway, and if it meant he could rub Thetheran's nose in the dirt, then it *was* what he wanted to do.

Now all he had to do was convince Kensher to let him do it.

# CHAPTER 26

"You know," Dumery remarked between bites of Pancha's baked pudding, "my father's a wealthy man."

"Oh?" Kensher said, not particularly interested. Kinner looked up from his plate, but said nothing.

Dumery nodded. "He'd pay well to buy me an apprenticeship, enough to cover all the costs with some left over."

Kensher shook his head. "No apprenticeship," he said. "I told you that. We have plenty of money as it is, and if we need more we just raise our prices; we don't need your father's gold." He scooped up another heaping spoonful.

Dumery looked down to hide his annoyance. He had thought he had a chance, that he would at least be able to put up an argument, but how could he counter that flat refusal?

He looked up again and glanced down the dinner table, taking in all the faces. Most of them, he knew, didn't understand Ethsharitic, so they had no idea what he and Kensher had just said. For all Dumery could tell, most of them might not even know that he *wanted* an apprenticeship.

And did all of them want to stay here and learn the family business? Maybe he could replace one, somehow.

He caught a glimpse of Wuller of Srigmor, the shepherd who had married Seldis of Aldagmor, the eldest granddaughter. *That* was a possibility—Wuller had married into the family, and there were still five other granddaughters, presumably all unmarried and probably not spoken for yet. There were not a lot of eligible suitors up here in the mountains.

There was Shatha, and Tarissa, and Kirsha, and Shanra, and Kinthera. Shanra and Kinthera were a few years older than Dumery was—not that that really mattered.

None of them particularly appealed to him, though. Seldis was pretty—but she was already married, and *much* too old.

And besides, he didn't really want to commit himself to marrying *anyone* yet.

Of course, he could lie and *say* that he wanted to marry Shanra; nobody would expect him to make good on that until he was sixteen, at the earliest, by which time he ought to know all there was to know about raising dragons for their blood.

But the knowledge wouldn't do him much good if he angered the owners of the only dragon farm in the World.

And besides, he didn't like the idea of lying about it. It wouldn't be proper to get an apprenticeship that way. And in all likelihood his lies wouldn't be believed in any case; these people weren't stupid, and they knew what he wanted, since he had foolishly admitted it already. They wouldn't accept him into the family just to give him an apprenticeship and they would know that was the *real* reason he wanted to marry in.

Besides, there was no guarantee that Shanra or any of the others would be interested in marrying *him,* now, was there?

No, marrying into the family was not going to be his answer. At least, not in and of itself.

If he could find some way to stay, then in fact he really might eventually marry one of the girls. After all, if he stayed here for a few years he wouldn't see any *other* girls, and sooner or later, he supposed, he would want to get married.

But that argument wasn't going to convince Kensher to let him stay, he was sure.

"And you really don't care if I tell all the wizards back in Ethshar that you people are running a farm here and not hunting dragons in the wild?" he asked.

Kinner blinked, Pancha flinched, and Kensher sighed.

"Not much," Kensher said. "The hunting story is a convenient fiction, and we've happy with it, but it's not really essential. We'd stay in business without it; we might need to negotiate a little with the Wizards' Guild, that's all." He put down his spoon. "Look, Dumery," he said. "Give it up. We don't need an apprentice here, and if we did, it wouldn't be a rich, spoiled city boy who was stupid enough to follow me home the way you did. And particularly not one who makes threats about revealing secrets."

Pancha flinched again. "Kenshi," she said, "don't be so harsh. It took courage and resourcefulness for him to come all the way up here by himself."

"Doesn't mean it was smart," Kensher said. "And resourceful or not, we do *not* need an apprentice!"

Kinner made a noise of agreement, and even Pancha couldn't argue with that.

Dumery often didn't know when to quit, but this time it finally sank in that he wasn't getting anywhere, and he finished his pudding in silence.

When he was done he sat staring at the empty plate, and inspiration struck. He looked up.

Pancha was clearing away the empty dishes, and Kinner had gone off somewhere with some of his younger grandchildren, but Kensher was still at the table, leaning back comfortably.

"What if I bought a dragon?" Dumery asked.

Kensher let out his breath in a whoosh, then leaned forward, startled.

*"What?"* he demanded.

"What if I bought a dragon?" Dumery repeated. "Or two, actually. They wouldn't have to be good ones; a couple of hatchlings you'd cull anyway would do just fine."

"We don't sell dragons," Kensher said, eyeing him suspiciously.

"You sell their blood," Dumery said. "What's the difference?"

"Plenty," Kensher said. "A bottle of blood never bit anyone's arm off."

"All right, so it's not the same," Dumery admitted. "Will you sell me a pair anyway?"

"A pair, is it? You mean you don't just want any two dragons, you want a male and female?"

"Well, yes," Dumery admitted, "that is what I had in mind."

Kensher stared at him for a moment, then leaned back in his

chair and said, "Boy, you're amazing. You must think I'm as dumb as you are! You want me to sell you a breeding pair so you can set yourself up your own little dragon farm and go into business in competition with us?"

That was, in fact, exactly what Dumery wanted, but it seemed impolitic to say so just now. Instead he sat silently frustrated, staring at Kensher.

"I have got to admit, Dumery, you are the stubbornest, most persistent lad I have ever met in my life," Kensher said, his tone almost admiring. "Even the dragons aren't as determined as you. But it doesn't matter. We are *not* going to set you up in the dragon-farming business, either here or in competition with us. We're going to send you home to your family, and hope you have the sense not to go and cause pointless trouble by telling where we live and what we do. Is that clear enough?"

Dumery reluctantly nodded. "It's clear," he said.

And in fact it *was* clear that the descendants of Sergeant Thar wouldn't help him intentionally.

Perhaps, though, they might be made to provide assistance without knowing it. As he carried his empty plate to the scullery Dumery was planning just how that might work.

It would involve lying and stealing and a good bit of danger, but he thought he could manage it.

Just a little while ago he had been reluctant to lie to Kensher and his family about wanting to marry Shanra, and here he was considering not just lying, but robbing them, as well.

Well, he was desperate. And this new scheme was much more likely to succeed, anyway, and it would be over much sooner, one way or the other.

There was a chance it would get him killed, but he refused to worry about that. It might work.

And if it worked, it would be well worth the risk.

# CHAPTER 27

*T eneria stared in disbelief at the pens.*

Dragons!

*Dozens* of dragons!

Big dragons, small dragons, red, blue, and green dragons!

She had never seen *any* dragon before, in her entire life, and here there were *dozens* of dragons..

What in the World *was* this place?

And what was Dumery doing here?

She lowered her pack to the ground, then scooped the sprig-gan off her shoulder and dropped it onto a nearby rock. She sat down, still staring at the farm, and tried to think.

As she did, she was aware once again of a sort of soft muttering in the back of her mind, as if someone were trying to sneak up on her, or was thinking loudly about her some-where nearby. The same uncomfortable sensation had come over her a few times on the way up into the mountains, and she didn't like it at all.

She had disliked it right from the start, but oddly, it had taken until the fourth time she felt it before she recognized it.

It was the Calling.

Witches weren't supposed to be susceptible to the Calling—but on the other hand, Adar had told her that people who got too close to the Warlock Stone could spontaneously become war-locks, and witchcraft and warlockry were apparently not all *that* different, after all. She knew that she had been born with a strong talent for witchcraft—Sella had told her as much. That was why Sella had been willing to take Teneria on as an ap-prentice, even though Teneria's parents couldn't pay the cus-tomary fee.

And if Teneria had the innate talent for witchcraft, why wouldn't she have the talent for warlockry, as well?

163

Even so, she might not have picked anything up, might not have sensed the Calling, if she hadn't spent those long, horrible hours focused on Adar's mind, trying to hold the Calling out. That had taught her what the Calling was, had attuned her to it.

She wasn't a warlock, even now, by any means; she could levitate things, of course, but it still tired her; it was still witchcraft, not warlockry.

Witch or warlock, though, she could feel that unpleasant mental touch, ever so lightly.

And it seemed to be growing more noticeable as she continued southward and eastward. She did not like the idea of venturing even farther in that direction.

But now she wouldn't have to. Dumery was here; despite the delays, she had finally caught up to him. And this, surely, was where he had been headed all along.

She could see why he hadn't wanted to tell the truth when his parents' hired wizard contacted him. That would have sounded *so* reassuring to his poor mother—"Oh, I'm hiking up into wild, dragon-infested, warlock-haunted mountains in Aldagmor, along what used to be the frontier of the old Northern Empire. I'll be up there in the freezing cold weather without any supplies or money, with nothing but the clothes on my back. I'm going to a secret menagerie of dragons up there."

And what in the World did Dumery *want* in this miserable, godsforsaken place, anyway? What business did a twelve-year-old boy have at an all-dragon zoo like this? Had he been tricked into coming here as dragon fodder?

No, that didn't make any sense; he was still alive, she could tell. And even if there were some reason to feed dragons boys instead of sheep or cattle, surely there were gullible boys to be found closer than Ethshar of the Spices.

Maybe the boy was on some errand for a wizard? Everybody knew he had been hounding half the magicians in the Wizards' Quarter for an apprenticeship; maybe he had settled for a job as a wizard's errand boy. Wizards seemed to take an unhealthy interested in dragons; she had certainly seen enough of them with dragons embroidered on robes, or with carved dragons adorning their shops.

Well, there were ways to find out what was going on. The simplest and best was to walk right up and ask.

If it turned out that her interest wasn't welcome, well, she was a witch; she could defend herself.

She marched down the path. Behind her the spriggan let out a small yip of dismay, which she ignored; it then scurried after her.

She reached the door, stopped, raised a fist, and knocked loudly. The spriggan grabbed her ankle and held on.

Even through the heavy oak, and even though she had never had any contact with the people on the other side, she could sense the astonishment within. She waited.

Eventually, the door creaked open an inch or so.

"Yes?" a handsome young woman asked, in Sardironese. "Can I help you?"

Teneria could see that the woman was thinking in Sardironese—hardly surprising, as they were still in Aldagmor. The witch was still not very comfortable with the local language, but she tried. "I am looking for Dumery of Shiphaven," she said, unhappily aware that she had spoken with a very thick Ethsharitic accent and that the spriggan was clinging to her leg, hampering any fast movement.

"Dumery?" the woman in the house replied, startled. Teneria saw that she knew exactly who Dumery of Shiphaven was; the mental image she conjured up matched Teneria's own perfectly.

"Yes," Teneria said, nodding. "Dumery."

"He hadn't told us he was expecting anyone," the woman said uncertainly. Teneria realized that she wasn't much older than herself.

"He wasn't expecting me," she said. "His . . . his . . ." She groped for the word.

Seeing Teneria's discomfort, the woman said, "I understand Ethsharitic, mostly."

Teneria noticed that she hadn't said so *in* Ethsharitic, so she kept her words as simple as she could. "His parents sent me," she said.

"Oh!" The confusion cleared from the woman's mind with miraculous speed. "Come in! I'm Seldis of Aldagmor; my parents and grandfather own this place. Come on in.'' She swung the door wide.

"Thank you," Teneria said, accepting the invitation. The spriggan, riding on her boot, came with her.

She found herself in a large, cluttered room, facing a horde of children and a handful of adults. One of the children she immediately recognized—Dumery of Shiphaven.

"Hello, Dumery," she said. "I'm Teneria. Your parents sent me."

"My parents?" the boy asked warily. "Not Thetheran?"

"Well—my mistress, actually. I'm still an apprentice. But your parents hired her." Teneria was uncomfortably aware of more than a dozen pairs of eyes watching the conversation closely, even though she could tell that only four of the listeners understood Ethsharitic—an old man with an arm missing, a big, powerful middle-aged man, a small, dark middle-aged woman, and Seldis.

Some of the children had spotted the spriggan and were pointing at it and whispering to one another. The little creature hopped off and ran off to hide under the furniture somewhere.

"They did?" Dumery asked. "Who *is* she, your mistress?"

"Sella the Witch," Teneria replied.

"My father hired a witch?" The boy believed her, she knew; he was just startled.

"I think your mother had more to do with it," she answered.

The middle-aged man had stepped forward; while Dumery groped for another question the man spoke, holding out a hand in greeting. "Welcome to our home, young lady," he said. "I am Kensher Kinner's son."

"Teneria of Fishertown." She bowed politely.

Dumery watched as this unexpected new arrival was introduced to all the inhabitants of the farmhouse, and as he watched he was trying to figure out what to do now.

He had never expected his parents to send someone after him; despite the dream Thetheran had sent he hadn't thought that they cared enough, or that his father would be willing to pay for it, and besides, why would they send someone when they had used the dream spell?

And quite aside from all that, how had this person *found* him?

She was an apprentice witch, of course, but he hadn't known that witches could do that.

Somehow, though, she *had* found him. Maybe that spriggan he had seen run under the sofa had had something to do with it, if that was the same one he had seen back at the Inn at the Bridge—after all, he knew even less about spriggans than he did about witches.

Just how it was done didn't really matter, though, since it *had* been done.

So now what?

What did this do to his plans?

It pretty much knocked them to pieces, he realized, unless he could either get rid of this Teneria, or get her over on his side, somehow. He had intended to take his leave of the farm, then sneak back at night and steal two hatchlings, as breeding stock for his own farm. If he was in a witch's care he couldn't very well carry out his scheme without her knowing about it.

Getting her over to his side—well, that would be ideal, certainly. A witch would be *extremely* useful.

However, he couldn't imagine any way it could be done. Getting rid of her should be far easier.

Just now, though, he wasn't sure how to do that, either.

It would require further thought.

Teneria, even as she committed the names of all the children to memory, was listening as best she could to Dumery's thoughts.

She couldn't get them exactly, but she knew he wasn't happy with her presence. He had been planning something and he didn't think she would approve.

This was something she would want to discuss with him. In private.

She smiled at Pancha and complimented her, in awkward Sardironese, on her fine collection of offspring. The mistress of the house smiled back.

She invited Teneria to stay for dinner, and for the night, and with an eye on Dumery, Teneria accepted.

# CHAPTER 28

*U*pon consideration, Teneria realized that effective privacy would not actually be all that hard to obtain, since the children spoke no Ethsharitic—only the adults had to be avoided. When Kensher and the older children were out checking on the livestock after dinner, and the younger children were playing with the spriggan, and Pancha was in the kitchen putting away dishes, a little judicious witchcraft allowed Teneria to get Dumery away from Kinner and Seldis.

Dumery hadn't really noticed yet that the two of them were alone in the front room until Teneria demanded, "All right, Dumery, what are you up to?"

Startled, Dumery said, "I don't know what you mean." He eyed the young woman he was beginning to think of as his captor and wondered how much she knew. The stories he had heard were vague on whether witches could read one's thoughts, or merely sense moods.

"I know you're up to *something*," she said. "I'm a witch, remember? Now, suppose you tell me all about it."

"All about *what?*" Dumery persisted, still unsure of his best course of action.

Teneria put her hands on her hips and glared at him. "You know what."

"No, I don't," Dumery said, trying to look puzzled.

Teneria let out an exasperated sigh. "All right, then," she said, "let's take it a step at a time. What are you doing up here in the mountains of Aldagmor, instead of safe at home with your parents?"

That was no secret anymore, so there was no harm in telling the truth. "I followed Kensher," Dumery said. "I wanted to arrange an apprenticeship with him. I saw him selling dragon's blood to Thetheran the Mage back in Ethshar, and I decided I wanted to get into the dragon's-blood business, too. So I followed him here and asked him.''

"And he turned you down," Teneria said. She could see that from Dumery's attitude and she could even see the reason—Kensher had eleven children of his own.

"That's right," Dumery agreed. "He turned me down."

"So now you're just going to go quietly home with me, I suppose," Teneria said sarcastically.

Dumery ignored the sarcasm and nodded, trying to look innocent.

Teneria was disgusted. "Right," she said. "You know perfectly well that that wasn't what you were planning at all."

"Well . . ."

"So what *were* you planning?"

Dumery stood obstinately silent.

Teneria sighed again. "Suppose," she said, "that your parents had instructed me to do whatever I can to see that you get what you came after, be it an apprenticeship or whatever. Would you still be standing there like that?"

"They didn't, did they?" He sounded very doubtful indeed.

"Not exactly," Teneria admitted. "But they *do* want you to be happy, Dumery, and to find a career you'll enjoy. I don't think they'd object to dragon-farming. Now, did you have some scheme for getting an apprenticeship dragon-farming, after all?"

"No," Dumery said. "There isn't any way. Kensher won't listen to me, and there aren't any other dragon-farmers."

Teneria was glad to see that Dumery was telling the truth. "So it's not that," she said. She eyed him carefully.

He was tall for his age, but very thin, with a very stubborn set to his jaw. His mind was not easily pried at—she could see at a glance that he was very closed and self-contained and could never have become a witch.

A thought struck her. The boy had been desperate to become a magician, and here he was in Aldagmor, where, she now knew, the source of one kind of magic was to be found. "Is it something to do with the Warlock Stone?" she asked.

"The what?" Dumery answered, baffled.

No, it wasn't that; Teneria could see that the boy had never heard the term before.

Back to other matters, then. "Something to do with dragons?" she asked.

He didn't answer, but he didn't have to.

"Dragons," she said. "Something to do with dragons." She considered him carefully.

"Not hunting them, I hope?" She had a rough idea how dangerous dragon-hunting might be; she could hardly say she'd fulfilled her task of seeing that Dumery was safe if she let him go off hunting the great beasts.

"No," he said, and she knew that he was telling the truth.

"It's something you feel guilty about, though," she said. That much was obvious. "Something dangerous?"

He shook his head.

Teneria frowned. That was a half-truth. Dumery thought it might be risky, somehow, but he didn't think it should be *really* dangerous. That didn't tell her much.

This was all very tiresome. He obviously wasn't going to tell her if he could possibly avoid doing so, and she couldn't read it from him, and it might take hours, or days, to guess it. She glowered at him for a moment, then changed her approach.

"Is there anything you wanted to ask *me?*" she asked.

Startled, Dumery studied her carefully and considered his response.

She was a witch, but he had only a vague idea of what sort of magic witches used—he had mostly heard of healings and divinations, and didn't know much about how those worked. He had always been more interested in wizardry and the other, more prestigious varieties of magic, not the rather plebian witchcraft. And she was a girl, almost a woman—he wasn't sure whether to consider her a grown-up or not.

She was working for his parents, so he had been thinking of her as being on their side, on the side of rules and regulations and authority, but might that be a mistake?

He couldn't very well ask her straight out "Are you going to stop me from committing a robbery?"

Maybe he could sort of feel her out, though. And there *was* something that he wondered about.

"What's the Warlock Stone?" he asked.

Teneria was caught off-guard and hesitated for a moment. Well, why not? What harm could it do?

"It's the source for all the warlocks' magic. It's somewhere in Aldagmor, to the southeast of here."

"Really?"

Teneria could clearly see the boy's sudden interest in this news, which was not at all what she had wanted. She sighed again.

"Listen, Dumery, forget it," she told him. "You can't get near it. No one can. It kills anyone who gets too close. *I* don't dare get much closer than I am right here and now—magicians are more susceptible."

"Oh," Dumery said. He thought that over.

He wasn't sure he believed her, but on the other hand, if it really *was* approachable, and if people knew where it was, and if it was really any use, then someone else would have gone there by now, and it would all be in the hands of others. After all, warlocks had been around since before he was born.

So that was out, and he was back to his former scheme.

"You're a witch, right?" he asked.

Teneria nodded. "An apprentice, anyway."

"Have you ever put a curse on anyone?" Maybe she wasn't a total goody-goody. Maybe she'd go along with a little adventure.

"No," she said, dashing his hopes, "witches don't do curses."

"They do in the stories. . ." Dumery began.

"All right," Teneria said, exasperated, "*I* don't do curses. And I never met a witch who did, either, but maybe there are some."

"Oh." Dumery shut up. It was clear to him that a person who wouldn't deal in curses was not the sort to go along with a burglary scheme.

Teneria glared at him. The boy was infuriating! And it appeared that she wasn't going to learn anything else useful from him.

"All right, look," she said, "whatever you've got in mind,

just forget it, all right? Tomorrow morning we're starting back down the mountain, taking you home to Ethshar. You can find an apprenticeship of some kind there.''

Dumery didn't answer.

They glowered at one another for a moment, then marched away in opposite directions.

Later that night, as the household began to settle down, Dumery considered the situation.

He had intended to take his leave, go down the mountain until he was out of sight, then slip back up at night.

He couldn't do that while in Teneria's care, though. He would have to make his move that very night, while everyone was asleep, before he and Teneria were thrown together for good.

He had also planned to flee down the trail to the river, the same way he had come, but now he decided against it. If he did that, Teneria would come after him and find him, almost certainly. She was a witch, after all, and had found him way up here in the mountains of Aldagmor.

He could escape her, though. He saw exactly how he could escape her. If he headed south or southeast, toward the War-lock Stone she had spoken of, she wouldn't dare follow. The thing would kill her.

It wouldn't kill *him*, though, because he wasn't a magician. Or at least, it wouldn't kill him unless he got really close, which he would try not to do.

And the possibility that he might stumble on the Stone by accident—well, that was a chance he'd take.

And if he did, who knew? Maybe Teneria was wrong and he would wind up a warlock after all.

It didn't seem very likely, though.

He hadn't really planned everything out yet, but there was no time to spare, with Teneria here. He would just have to improvise, deal with problems as they arose.

As soon as he was sure everyone was asleep, he would go.

He lay back and waited.

# CHAPTER 29

*D*umery *crept down the stairs with his pack on his arm,* walking to one side to lessen the chance of creaking, and listening intently for any sign that someone else was still awake—someone like Teneria, for example.

He heard nothing but the wind outside. Apparently witches slept just as soundly as anybody else.

Cautiously, he made his way down the hall and through the rear storage room to the back door, the one that led out to the dragon pens.

It was barred, with three heavy bars—Dumery assumed that that was just to keep dragons out, should one escape from its cage. He looked the bars over carefully.

They were padlocked in place, and the keys were nowhere in sight.

He had half expected that. With a shrug, he turned and made his way, slowly and cautiously, back through the house to the front door.

That had an ordinary bolt and a hook latch; he threw the bolt, lifted the latch, and then, very slowly, eased the door open and slipped out.

Both moons were high overhead, the lesser just passing the greater, and between them they gave enough light that Dumery could see where he was going. He made his way up the path between the flower beds and through the garden, back over the rocky shoulder of the mountain, until he could see the forest spread out below, black in the moonslight.

The weather had finally warmed somewhat in the last day or so, and the winds were relatively calm, for once. Moonslight sparkled eerily from snowcaps on distant peaks, and the moons' two colors edged shadows with pink and orange. It was a beautiful night. Dumery could easily have made his way downslope and into the woods without fear of stumbling or losing his way.

That was if he were heading downslope, though, and in point of fact he had no intention of doing so.

Rather, he intended to circle around the house so as to get at the dragon pens.

Accordingly, as soon as he was certain he was out of sight, should someone wake and glance out an upstairs windows, he turned left off the path and began cutting cross-country, through the pastures where the cattle that the dragons ate grazed.

At first he had intended simply to circle around to the back of the house by the shortest possible route, but he encountered an obstacle he hadn't known about—a fissure, separating the pasture from the dragon pens. The house appeared to have been built directly atop it.

He studied it for a moment. It was deep and wide, and the plank bridge that the people and cattle presumably used to cross it was drawn up on the other side. One end ran right up to the foundations of the farmhouse.

He supposed it kept the dragons and cattle from approaching each other too closely and he wished he had noticed it before.

It was too wide to leap, in the dark, and the lower end was impassable because of the farmhouse. He would have to go around the upper end.

That took him up out of the pasture, over the fence, and into the wilderness beyond.

There was no trail at all this way, and the terrain was rough; stretches of bare, jagged stone were interspersed with moss, lichen, gravel, and a few struggling pines. Dumery had to pick his footing carefully, and every so often a rock or chunk of moss would slide out from underneath him and send him sprawling. He cut his chin, bruised and scraped the palms of both hands, and twisted his left wrist painfully, but he made steady progress.

His biggest worry wasn't falling into the fissure—he kept a healthy distance between him and that—nor falling off the mountain—for the most part the slopes were not so steep as to make that a real danger—but the possibility of encountering an escaped dragon. Despite what Kensher had said, Dumery suspected that there were probably quite a number of them in the vicinity, gone wild.

He couldn't decide whether they would be more likely to leave the area completely and avoid the place where they had suffered in captivity, or whether they would hang around the only home they had ever known.

He tended toward the former theory, not just because it was reassuring, but because he remembered those pitiful broken wings hanging down across the hatchlings' flanks. If he'd had something equally unpleasant done to him, such as a broken arm or two, he certainly would never again want to go anywhere near the place it had happened.

But he wasn't a dragon, of course, and he didn't know how dragons thought about these things. So he struggled onward and tried not to worry about it.

The lesser moon was down, and the greater sinking fast when he finally scrambled around a towering boulder and found himself in sight of the back row of dragon pens, with the farmhouse just barely visible beyond them.

He smiled, satisfied, and crept down toward the pens, moving as silently as he knew how. He ignored the curious glances some of the dragons gave him. Several of the sharp-eyed creatures were awake, and some had spotted him as soon as he emerged from behind the boulder into sight of the farm, but they hadn't done anything about it. There was no reason they should.

They weren't watching him constantly, but they certainly knew where he was and cast an occasional glance at him.

The bigger ones did, at any rate; the yearlings didn't seem to have noticed anything, and he couldn't even see the hatchlings from where he was.

The hatchlings, however, were what he was interested in. If he could sneak off with a pair of them, one of each sex, then he could start his *own* farm, and to hell with Kensher and his brood.

He had planned it out as best he could while he was convalescing, and although he never got another real tour after that first one and had had to hurry everything up drastically when Teneria showed up, he had had chances to watch out the window when the hatchlings got fed, and had asked a few important questions, such as "How do you tell them apart? Male and female, I mean."

He hadn't gotten a good explanation, really, but in the ensuing conversation he had been told that the black one, the red one, and the reddish-gold one were all male, while the two blue-green ones were both female. The green ones included four males and two females.

He intended to ignore the green ones, since he couldn't tell them apart, and grab a blue-green one and one of the others. He figured that if he held them by the neck, one in each hand, they wouldn't be able to bite him—and he just hoped they wouldn't claw him. Hauling two four-foot, forty-pound dragons was gong to be quite difficult enough without getting clawed up.

He hoped he could manage it. It would be tough, but if he got away with it he would be set for life.

He had watched when the hatchlings were fed and watered and when Seldis had given them their bath—she had climbed up on top of the cage and poured buckets of water in through the bars, and then had gone into the cage with another bucket and scrub brush to do a final inspection and touch-up. Wuller had gone in with her, carrying a sharp prod, and two of the others, Kinner the Younger and Korun, had stood at the door of the cage as backup, but the dragons hadn't given her any trouble.

And watching that, Dumery had seen that the latch on the cage didn't need a key. He hadn't gotten a good look at just how it worked, but he was sure no one had used a key, or anything but fingers, to work it.

And the calm ease with which Seldis had handled the hatchlings had been very encouraging. They were used to human touch.

Dumery thought he could manage it—get it there, grab the dragons, and get out again, and then hide somewhere in the forest, work his way south and west, back out of the mountains and back toward civilization. Teneria wouldn't dare follow him if he went south, near the Warlock Stone.

He hadn't worked out all the details, of course, but the *hard* part, he was sure, would be getting the dragons. Once he had his breeding pair he would worry about details, such as where he was going to keep them, and how he was going to get them there.

First things first, he told himself.

He reached the outer fence and discovered that the very first step—getting back into the farm—was going to be harder than he had thought at first. This was not an easy fence to climb. It was nine or ten feet high, with black iron uprights set a few inches apart—that much he had known already.

He had not, however, paid much attention to the fact that there were only two crosspieces holding the uprights together, one nearly at ground level and the other near the top. The uprights were far enough apart that he couldn't brace his foot between two of them, but close enough together that he couldn't squeeze through.

And climbing the uprights themselves, while possible, wasn't going to be easy, because they weren't round, easy-to-grasp rods. They were triangular, with concave faces, so that the edges were sharp.

He sighed, grabbed hold of two uprights, and started climbing.

The metal cut into his palms and his fingers; if he clung tightly enough to pull himself up the edges cut more deeply.

And then he felt himself starting to slide back down; the smooth metal didn't give him enough friction to hold. The edges were cutting more than ever as his hands slid down them.

He let go and fell back to the ground, frustrated. He looked at his hands.

The palm of his left hand was bleeding sluggishly; the fingers, and his right hand, were marked with red pressure lines, but the skin hadn't been broken.

He swore, using every foul word he'd ever heard the sailors on his father's ships use, and wiped the blood off on the grass.

That, he told himself, was a truly *vicious* fence! Why had they made it that way?

He supposed that it was really intended to prevent dragons from getting out, rather than to keep him from getting in, but it seemed to work quite well either way.

On the other hand, he thought, he was smarter than any dragon, and the dearth of crosspieces gave him an idea. If he could find something and wedge it between two of the bars, he should be able to bend them farther apart and squeeze through. After all, he was thin enough, particularly after his recent adventures in reaching this point. The bars were iron, not steel—iron was cheaper and lasted better in the open weather, since steel would rust away. Iron, however, was easier to bend, and the bars weren't that thick, no more than an inch or two through.

He looked around, but he was standing on bare rock. His only real tool was his belt knife, and that wouldn't do.

The greater moon's light was already starting to fade, and he decided that speed was more important than any other consideration; he picked up a handy rock, roughly the size of his head, and jammed it into the fence.

It went right through.

He swore again, and picked up another, larger rock.

This one took an effort to hoist up, but at least it didn't go right through the bars. One end of it did. He braced it up with one hand and hammered at it with the other.

The fence jangled loudly at the impact, and he hurt his hand, but the bars didn't yield.

A dragon roared at him from one of the pens, but in the darkness he couldn't make out exactly which one it was.

He snarled in reply, then with one hand holding his wedge-rock in place, he picked up another and used it as a hammer, pounding at the wedge-rock with it.

The fence rang and buzzed at the impact, and the dragons bellowed in reply—which pleased Dumery, as he judged that the draconic racket would drown out the noise the fence was making.

Then one bar started to give, and Dumery pounded harder, holding his improvised hammer in both hands.

With a loud snap, the rock suddenly fell through the fence, and Dumery blinked, startled. The bar hadn't bent that far yet!

He looked again, and realized that the bar had snapped off at the bottom. He pushed at it, and it swung freely.

Delighted, he shoved it to one side and squeezed sideways through the opening.

Now all he had to do was to get to the hatchling cage, get inside, grab two dragons—a male and a female—drag them out, close the cage behind him, drag the dragons over and out through the fence, and run and hide.

Oh, sure, that was all. He grimaced slightly and wondered if maybe he was being a little overconfident.

It also occurred to him that he did *not* want to close the cage behind him. If all twelve hatchlings got loose the resulting confusion would keep the farmers much busier, which would be so much the better for him.

He trotted along the fence, around the largest pen, ignoring the dragons that were staring at him. His toe caught on a rock and he stumbled, which elicited a weird hooting from one of the dragons, but he caught himself and hurried on.

The dim orange moonlight was fading, and he didn't want to stumble over a cliff in the dark; he had to hurry!

# CHAPTER 30

*T*he latch was a black lump in the dimness, and he poked at it in growing frustration.

How in the World did the damn thing work?

It was like no latch he had ever seen before. There was no simple bar to lift, no lever to pull, and no knob to turn; instead two thumb-size stubs protruded from the top of a tangle of ironmongery that Dumery could make no sense of. He tried pushing first one stub, and then the other; both resisted, but either one could be moved. Neither one seemed to do much of anything.

Annoyed beyond reason, he bashed at the thing with his fist, and that didn't help either. It made the cage door rattle against the frame, but the latch stayed closed.

A dragon snorted somewhere nearby; Dumery didn't look up. Instead he grabbed each stub in one hand and tried working both at once, to see what would happen.

Sliding both to the right didn't work, nor did both to the left, but when he pushed them together in the middle he heard a clank, and the door swung open.

Dumery smiled.

A dozen little dragons stared up at him from inside the cage, their gleaming eyes unreadable. He stared back. The colors were harder to distinguish in the gloom than he had expected—the orange light of the greater moon turned both green and blue-green to a murky, dim, nameless color. He was about to step into the cage for a closer look when he heard the growl of a larger dragon. He turned away from all those staring little eyes to see if anyone in the house had noticed the noise, or had just happened to be looking.

He found himself looking directly into another, much larger pair of draconic eyes.

He blinked and caught his breath.

One of the big dragons was loose and standing not ten feet away, its long neck extended so that its head was mere inches from his own.

It growled again.

One of the hatchlings hissed and snapped at Dumery's leg; Dumery snatched the threatened limb away and started to kick at the little beast, then reconsidered as he felt the big dragon's hot breath on his shoulder.

Snatching up two of the hatchlings while this monster watched did not seem like a viable plan. In a hopeless attempt to look innocent, Dumery managed a sickly smile and started to close the door of the cage. He stopped abruptly when one of the hatchlings shrieked; he had caught its neck and one wing in the door.

He decided to leave the door open after all and to just forget about the hatchlings.

In fact, he decided to forget about everything, except leaving as quickly as possible. He began backing away, watching the big dragon carefully.

His foot landed on something slick, and a hatchling yowled. Stepping quickly aside, Dumery saw that one of them, the black one, was out of the cage already, and he had just stepped on one of its dragging wings.

The big dragon roared angrily at him.

Dumery didn't dare turn away and he found himself with a clear view of a dark mouth lined with hundreds of extremely sharp teeth; foul breath, redolent of rotting meat, swept over him, and his ears rang.

A window swung open in the farmhouse.

"Who's there?" someone called.

Dumery wasn't stupid enough to answer that, but the big dragon turned away for a moment, distracted, and Dumery seized the opportunity. He spun on his heel and ran, narrowly avoiding tripping over the black hatchling.

As he ran, he heard a man's voice shouting, "*Hai,* dragon! What is it? Guard, boy, guard!"

Dumery ran for the loose upright in the fence, not worrying about what that meant, not worrying about anything except whether that huge, angry dragon was following him. He didn't see it start after him, nor did he see it stop when it heard the order to guard. He didn't see it return, disgruntled, to the door of the hatchling cage, where it began snatching up errant dragonets by their tails and tossing them back into their pen.

Dumery didn't dare look back as he groped along the fence in the dark, feeling for the broken bar, but at last he found it and squeezed through. He stumbled on until he rounded the boulder and was out of sight of the farm.

There he fell to the ground, panting.

After a moment he felt sufficiently recovered to sit up, look around, and listen.

He heard dragons bellowing, but that was off in the distance somewhere; there was no sign of pursuit. The lesser moon was up again, looking even more pinkish than usual and half obscured by a wisp of cloud. The greater moon's glow had faded to a mere tinge in the west, and no more stars were visible through the gathering mist and cloud.

All Dumery could see was rock and moss and sky.

He sat and gathered his wits.

It appeared that Kensher and company had a line of defense they hadn't mentioned—trained watch-dragons. Or one watch-dragon, anyway. That hardly seemed fair.

But then, they weren't *trying* to be fair—they were trying to defend themselves.

Against what? Dumery wondered. What was there out here in the middle of nowhere that called for that sort of defense?

Or was it to keep the dragons in?

Would a dragon, even a trained one, help in imprisoning its own kind?

Well, yes, Dumery thought, it probably would. People served as jailers willingly enough, didn't they?

Whatever the watch-dragon was there for, it was there, and it had kept him from getting his hatchlings. The exact reason for its presence didn't seem anywhere near as important as the *fact* of its presence.

His burglary attempt was a failure; he hadn't gotten his breeding pair.

Had Kensher guessed what had happened? Would he be guarding against another attempt? Would Teneria know what was going on?

Well, the ground was so rocky that there would be no footprints to show that an unauthorized human being had been there. The watch-dragon wouldn't be able to say anything—would it?

No, Dumery just couldn't believe that Kensher would keep a talking dragon around. And that one had growled and roared, but shown no signs of any greater vocal ability than that. It also wasn't any bigger than some of the dragons in the cages.

So it couldn't talk and say it had seen Dumery. The only evidence of his presence would be the broken fence—if that was noticed—and the open cage door.

That was quite an extensive fence, and there were a great many uprights in it; one broken one might well go unnoticed. It would almost certainly not be found until daylight, at the very least, not unless someone walked the entire fence with a lantern.

Of course, someone might do just that, Dumery had to admit.

And there was that witch. He had no idea what she might see, with her magic, or what she might do about it.

He decided that he would assume that she wouldn't know anything more than anybody else. After all, what did she know about dragons or burglars? Neither one had anything to do with witchcraft. So he would ignore her for now, and assume that she would go along with whatever the others thought.

If he was lucky, they would see the open cage door and would think that one of the hatchlings had somehow opened it, or that whoever was last in there hadn't closed it properly, and that what the watch-dragon had spotted was hatchlings getting loose.

After all, could they really expect intruders up *here?*

Almost certainly they'd just think it was an accidentally opened cage that caused the fuss.

In that case, once everyone had settled down again, Dumery would be able to sneak back into the house. Or even sneak back to the pens and try again.

He had to think about that. If he was going to make a second attempt it would be best to do it tonight, rather than waiting, because the longer he waited the more time they would have to find the break in the fence.

There was the problem of the watch-dragon, however. Did the creature ever sleep, or was it constantly on guard? Was there any way he could elude it, or fool it into thinking he belonged there?

This was a matter that required some thought. Besides, it would take sometime for everything to settle back to normal, and there was the darkness to worry about—the lesser moon was still low and didn't give all that much light in any case. Dumery decided that he would wait until everyone had had time to calm down, and then would decide whether to make another try, or to slip back into the house and pretend he had slept through all the excitement.

For now, he would wait. He settled down, making himself as comfortable as he could on the hard stone.

He had no intention of sleeping, but all the same, within minutes, he was asleep.

When he awoke the sun was warm on the bare stone and he realized with a start that he had missed his chance. The sun was well up in the east, peering down at him over the peak of the mountain—half the morning was gone. Kensher and his family would be out and about; they might well have found the break in the fence. They would surely have all the hatchlings back in their cage and might have put a lock on it. The watch-dragon would surely be awake.

And he had missed his chance to get back into the house. They would surely have noticed his absence by now.

In fact, that Teneria might already be looking for him, brewing up her spells or whatever she did. She might come upon him at any moment; if she had followed him to the farm from all the way back in Ethshar, finding him now should be easy.

He sat up and considered.

She hadn't found him yet, though. Maybe she wasn't looking, or maybe something had gone wrong with her witchcraft.

If she didn't find him, he could slip away, hide somewhere, wait until nightfall, and then try again; he could break the fence again, if it had been repaired.

But how could he get past the watch-dragon?

And looking at the situation in the light of day, how would he get two squirming hatchlings out through the fence and down the mountain?

And what if one of the hatchlings turned out to be a fire-breather?

It was a good thing that Kensher didn't raise fliers or fire-breathers, even as watch-dragons. If the watch-dragon had been a fire-breather, Dumery realized, he might have been dead by now, a charred corpse lying on the stone, instead of alive and well. If the watch-dragon could fly it might have pursued him past the fence—and he hadn't gone very far, had he? Around that boulder and across maybe fifty feet of open ground lay the fence; surely the dragon could have tracked him that far.

He was glad that Kensher hadn't thought to let the dragon out to come after him with it.

That assumed, of course, that dragons could track, like dogs or cats, and really, Dumery didn't know for certain that they could. And Kensher probably had good reasons for not letting the watch-dragon out; could he control the beast outside the fence?

Maybe the fence was there to keep the watch-dragon in, more than anything else.

Whether dragons could track people or not, witches surely could; why hadn't Teneria found him yet?

And while all this speculation was very interesting, it wasn't getting him any closer to setting up his own dragon-breeding operation.

He sat and thought, uncomfortably aware that Teneria might appear at any moment.

He devised scheme after scheme for stealing a pair of hatchlings, but they all fell apart upon close inspection. He could think of no practical way to deal with the watch-dragon, or with Kensher and his family if he tried to sneak in when the dragon wasn't on duty. He had no way of killing a dragon that size.

Besides, killing it seemed a bit extreme. It was Kensher's dragon.

It hadn't been that hard to talk himself into stealing a couple of hatchlings; after all, Kensher had lots of them, and most of them were destined to be slaughtered in a year or so anyway. The watch-dragon, though, was fifteen or twenty feet long and must be three or four years old, at least. Kensher had clearly put considerable effort into training it, judging by the way it had behaved—and Dumery was grateful for that training, because without it the monster might have gone ahead and eaten him.

He was also grateful to Kensher and the rest of the family for taking him in when he turned upon their doorstep. Yes, it was just normal hospitality to take him in and give him a meal, but even that much wasn't something everybody would bother with, and they had gone farther than that, giving him days to regain his strength, feeding him generously, and giving him clothes and supplies for the journey home.

He began to be ashamed of himself for plotting to rob the people who had saved his life. Was he *that* low a person? Was he *that* desperate to get hold of a couple of dragons?

He shook his head. It wasn't right. He had let his obsessions get the better of him. He had done Kensher quite enough harm already. He had repaid kindness and succor with threats, attempted blackmail, burglary, and a broken fence. He would do no more harm in return for good.

It was time to get away from Kensher and his farm.

It was time to go home.

For one thing, he didn't really want to get caught.

Ostensibly, all he had to do was loop back around the way he had come and head on down the trail to the river.

There was a problem with that, however. A problem named Teneria.

He was sure that she would know what he had done. She

would know that he had tried to steal those hatchlings. If she went home with him she would probably tell someone, like his parents. And even if she didn't, she would certainly be keeping a close eye on him every step of the way home.

He didn't think he could face that.

And for that matter, did he really know anything about her? *Had* his parents sent her? It didn't seem like them. After all, they knew he was all right; they'd talked to him in that silly dream Thetheran had sent.

Maybe someone else had sent her, or she had come on her own. Maybe the magicians, including the witches, were all out to get him.

Was she really a witch, though? He hadn't seen her work any magic. She had found him, somehow, which was impressive, and she seemed to be able to tell lies from truth with phenomenal accuracy, but neither one proved she was actually the witch she said she was. He hadn't seen her fly or anything.

But even if she was exactly what she claimed to be, he really didn't want to go home with her, having her there gloating over him the whole time.

He would find his *own* way home—overland, not by the river. And south, where the witch wouldn't dare follow, if she was really a witch.

And if she hadn't lied about the Warlock Stone.

He didn't really think she had. He set out down the slope, to the southeast.

As he walked, he considered.

True, he didn't want to rob Kensher and he couldn't think of any way to do it in any case, but did that *really* mean he had to just give up and go home?

He still wanted to do something about his thwarted ambitions. He couldn't be a wizard, he had established that. And he couldn't seem to find an apprenticeship in any other branch of magic, either.

Controlling a supply of dragon's blood would let him lord it over the wizards. He couldn't wangle an apprenticeship in the dragon-farming business, that was clear, and he couldn't see any way to get hold of any of Kensher's livestock to set up his own farm—but were those the only possibilities?

All he needed was a pair of dragons, and while Kensher

might have the only dragon farm in the World, he didn't have all the dragons in the World, by any means. There were plenty of dragons out there.

Wild dragons.

Dragon-hunting as a career didn't sound very promising, though. He remembered the sight of that gaping, tooth-lined maw when the watch-dragon had roared at him, and Kensher had said that the farm dragons were nowhere near as big as dragons *could* get. Presumably there were wild dragons that were much bigger and fiercer.

But what if he were to find and capture a pair of *baby* dragons? Or better yet, find unhatched eggs? It happened; he had seen dragons in the Arena that had been hatched in captivity.

That would be perfect.

But how could he hope to find them? He looked out over the edge of the cliff he was skirting and saw forest stretching to the hilly southern horizon.

That was a lot of countryside, and dragons might be anywhere—or nowhere— in it.

He could *look*, though, couldn't he?

If he did, he might search forever without finding anything. Or he might starve to death, or get killed by a wild dragon, or by wolves or bandits or something.

On the other hand, who knew *what* he might find?

Wolves, pitfalls, bandits—or a dragon's lair.

Wolves, pitfalls, and bandits were probably far more likely, and if he *did* find a dragon's lair it might well have a mother dragon at home, guarding her young.

That was a good way to get killed, finding an occupied lair.

No, the thing to do was to go home, to his own home, back in Ethshar, and then see if he could somehow buy a pair of dragon eggs.

A thought struck him. If he demanded that as his patrimony, would his father cooperate?

He *should*, Dumery thought. After all, Doran hadn't come through with the promised apprenticeship to a wizard. Millennium-old tradition said that every child was entitled, between his or her twelfth and thirteenth birthdays, to demand that his or her parents provide some way to establish a future career—arrange a profitable marriage or an apprenticeship, guarantee an inheritance, *something*. Demanding a pair of dragon eggs was unusual, but it ought to qualify.

That, then, was what he would do. He would go home and demand a pair of eggs.

All he had to do was find the way.

He knew he was somewhere in Aldagmor, in the Baronies of Sardiron. That meant that he was far to the north of Ethshar of the Spices. And he was east of the Great River, since he had gone ashore on the eastern bank, while all the cities of Ethshar were more or less to the west of the river's mouth.

Ethshar of the Spices was actually south or maybe southeast of the river's mouth, because of the way the river and the coastline wiggled about, but it was effectively on the western side all the same.

If he headed west he would eventually come to the Great Rive, but that would mean cutting directly across all those ridges, and then finding transportation downstream, and Teneria might well catch up to him—there was nothing she feared in the west. On the other hand, if he headed due south he would eventually reach either the Great River—much farther downstream—or the Gulf of the East, or if worst came to worst, the southern edge of the World. And he would be passing too close to the Warlock Stone for Teneria.

He certainly hoped he wouldn't have to go anything like as far as the edge of the World. It seemed unlikely that he would.

If he arrived at the river he could follow it downstream, either on foot or by boat, and once he reached Azrad's Bridge he would have no trouble finding his way home.

If he reached the Gulf he could follow the coast west to the river's mouth, then up to Azrad's Bridge. If the gods were nasty and he reached the edge of the World, he could head west to the sea, and then take ship home, or follow the coast around to the river's mouth.

So he would head south, and when due south wasn't practical he would veer to the west, and sooner or later he would reach civilization, or the Great River, or something else helpful.

Accordingly, he looked up at the sun, which was almost

directly overhead now, and then around at the mountains, and estimated which direction must be south.

This was turning out to be far more of an adventure than he had expected when he went up to Westgate Market to seek inspiration. He stepped out boldly, stumbled over an exposed root, fell, picked himself up, and marched on, sighing.

While Dumery made his decision, Teneria had finally gotten everything straightened out. The chaos of the farm family's efforts to round up the escaped hatchlings and get everything back to normal had confused and delayed her, and she had not worried at first about exactly what had occurred, but only about straightening out the current mess. She had offered to help, but had been turned down—apparently these people did not entirely trust her.

That was not really surprising, under the circumstances. Her unexpected appearance the day before did look as if it might be connected with the night's disruptions.

And the nature of those disruptions was pretty clear; the reports of the various family members, combined with what her own senses and witchcraft told her, made it all plain.

Dumery had slipped out in the middle of the night, had circled around to the back of the farm, and had then broken into a cage of hatchling dragons. Kensher assumed that the boy had intended to steal a breeding pair, so as to start his own dragon farm, and Teneria had to admit that it was a very convincing theory.

However, the watch-dragon, which Dumery hadn't known about, had caught him and ruined his plans.

When Teneria first heard that, she was afraid that the dragon had eaten Dumery, which would not only have been regrettable in itself, but would mean that she had failed in her task of keeping him safe. Fortunately, Kinner the Younger was able to reassure her—the watch-dragon hadn't eaten anybody. There was no blood anywhere.

Besides, when Teneria stopped and concentrated, she could sense that Dumery was still alive.

After the farmers had rounded up all the dragons they could find and had taken inventory they concluded that only one of the hatchlings was missing, not a breeding pair, and it was entirely possible that that one, a rather feisty black one, had slipped away by itself in the confusion, rather than having been carted off. Spotting a black dragon in the dark would not be easy.

She considered offering to track it down for Kensher, but she was unsure she would be able to deliver. Dragons, especially young dragons, didn't seem to leave much in the way of psychic traces.

Besides, the dragons weren't her problem—Dumery was. She was not particularly enamored of the ungrateful little would-be thief, but she was supposed to see him safely home.

Once the eleven hatchlings had been rounded up and secured, and once she had used a little witchcraft to convince Pancha that she was not Dumery's co-conspirator and that it was safe to let her out of her room and out of the house, Teneria set out on the business of tracking Dumery down.

She followed his trail around the mountain, across the pastures, and through the dragon pens, and back out to the flat, stony area behind the boulder.

There she stopped.

The damned fool of a boy hadn't gone back to the trail. Instead he had set out due south, into the wilderness. She looked down the slope after him, peering into the gloom of the forest, her supernatural senses extended.

Something muttered blackly in the back of her mind, something harsh and alien and almost seductive, something that had drawn Adar away forever.

The Calling.

That was *it*, she told herself. That was the pebble that sank the barge. To Hell with Dumery of Shiphaven. To Hell with Sella, if she dared to criticize Teneria for her failure.

She had followed the boy halfway across the World, up the Great River, and across most of Aldagmor, but she was *not* going to walk out into the uncharted wilderness, where escaped dragons roamed free and something apparently ate warlocks alive, something that seemed to intend to eat *her* alive, as well.

She had had quite enough. She was going home. She was going home by the same route she had come, though without the aerial detour from the Blasted Pine.

And maybe, when she got back home to Ethshar, she could

contact some of the local warlocks to see if something couldn't be done about the Calling.

# CHAPTER 31

*A*t least, Dumery told himself, it was warmer once he got down off the mountain. And the forest could be very beautiful—the sunlight spilling down through the trees, the branches stirring in the breeze with a whisper like the waves of a distant sea, and the squirrels and chipmunks darting about in the treetops and underbrush every so often, like little flickers of fur.

The ground was rougher than he had expected, though. He hadn't realized just how much difference having a trail, any trail, underfoot actually made. He was sure that he wasn't making very good time at all.

He had the horrible suspicion, the first night, that he hadn't gotten more than a league or so from the dragon farm. He wrapped himself tightly in the thick woolen blanket Pancha had given him, which he had surreptitiously stuffed in his pack, and huddled against a tree, hoping that there were no night-prowling predators in the area. Dragons, he was fairly certain, were basically diurnal, but didn't wolves hunt at night? He wasn't sure. And of course, nightwalkers were all of necessity nocturnal, but he had never heard of any of them in the north; they were found in the Small Kingdoms, according to the tales his mother had told him.

Of course, he didn't know how far they might roam, or even how far he was from the northernmost of the Small Kingdoms.

Something, probably a bird, shrieked weirdly in the distance, and Dumery tried to make himself smaller. He was a city boy; this sort of thing was not his idea of a good time. Going north he had at least been on trails and usually within a mile or less of some sort of human habitation, but here, for all he knew, there wasn't another human being for a league or more in every direction.

He lay curled up in a ball, one hand on the hilt of his belt knife, while he eyed the surrounding trees suspiciously, trying to see by the feeble light of the cloud-smudged moons until exhaustion got the better of him and he fell asleep.

The second day of the journey he was stiff and sore from sleeping all tensed as he had, and that made walking even worse. He took frequent rest stops, telling himself there was no real hurry. He didn't need to catch up to anybody now; he was just going home and he could take his time. He still had months before his thirteenth birthday, months in which to make his demand for a pair of dragon eggs.

On the other hand, his trail rations were already running low, and traveling cross-country meant that he wouldn't pass any inns. When this fact sank in, after lunch, he tried to pick up his pace a little.

When he settled for the night this time he tried to find a sheltered spot where he could stretch out, to prevent the sort of cramping he had suffered that morning. He found what seemed like a good spot, but when he lay down he found that a knob of pine root dug into the small of his back. After shifting about in unsuccessful attempts to dodge it he finally gave up and moved to a nearby corner that looked much more crowded, but which in fact proved to be quite comfortable.

He was sleeping soundly and peacefully when the dream came.

He was home, in the front hall of his parents' house, and Thetheran the Mage was standing there before him.

"Hello," Thetheran said. "This is another magic dream. Your parents haven't heard from you in quite some time, and they're worried. They even sent someone after you, an apprentice witch, but we haven't heard from her, and I take it she hasn't found you. Are you all right, Dumery?"

"I'm fine," he answered, a little defensively. It was somewhat reassuring to know that Teneria hadn't reported in. "I'm on my way home. The apprenticeship didn't work out. I have another plan, though, one that I think they'll be happier with."

"What sort of a plan?" Thetheran asked.

"That's none of *your* business, wizard!" Dumery noticed that he was bolder in these dreams than he was when he was awake and wondered if it was some side effect of the spell.

"All right, then," Thetheran said. "There's no need to be rude. I'm just asking on behalf of your parents—I'm sure they'd want to know. When do you expect to be home?"

That was an awkward question, but reasonable enough. Dumery hesitated and then said, "I'm not sure. I'm traveling overland from Aldagmor and I don't know how long a journey it is." He was annoyed at his own inability to give a clear answer and he turned that irritation on his questioner. "You tell them that I'm safe and on my way," he shouted. "That's enough!" He waved angrily, and to his surprise a wind swept Thetheran off his feet and blew him back down the hallway into the kitchen and out of sight.

Dumery looked foolishly at his upraised hand. "Did I do that?' he asked.

A great grinning mouth suddenly appeared on the wall next to him. "You might say so," it said. "Thetheran's spell is slipping—it's not one he's done very often, and he didn't get it quite right this time. He's losing control of the dream. It's turning into just an ordinary dream, rather than a wizardly one. He managed to send me here anyway, but I'm afraid that the two of you aren't really talking to each other any more."

Dumery stared at it. "Why would I dream *you?*" he said.

The mouth vanished without answering, leaving Dumery alone in the house. He started up the stairs, feeling less real every moment; a huge green dragon thrust its head out the door of Dessa's bedroom at him, and he turned and fled, the dragon's head pursuing on a neck that stretched longer and longer, without end, and from there on the dream turned into an ordinary, if distressing, nightmare, full of fangs and claws and dark hallways.

In fact, when he awoke and blinked away grit he wasn't sure whether the magical part of the dream had been genuine, or whether he might have dreamed that by himself.

He assumed it was genuine, though. That meant that they were still thinking about him, back home, and now they'd be expecting him. He really hadn't anticipated that they would go to all this trouble over him—wizard's spells and witch's apprentices and all. He sighed, brushed himself off, and got on with the business of walking interminably south.

Around midmorning he was feeling fairly cheerful—his parents were concerned about him, which might not seem like much, but it was something. And the weather was beautiful—it had been an unusually dry spring so far, which undoubtedly had all the farmers worried, but which made for easy traveling.

He casually dodged a malodorous object that lay more or less in his path, and then stopped.

He turned and took another look.

Whatever sort of beast had left that was *big*. And it was fresh, too. His good cheer faded abruptly at the thought of large, hostile animals in the area.

There was something familiar about the stuff, too, both appearance and odor. He studied it for a moment, then looked around uneasily.

Something had scraped that big oak tree there. He stepped over and investigated.

Two or three tiny flakes of red-gold scale clung to the rough bark. They were unmistakable.

A dragon. A wild dragon had passed by here, quite recently—a good-size one.

He was torn by two powerful and conflicting urges.

First, here was a dragon, and quite possibly a female, and a female might have eggs or hatchlings nearby, and it was too good an opportunity to ignore. The gods had sent him this chance. He should follow the trail—and yes, there was a visible trail through the underbrush—and track the beast to its lair and see what the situation was. This might be the only chance he would ever have to realize his dream of capturing dragons he could raise as his own, to start a dragon farm and get rich selling dragon's blood and rubbing the wizards' noses in it. His father might not be able to buy dragon eggs, or might not get both sexes, but he might be able to just pick up a couple himself if he followed that trail.

On the other hand, here was a *dragon*, and dragons were flesheaters, by all accounts and by the evidence at the farm perfectly willing to settle for eating people if they couldn't find anything tastier. It was a fairly large dragon, too, no mere hatchling—the scale fragments on the oak were level with the top of Dumery's head, and presumably came from the beast's flank. An animal defending its nest was likely to be particularly vicious, and dragons had remarkable teeth and claws. This was no half-tame farm dragon, either, but a wild dragon, which might breathe fire and might be able to fly—it could be lurking overhead, waiting to pounce, even as he stood and debated with himself.

He looked up quickly and scanned the treetops, but saw no sign of a large red-gold dragon anywhere.

The gods might have sent him this opportunity—but he was an Ethsharite. He knew the proverb "Trusting the gods is no better than throwing dice." The gods were powerful and benevolent, but that didn't necessarily mean that everything they did would work out for the best. If he went after the dragon, the gods probably wouldn't help him fight it, or escape from it, or rob it. If it *was* some god doing him a favor, just putting the dragon in his path was probably the extent of it, he couldn't hope for any further protection. The gods could be whimsical and they generally kept their meddling to a minimum.

If there *were* eggs or hatchlings, he would have to steal them from their mother, and the mother was likely to object strenuously to that. He would do best to kill the mother, if he possibly could—but how could a twelve-year-old boy kill a grown dragon? He didn't even have a sword or a shield, just his belt knife.

For that matter, if there were hatchlings, how could he hope to capture them and get them back to Ethshar? He had no tools, no rope, no sacks or nets, he was tired and footsore, and he didn't really know where he was. He was in no shape to handle even hatchling dragons.

Eggs, though—if he could slip a couple of eggs out when the mother dragon wasn't home, he could wrap them in the blanket and carry them that way.

Or if there were no eggs, at the very least he could see where the lair was, what it looked like, and maybe he would be able to find his way back to it later, when he was better equipped.

He would go and take a look, anyway, and hope that he didn't encounter the dragon.

That brought up the question of whether the dragon, when it passed through, had been going *to* its lair or *from* its lair.

It was still morning; Dumery guessed that it was going *from* its lair and therefore he wanted to backtrack, rather than follow the beast.

Besides, this way he was far less likely to wind up as the dragon's lunch.

He knew he was being reckless following the dragon's path in *either* direction, but after all, one couldn't be a great hero or become fabulously wealthy without taking *some* risks.

He studied the scraped bark, the trampled underbrush, and turned eastward, back the way the dragon had come.

# CHAPTER 32

*A*s he walked, Dumery wondered just what he was actually looking for. He had never seen a wild dragon's lair. In the stories, dragons lived in caves, or forgotten crypts, or ancient tombs, or abandoned castles, or at the very least on rocky mountain ledges, and he wasn't *in* the mountains anymore, just in rolling wooded hills, where it seemed very unlikely that he would find caves, castles, or crypts.

What if the beast lived in a concealed pit, like a hunter's trap? He might fall into it and wind up as an evening snack.

What if it *had* no lair, but just roamed about from place to place? He could wander on indefinitely, in that case—and he was going the wrong direction to get home.

He decided to give it until sundown and if he hadn't found the lair by then he would turn around and head southwest.

At least the dragon hadn't tried to hide its path; it had just marched on, more or less in a straight line, without worrying about obstacles.

He crossed a boggy area where he found a few clawprints,

and he almost reconsidered what he was doing; this was no ten-foot yearling. The claws were as long as his arm.

On the other hand, it was going in the other direction. If he turned around now, for all he knew he'd meet it coming back.

He wondered why it was walking, rather than flying. He mulled that over for a time, and a suspicion arose that he might be dealing with one of the escapees from Kensher's farm. Its wings could well have failed to heal properly after deliberately being broken each year for two or three years, leaving it too weak to fly. Or maybe it had just gotten accustomed to walking. Was flying something a dragon had to learn young, or not at all, perhaps?

It didn't really matter; he pressed on.

One pleasant thing he noticed about following the dragon's trail was that he didn't need to worry much about tripping over branches or catching his tunic on thorns—the dragon had stomped all such obstacles flat. He marveled at just how mashed some of the brush was.

He looked up from a pile of shattered twigs that had once been a rhododendron and spotted something in the distance.

At first he took it for a fallen tree, and then for several fallen trees, and he wondered whether the dragon had knocked them down, or whether some storm had left them there.

As he approached, though, he realized that these were not just downed trees. No storm knocked trees into stacks.

*Something* had stacked up whole trees like kindling for a fire. Something had yanked them up by the roots and then laid them in a rough approximation of a circle, piling them up so that the roots and branches interwove and held them in place, forming a great wooden ring at least ten feet high—probably more, Dumery thought, looking up at the massive barrier.

It looked a little like a gigantic bird's nest, using fifty-foot trees instead of five-inch twigs.

Dumery hadn't really been thinking in terms of a *nest*, despite the winged, egg-laying nature of the best, but this was obviously the dragon's lair.

This, he thought as he looked at the huge trees used as building material, could be dangerous. Suddenly wary, he crouched down and crept closer, moving as silently as he could, mentally cursing the twigs and leaves that crunched and rustled underfoot.

What if the dragon had returned by another route? What if its mate was in there? What if it had young—not hatchlings, but yearlings, big enough to dismember and devour a full-grown cow—or a half-grown boy?

Dumery inched closer.

The trees were not stacked very tightly; Dumery could see daylight through some of the gaps between them. He decided that he could sneak up and look through one of those chinks and see whether there were any eggs or hatchlings in there.

As he drew nearer he moved ever more slowly, taking his time with every step, struggling to minimize the sound he made, but finally he reached the wooden walls of the nest.

By stooping slightly he could peer between two of the massive logs; he stooped and peered.

The inside of the nest was a sunny, treeless, bowl-shaped enclosure—a bowl full of dragons.

Most of them he took to be yearlings—he counted four, three of them various shades of green and the fourth a brilliant red, which were eight or ten or twelve feet long. It was hard to judge lengths when the only background was uprooted trees, which could be almost any size, but he was fairly sure that those four were yearlings.

One larger one, with gleaming sea-blue scales that faded to a fishbelly white along its underside, was curled up in the sun; Dumery estimated that, uncurled, it would be at least a fifteen-footer, probably more.

And he could hear, but not see, something stirring about just below the crack he was looking through. He was pressing his forehead up against a log, trying to get a better angle, when the rustling of leaves abruptly stopped. A head popped up into view.

There, staring at him through the crack, was a hatchling dragon, a black one, with golden, slit-pupiled eyes.

It looked *exactly* like the black one back at Kensher's farm.

It blinked at him and hissed loudly, thrusting out its long dark red-forked tongue.

Dumery sat down abruptly, dropping out of the little creature's line of sight.

The hissing stopped; the dragon was silent. Dumery wondered what it was doing. Was it waiting for him to reappear? Was it going on about its business?

Getting spotted hadn't been in his plans. If that little nuisance had some way of communicating to the other, bigger dragons that there was a human being snooping around uninvited, Dumery might well wind up as dragon food.

He cowered, crawling down beside the bottommost log and making himself as inconspicuous as possible.

He listened and heard no more hissing, no roaring or bellowing or growling

That *probably* meant that he was safe enough.

Still, he waited.

While he waited he thought about that black hatchling.

If that was the same one he'd seen at the farm, it was a healthy, spirited little beast. If he could capture it somehow, take it home with him, he'd have half the pair he needed.

How in the World had it ever gotten here, though? True, when he fled the farm it had been out of the cage and running about loose, and it might be small enough to have squeezed out through the fence the same place he did, but how could it possibly have come all this way and wound up in this other dragon's nest?

And who were all these other dragons, anyway, and how did they relate to the one whose trail he had followed? Was the big blue one the mate of the one that made the trail and these others their offspring?

That would make sense, but it didn't explain the hatchling. Dragons never hatched just one egg.

Of course, maybe there were other hatchlings he hadn't seen. He hadn't gotten a very good look at the entire nest.

Suppose, though, that the yearlings were the young of the blue one and the wandering red one, and that the black hatchling had escaped from the farm and somehow found its way here, seeking out its own kind?

In that case, would the other dragons really object if he captured the little one?

How could he capture it, though? He had no chains or rope, no sacks or restraints of any kind. All he had was his belt knife and the borrowed—no, stolen—blanket and a dwindling supply of trail food.

That and his bare hands.

That wasn't really enough, and he knew it.

Still, that hatchling—*was* it the one he had seen at the farm? *Were* there any other hatchlings in there?

He still heard nothing alarming from inside the barrier; apparently he was safe, for the moment. He crawled out of concealment and inched along the outside of the nest, looking for another vantage point.

About a fourth of the way around he found an opening level with his chest that seemed wider than most; it looked as if he could lean through it and look around.

Cautiously he did just that, slipping his head between the logs, his hands to either side.

The wall was thicker here than he had realized, and he pulled himself forward, into the gap. His feet left the ground, and he tugged himself along with his hands.

The problem was that this section of the barrier was two trees thick, and the inner layer was made of very large trees indeed. He slipped through the outer wall, and then had to work his way along the trunk of a gigantic oak until he found an opening in the inner wall, an opening into the bowl-shape enclosure itself.

He lay along the oak and slipped his head through the gap, into the nest.

The big blue dragon was still sound asleep, over on the far side. The four yearlings were entirely concerned with each other—they were arguing, or playing, or doing *something* that involved twisting their long necks about one another and tugging back and forth.

Dumery spotted the hatchling off to the side, and just as he did, it spotted him.

It came slithering over the thick layer of broken branches that lined the sides of the bowl, its tail winding back and forth like a snake, its broken wings hanging down and brushing across the shattered wood.

The broken wings convinced Dumery—this *had* to be the same hatchling he had seen at the farm!

He hesitated, debating whether he should pull back and get back out of sight before the creature reached him. That would certainly be the safe and sensible thing to do.

It didn't look hostile, though, merely interested. He watched it approach until it was just a few feet away, looking up at him.

He looked down at it, and at the tree branches beneath it, and he suddenly noticed that many of tree branches were white, rather than gray or brown.

Wood isn't white, Dumery told himself. He leaned forward to get a better look.

Those white things, he realized, weren't branches.

They were bones.

This graphic reminder that dragons were carnivores convinced him that it was time to leave; he started to shift his hands, which were positioned for sliding forward.

Just then a titanic booming sounded, and the sky overhead darkened. Startled, Dumery looked up.

At first he saw only an immense darkness, but then his eyes adjusted and the thing dropped lower and he realized what it was.

A dragon, the biggest dragon he had ever seen, bigger than any dragon he had ever even imagined, was flying overhead. Its great translucent green wings hid the sky, its head blotted out the sun, its body was like a flying mountain, dark with shadow. Something dangled from its jaws, and its talons held squirming objects that Dumery didn't have time to recognize.

Those tremendous wings flapped, and the booming sounded again; a great wind swept down into Dumery's face, blinding him for a moment. He blinked and wiped at his eyes and came within a inch or two of losing his balance and sliding down into the nest.

By the time he had recovered himself the dragon had dropped the load it had been carrying, and three large brown steers had fallen thunderously to the ground.

The four yearlings immediately leaped upon them, the blue dragon—Dumery could scarcely continue to think of it as the *big* dragon, under the circumstances—close behind.

The hatchling paid no attention to this bounty from the heavens; it was staring at Dumery.

Dumery stared back, then looked quickly up as the shadows deepened.

The big dragon, having delivered its cargo, was coming to rest, settling down into the nest. Dumery could see now that its scales were a rich emerald green on its back, legs, head, neck, and tail, while its chest and belly were golden yellow.

It was immense, easily larger than all the other dragons put together. The head alone was as large as a yearling's body, the neck as long from jaw to collarbone as the blue dragon was from nose to tail. The talons on the foreclaws were at least as big around as Dumery's thighs, the claws themselves as big as his entire body.

Those talons looked as sharp as spear points, nonetheless.

There was also a look of age and maturity about this creature, a more hard-edged and finished look, rougher and more worn than any other dragon Dumery had ever seen; by comparison, even the biggest back at the farm appeared as soft and harmless as infants.

It struck Dumery that the fact that it was green rather than red-gold meant it wasn't the one whose trail he had followed, and any scales it lost against trees would have been much higher up than the traces he had found. That hardly mattered, under the circumstances.

The yearlings looked up and began scampering—Dumery had never imagined ten-foot dragons could scamper, but there was no other word for it—out of the way of the descending behemoth, dragging the freshly killed cattle with them.

The huge dragon landed lightly in the center of the bowl, touching down first with its foreclaws and then its hind ones, facing toward the blue dragon. The tail snaked down into a graceful coil. The gigantic wings stretched, shuddered, and then with a sudden snapping motion and a deafening slap, folded against the broad green-scaled back.

The wind from that action dislodged Dumery from his perch, and with a great crunching and rattling of dead branches and dry bones, he tumbled down into the nest.

# CHAPTER 33

*The hatchling hissed and thrashed its tail like an angry cat;* the yearlings and the blue dragons, busy as they were with their feasting, paid no attention.

The gargantuan green dragon swung its head around to see what the commotion was about, and two huge golden slit-pupiled eyes focused on Dumery.

Dumery scrambled back, snatching at his belt knife, but as the great head drew closer and closer he realized that even with a strong man's arm behind it, let alone his own far weaker muscles, his pitiful little tool—even calling it a weapon was an exaggeration—wouldn't so much as scratch this creature's armored hide.

He'd wanted dragons, he thought bitterly—well, now he had plenty of dragons, in all sizes and colors, and they were about to be the death of him. He would be swallowed by the big one in a single gulp, or ripped into shreds and devoured by the yearlings, or gnawed on by the hatchling. He would never raise dragons, never have a farm of his own, never rub Thetheran's nose in the dirt, never see his family again, never see Ethshar again, never grow up to be a man.

He would be eaten by dragons. He would be nothing but dragon fodder.

He should have just gone with Teneria.

The ponderous jaws began to open, and sudden inspiration struck Dumery.

This creature was surely the one that had built this nest and that had put at least some of the other dragons in it, giving them a place of safety, a home, a nest. It had brought them food. It cared for them. It might be the mother or father of some of them.

He rolled over and dove for the black hatchling, catching it off guard. He came up with his left arm clamped around its throat, his right hand holding his knife under its jaw.

"I'll cut the little bugger's throat if you come any closer!" he shouted.

The black dragon squirmed, one foreclaw gouging Dumery's leg, but it stopped when it felt the prick of the blade.

The great green dragon's gleaming golden eyes blinked, thick horny lids sliding down across them and then flicking back up.

"Very well," the beast said, in a voice like an avalanche, "then I shan't come any closer."

Dumery's mouth fell open.

He had known that dragons could talk, at least in theory— but theory wasn't reality. All the dragons he had seen so far had been treated as mere beasts and had behaved as mere beasts, either caged and subdued or wild and dangerous. Even given the far greater size and obvious relative maturity of this monster, he hadn't expected speech; where could it have learned Ethsharitic, out here in the forests of Aldagmor?

Still, it had clearly spoken, and spoken clearly.

For a moment Dumery stood, the black dragon's head clutched to his chest, and the knife at its throat, while those huge golden eyes watched him, the gigantic dragon's expression completely unreadable.

His own throat was dry; he swallowed.

"If you would be so kind as to release the hatchling?" the tremendous rumbling voice said.

The hatchling reacted to this by scrabbling viciously, shredding the right leg of Dumery's breeches and drawing three deep scratches down his thigh. He squeezed its neck more tightly, and it stopped.

"You'll eat me if I let it go," he said.

"Nay, I shall not," the great dragon replied. "I feasted well ere I fetched the kine for these younglings and I've no appetite left in me. I'll swear not to harm you, if you'll in turn swear not to harm these infants here gathered."

Dumery glanced down from those eyes and saw the other five dragons watching with interest.

"You've got to promise to keep the others away from me, too," he said.

"Surely," the dragon agreed. It turned its immense head and hissed, a sound like storm-driven waves breaking across the docks of Ethshar; the yearlings and the blue dragon backed away to the far side of the nest, thoroughly cowed.

Then the head swung back to face Dumery.

"Release the youngling, then," the dragon said.

Still reluctant, Dumery looked down at the black hatchling. It glared up at him with its yellow-golden eyes and squirmed again, but this time its foreclaws missed his leg.

He dropped his knife and took the little beast's neck in both hands, then flung it aside, stepping back away from it as he did so.

The dragon tumbled, then scrambled to its feet and started back toward Dumery, hissing, its neck weaving like a snake preparing to strike.

The adult dragon hissed in reply, loud as an ocean; startled, the hatchling stopped in its tracks, turned its head, and stared up at its guardian.

The big dragon bent down and picked the infant up, grasping it gently in its gigantic maw and depositing it, unhurt, with the others.

Then it turned back to Dumery.

"You swore," Dumery said nervously.

"Aye, I swore I'd not harm you and I shan't. Speak, then, manling, and tell me what has brought you hither. Why have you come to my nesting and keeping?"

The beast spoke Ethsharitic very clearly, but also very oddly. Its words were accented strangely, consonants enunciated far more clearly than Dumery was accustomed to, and some of the words it used struck him as curiously old-fashioned. Dumery tried to make sense of the dragon's question. Did it mean why was he here in the area, or what was he doing in the nest?

He decided it must mean the latter.

"It was an accident," he said, defensively. "I was just curious about what was in here, so I was looking through the logs, and the wind from your wings knocked me down inside."

"Ah, and what was a lad from Ethshar, for I note your use of the Old Tongue as spoken in that land, what was a lad from Ethshar doing in the wildernesses here, where few men dare venture, save the warlocks bound to their fate?"

This sentence was too much for the boy, with its warlocks and tongues and ventures.

"What?" he asked.

The dragon made a noise in its throat that reminded Dumery of a heavy bucket dropped into a very deep well. "Are my words hard on your ears, then? I confess, I must strain to apprehend some of your own pronunciations."

Hopelessly Dumery repeated, "What?"

The dragon eyed him warily, then asked, "Do you have trouble understanding my words, lad?"

Dumery nodded. "Yes," he said nervously.

"And I yours," the beast said. "I fear our common language has changed since last I had occasion to speak it."

"And you use big words," Dumery said.

The beast snorted in amusement, and the gust of hot, fetid air nearly knocked Dumery off his feet. "Aye," it said, "surely I do, by the standards of a lad as young as yourself. I forget myself. Well, then, I shall attempt to limit myself to simpler words, and my apologies to you, boy, for my inconsideration."

Dumery just stared.

"Now then, boy, why is an Ethsharite in this vicinity?"

"I . . . I was on my way home."

"Ah? Whence, that your route led through these wilds?"

"What?"

"Where had you been, lad?"

"Oh. In Aldagmor."

The dragon made the bucket-in-a-well noise again—could it be a chuckle? Dumery hoped it was that, and not something more ominous. The dragon said, "Verily, lad, still are you in Aldagmor, as they call this land, and indeed at its very heart and namesake. Mean you that you were at the keep of him who falsely claims to rule here, him styled Baron of Aldagmor?"

"No," Dumery said. He hesitated, then asked plaintively, "Um . . . smaller words, please?"

"Forgive me, child," the dragon said, with what Dumery took for a sort of smile. " 'Tis such a pleasure to speak to a human again, after all these years with none but foolish young dragons to hear me, that I find myself wrapping my tongue around the richest and finest words that strike me, the better to savor the experience. I've had none with whom to hold converse for thirty years or more save younglings of my own kind, taught to speak by myself, so that I've but heard my own words prattled back to me, and poorly, at that. This drought has been hard and long on my ears, so that I would now drink deeply indeed from the font before me. Is't truly hardship for you, then, to follow my thoughts?'' It looked at Dumery's bewildered expression. "Ah, I see it is, and again I would beg pardon." The beast paused, clearly thinking, its head cocked slightly to one side. Then it spoke again.

"I shall try to use smaller words. Were you visiting the Baron of Aldagmor?"

"No," Dumery said. He debated whether to volunteer more information, and if so, whether to tell the truth.

"You are surely a reluctant font, which needs must be pumped," the dragon remarked. "Where, then were you, if not at the castle?"

"I applied for an apprenticeship," Dumery said. "I was turned down and I lost my way and I knew that if I headed south, I'd eventually come to the river or the sea."

"And in truth you might, but had none warned you of the perils of such a journey? This land is counted accursed by many of your kind, boy, and indeed I myself am a portion of that curse, though of late only the lesser portion." It saw Dumery's helpless expression and said, " 'Tis dangerous, lad! Did no one tell you?"

"No," Dumery said. He was beginning to accustom himself to the beast's manner.

"Well, 'tis. Truly, it is. Aside from the presence of myself and my kind, this is the land where warlocks vanish, where ordinary folk may become warlocks, to vanish in their turn. All this, and the more usual hazards of any wilderness, as well."

"I didn't know," Dumery said. It seemed the simplest reply, under the circumstances, and after all, he hadn't *known* there were wild dragons, or that the Warlock Stone was real and dangerous, if it really was.

"And did you make this journey unaccompanied, with none to aid you?" the dragon asked. "No father, nor mother, nor sib, nor comrade, to see you safe to your destination?"

"No," Dumery said, "just me. My father didn't approve."

"Ah," the dragon said, in a curiously sympathetic tone, "an

outcast from the bosom of family, are you? So was I, once, these few centuries past, to a way of thinking. What name do you go by, lad?''

"Dumery," Dumery said. "Dumery of Shiphaven."

"A fine name, it seems to me, a fine name. No patronymic, then, but merely a residence?''

"I'm the third son," Dumery said in explanation. He didn't mention that patronymics were out of fashion in Ethshar.

"Ah. Well, then, Dumery of Shiphaven, I have been known, and know myself as, Aldagon, which is in the speech of the lost ancients 'She Who Is Great Among Dragons,' or so I was once told. Some have called me Aldagon of Aldagmor, but that strikes me ill, since the land's named for me."

"It is?" the boy asked, startled.

"Aye," the creature said. "Aldagmor means, clearly, 'the Mountains of Aldagon,' and the Aldagon so named is myself. I was here ere this land had *any* name in our common tongue." Aldagon turned its—or rather, *her* head slightly and squinted at Dumery. "Meseems we've wandered afield in our converse, lad. I was asking whence you came, and why, and we've rambled off to names and whatnot whilst I have no sound reply from you."

Dumery said nothing—not because he was stubborn or reluctant, but only because he didn't know what to say.

Aldagon let out a long, earth-shaking draconic sigh. "Speak, lad, tell me the tale entire, in whatever words and manner that you choose, but you tell it all. How came you here?"

Dumery hesitated, but then explained, in awkward and stumbling sentences, that he had wanted to see dragons, and that he had seen Kensher Kinner's son in Ethshar, and had followed him home to the dragon farm. There he had asked for an apprenticeship, had been refused, and had left in despair, only to lose the trail and head south, cross-country, toward Ethshar.

That was the tale as he told it, and Aldagon accepted it. No mention was made of burglaries or witches.

"You sought dragons, you say, and indeed you've found a surfeit of them, I'd venture—first came you to that accursed and damnable farm and now to my nesting, where you find us all." She flexed a wing slightly to indicate the half-dozen young dragons huddled on the far side of the lair.

Dumery nodded.

"Meseems you have an unusual favoring of fortune, to chance upon so many. In truth, I am not often to be found here; my common dwelling is to the east, beyond the mountains, where I'm little troubled by your kind. I take pleasure in converse with humans, but alas, few care to join me so; the more likely occurrence, should I appear amongst them, is a flurry of spears or spells, flung hither and yon for fear of me."

Dumery gulped and ventured, "Well, you *do* eat people, don't you?"

"Nay," she replied with a shake of her head. "I've not tasted man—nor woman, nor child—for these two centuries and more, not since the Great War ended."

"Oh." The idea that this creature had been around during the Great War seemed absurd at first, but then Dumery looked at it again. Aldagon was immense, her head alone a good bit bigger than a farmer's wagon. She had certainly needed a very long time to grow to such a size.

And she was clearly old. Her scales were thick and overlapped each other heavily, while the edges were all worn smooth. Her teeth were huge, but they, too, looked worn.

And if she had really been around back then it made her claim that Aldagmor had been named for her more reasonable, too—Dumery was rather vague on the details, but he thought that Aldagmor, like most of the rest of Sardiron, might have been part of the Northern Empire, so it wouldn't have had any name that ordinary people could use until after the war was won.

"Were you really around during the war?" he asked.

"Oh, aye, of course," Aldagon said. "I was born and bred for the war, these four hundred years past. I was hatched on just such a farm as you saw, though not that very one—the Ethsharite forces had not penetrated so far in my time. I was trained from the egg to fight and fly in the service of the Holy Kingdom of Ethshar, against the minions of the Empire, and for a century I burned the towns and camps of the Northerners, slew their sorcerers and the sorcerous beasts sent against me, and devoured whatever Northern soldiery I could find. I took many a blow in that service, and with damnably little in recompense."

"Really?" Dumery asked.

"Aye, really," Aldagon said. "Oh, at first I was but a beast, rampaging where my masters sent me, at the behest of a half-trained fool whose handsigns I had been made to recognize, but when I had at last learned to speak I began to operate more freely, to take orders too complex for a beast, to fetch back what news I could, and my masters sent me ever farther afield in pursuit of sundry military goals. And what did I ever receive for my pains, but shouted commands, scant provisions—for they wanted me always hungry, the better to feed on the foe—and the occasional whack on the snout?"

Dumery made a wordless noise of sympathy. Aldagon nodded.

"At last I thought better of it," she continued. "I betook me across these mountains and made my home upon their eastern slopes, where I could dine in peace upon the abundant wildlife and the stray Northern patrol that ventured by."

"And you've been there ever since?" Dumery asked.

"That I have, save when the whimsy takes me, and I stray back this way, seeking a taste of beef, or to rescue a handful of my fellows from that foul farm where you were turned away." Again Aldagon gestured toward the young dragons.

"Oh," Dumery said. "They didn't just escape?"

"Nay, I brought them forth—save that one hatchling, he of the black scales, whom I found wandering the mountaintop behind the farm, lost and alone. I know not how he came there." She made a motion with her neck and shoulders that bore an uncanny resemblance to a shrug.

"Oh," Dumery admitted, "I think that was my fault."

# CHAPTER 34

*Aldagon eyed Dumery with interest.*

"Speak, child," she said. "Tell me how you came to send this youngling roaming free."

Dumery cleared his throat uneasily, stalling for time to think about what he wanted to tell this gigantic beast. Despite its oath, he still feared that if he said the wrong thing he might be roasted, eaten, or both—after all, a fit of temper would only need to last an instant for a dragon as large as this one to kill him.

"First," he said, "tell me about rescuing the others."

"There's little to tell," Aldagon said, lashing her tail slightly and sending dry bones and broken branches flying. "I came upon that farm in the waning days of the war, when I chanced to be flying over the area and saw dragons beneath. Mine is a lonely life, lad, so I descended, only to see that my fellows were penned up like beasts, as had I been in my youth. I realized that it was but another breeding farm and paid it no more heed—I had no wish to interfere in the Ethsharitic war effort.

"But then came rumors of peace, and I wondered what was to become of dragons, when they were needed no more in the great conflict, so I took to flying over that establishment every few days.

"To my confusion, I saw few changes. Still were there dragons penned there, and still did humans tend them, and assist in breeding them, and watch carefully over the hatchlings.

"But in time I did notice that all was not as it had been. Many of the hatchlings were slain, and yearlings as well. Those that reached an age to be trained were *not* trained, but were

211

slaughtered instead. Wings were broken and broken again, and I know not why. It seemed to me that this camp had become a mere prison, with no sound reason to continue.

"I mused upon this and considered what action I should take. The thought that I might destroy the establishment and free my fellows occurred to me, but I pursued it not—surely some sound and logical reason existed for its continuance, and had I obliterated it I might be doing great harm, in some way I failed to comprehend. I might well, I thought, by such an action, have given your fellow men reason to hunt me down and slay me—something that none ever troubled to seriously attempt, though my presence was widely known. I bothered few, and the task of exterminating me, while certainly within the abilities of your kind, was apparently deemed to be not worth the effort required. Had I destroyed the camp, though, perchance that had provided the impetus needed to send wizards against me with spells sufficient to the task."

*"Are* there spells that could kill you?" Dumery asked.

"Oh, assuredly," Aldagon replied. She continued. "Thus it was, though, that I knew of that iniquitous place, yet feared to demolish it. Instead, I ventured near and snatched free one of the largest dragons, whilst no humans watched. I sought to question him, but alas, the poor thing was still only a beast, with no powers of speech and little thought beyond his belly. So no greater purpose was served by my effort."

Dumery nodded his understanding.

"I noted that no retaliation was made against me for his freedom, though," Aldagon went on. "No embassy was sent, no traps set, and no spells cast. It seemed to me that though I dared not blast the farm to rubble, I might even so save some of its inhabitants from the abattoir, and the humans would not trouble to stop me, should I keep my depredations minor. And in fact, such has proved true—though I have returned every few years and carried off as many as a half score of dragons at a time, as yet have they done naught to deter me."

She made an odd noise in her throat, then continued. "I confess, 'twas for the most part loneliness that drove me to these rescues, more than altruism, for I had hoped to enjoy the company of my own kind again, as I had not since I fled my duties long before. In that I was sorely disappointed, for the infants I have saved from slaughter are none of them capable of speech, and most perish ere they learn.'' She glanced around the nest. "I see, certes, that the one I called Kuprik has fled the lair, no doubt seeking the food that I would have brought him, had he but waited.''

"Was that a big red and gold one?'' Dumery asked. "I mean, not *big*, not like you, but bigger than most of those.''

"Indeed he was,'' Aldagon answered, startled. "Saw you such a one?''

Dumery shook his head. "No,'' he said, "but I followed his trail back here. He left some scales on a tree he scraped against, so I knew what color he was.''

"Ah, well,'' Aldagon said, "and had you seen him he would most likely have devoured you. A shame, that he's gone, for he was the eldest and largest I had here, and knew a few words, as none of these others yet do.'' She sighed.

"Couldn't you follow him and bring him back?''

She shook her head, and Dumery got dizzy just watching it swing. "Nay, how could I know whither he's fled? And am I a jailer, in my turn, to keep him pent against his will? Neither jailer nor mother, but only a friend and tutor, and with other charges who must be tended, leaving little time to pursue those who refuse my care.''

Dumery blinked. "But . . . you said you'd rescued a lot of dragons. If you've been doing it since just after the war, that's two hundred years! You must have rescued *hundreds* of dragons. Where *are* they all?''

"How am *I* to know?'' Aldagon snapped angrily; Dumery cowered a little, involuntarily. Then the great dragon calmed and said, "I fear, though, that most have long since perished. I have seen them fight amongst themselves, aye, and even battle to the death over a scrawny bullock ere I could intervene. I have seen them slain by men armed with swords and spells, their heads and tails fetched away as trophies of the fight. I have found their starved bodies, little but skin stretched on bone, dead of hunger, for most never learned to hunt properly—the foolish creatures have been accustomed to having their food fetched to them. I have found them dead in a hundred ways, of falls and drowning and fire, sword and spear and spell, choking and poison and traps, claws and teeth and fangs. Few have lived long enough to learn speech, and none long enough to learn sense.'' She twitched her tail. ''Which may be all for the best, in truth, for if dragons were wiser when young and survived in greater numbers, the entirety of the World might now be covered with dragons.''

Dumery shuddered at the thought, and for a moment the two simply stood looking at one another.

''It occurs to me,'' Aldagon said, staring at Dumery, ''that your presence here may bring me the answer to a mystery, to wit, the continued existence of that farm. Is't maintained only lest there be another war, and dragons recalled to service? If so, it seems to me that they are doing their job but poorly, as they train them not, neither do they permit them to attain a size that would allow them to be effective in combat. Why, then, do they continue, breeding the poor little beasts and then slaying them? And you have not answered my question, as to the part you played in the liberation of little Pish. Might there be some link betwixt these two?''

''Well,'' Dumery said, ''you might say so . . .'' He hesitated, trying to think what to say, and the hesitation grew into an awkward silence. ''I mean . . .'' He let his voice trail off.

''Speak to the point, Dumery of Shiphaven,'' Aldagon said irritably, ''ere my temper bests my honor.''

''I'll try,'' Dumery said. ''I . . . I let the black dragon out because I was trying to steal it.''

''Steal Pish?'' Aldagon asked, startled. ''Whatever for?''

''I wanted him and a female, a breeding pair, so I could start my *own* farm.'' Dumery suddenly found himself fighting back tears, and though he succeeded in that effort, words began to spill out instead. ''I didn't mean any harm and I wouldn't have broken their wings that way, I think it's cruel, and I'd be good to them, and . . .''

''Peace, lad, and fear not,'' Aldagon told him, holding up a foreclaw.

Dumery gulped, and regained control of himself.

''I'm sorry,'' he said.

''Lad, you've no need to apologize,'' Aldagon said kindly. ''Think you I know not that I am a thing of terror to you? Think you I expect a mere child to have courage to face me without fright, or the wit to charm me, or the wisdom to know wrong from right, when your elder fellows do not? You saw a farm where dragons were treated as cattle, and you knew naught of dragons but what you saw there, so why should I think the less of you for wishing to keep dragons yourself, as if they were only cattle?"

Dumery swallowed again and attempted to smile.

"There, lad, that's better! Now, tell me, what use are these infants, that they have been raised there these two centuries, and that you would have your own?"

"Blood," Dumery explained.

Aldagon blinked, and Dumery was surprised just how puzzled a dragon's relatively immobile features could look.

"Dragon's blood," he elaborated.

"I had not supposed you meant chicken blood," Aldagon retorted, "nor fish oils nor insect's ichor. Of what use to them is dragon's blood?"

"For magic," Dumery said. "Wizards use it in their spells. Almost all the good spells need dragon's blood."

Aldagon frowned. "Do they?" she asked. "Do they indeed?"

Dumery nodded. "I think so," he said. "I wanted to be a wizard, but it's all secret. You have to be an apprentice to learn anything, and then join the Wizards' Guild and swear secrecy, so nobody really knows but wizards. I wanted to be a wizard, but they all turned me down; nobody would take me on as an apprentice. And then I saw Kensher selling dragon's blood, and the wizards had to pay any price he asked, and I thought . . ."

"You thought that you would take a petty revenge," Aldagon finished for him.

Dumery nodded, shamefaced.

"Well, ho, boy, I expect no better from one of your years, so you needn't look so woeful. You've done no wrong that I can see—save, wait, you sought to *steal* Pish and his mate?"

Dumery nodded again. "They wouldn't take me on as an apprentice there, either."

"Nor sell you a pair?"

"No, of course not," Dumery replied.

Aldagon blinked. "Why not?"

"Because that would break their monopoly," Dumery explained. "That's the only dragon farm left in the World."

"Is it, in truth?" Aldagon rocked back on her four heels at this news and eyed Dumery with renewed interest.

Dumery nodded.

"And they bleed the little dragons and sell the blood?" Aldagon asked. "Well, I suppose 'tis no worse than some other wizardly ingredients—now that I think back all these long years I seem to recall wizards calling for virgin's tears and lizard skulls and the hair of unborn babes, and other such things, and dragons are said to be magical in nature—though the gods know *I* have no magic, else I could scarcely live here, so close to the Warlock Stone!" She mused, while Dumery absorbed this new mention of the Warlock Stone. Was it really close by?

"Do you know," Aldagon said at last, "I believe I remember, when I was very young, that at times wizards drew *my* blood. The memories are very dim, after so long a time, but meseems they are truly there, that I do recall such a thing. The drawings stopped, of course, when first I went to fight and had need of my full strength. So they carry that on and bleed the dragons at the farm?"

Dumery nodded. Then he stopped. She didn't understand, he realized. And she *should* understand—these were her kin they were discussing. He swallowed and said, "They kill them and drain the blood. They cut the dragons' throats."

Aldagon reared back, her head flying upward. *"Kill* them? Kill them? *Do* they so? Is *that* why they breed so many and kill them so young?"

Dumery squeezed back against the hard logs of the nest wall. "Yes," he said.

"Why, those foul, treacherous fools!" Aldagon roared, so loud that Dumery thought his ears would burst inward into his skull. "What need, to *kill* the poor things? Those barbaric idiots! Any pinprick will draw blood; what need to open their throats? What need to slay them?" She stamped about, her tail thrashing, and the smaller dragons scattered in terror, while Dumery readied himself to climb back through the gap between the logs.

*"Idiots!"* Aldagon roared, spewing forth a huge gout of flame, the single word so loud that the ground shook, and wind rustled the leaves in the surrounding trees for several seconds.

Finally, though, the great dragon calmed herself and sought out Dumery once again.

He stood with his back pressed against the rough, peeling bark, trying not to cower too obviously, and faced her as she lowered her head toward him.

"Tell me, boy," she said, so loudly that Dumery's ears rang, "did *you* intend to slaughter them so, had you your own farm?"

Dumery had sense enough to lie. "No," he said, shaking his head, "of course not!"

She glared at him suspiciously. Then she turned away. "Oh, foul creatures," she muttered, more loudly than Dumery could shout, "to slaughter them so needlessly! Would that I had smashed that den of evil long since! Would that I . . . but shall I, now, then?" She turned, head raised, and looked north, her tail lashing, sending up showers of broken wood and bone. "Nay, they would summon their clients, all those wizards who purchased hatchlings' lifeblood, to turn their spells against me . . ."

Dumery watched this display of draconic fury, marveling, and very glad indeed that Aldagon had managed to keep her word and hadn't killed him in her first burst of anger.

He sympathized with her, really. The farm's methods did seem unnecessarily cruel. The memory of all those hatchlings dragging their poor broken wings around the cage was still fresh. But what could anyone do?

Inspiration struck.

*"Hai!"* he shouted. "Aldagon!"

She ignored him.

"I have an idea," he called. *"Aldagon!"*

She turned. "Manling," she growled, "you'd be well advised not to draw my attention just now."

"But I have an *idea*," he insisted. "A way to put the farm out of business!"

She blinked, paused her thrashing, and lowered her head to look at him more closely.

"Manling," she said, "your idea had better be *good*."

# CHAPTER 35

*A*ldagon *sat and considered, the tip of her tail twitching* slightly.

"I don't know," she said doubtfully.

"It'll work," Dumery insisted. "It'll work fine. We'll just undercut their prices. My father's a merchant, I know how it's done!"

"I don't know," Aldagon repeated.

"Look, Aldagon," Dumery said, "how big are you? What do you weight?"

"How am I to know?" She looked back along her gleaming, green-scaled body, past the dark-green wings and the four great hunched legs and out along her tail. "Forty yards, perhaps, from head to tail? Seventy, eighty, ninety tons?"

Dumery nodded. "Say it's eighty tons," he said. "I think that's the important part. Well, the farm has, what, a dozen dragons a year to . . . um . . . I was going to say harvest, but that's not the right word."

"To slaughter," Aldagon said. "And betimes it's a score.".

"All right, twenty. Well, they aren't any bigger then twenty feet long, ever—Kensher told me that was a rule his family had always lived by, ever since the war ended. And a twenty-foot dragon weighs maybe a ton, he said."

Aldagon nodded. "About that. Betimes a plump one could be a ton and a half." She considered, then added, "A *very* plump one."

"Well, then," Dumery said, "say twenty dragons at a ton and a half apiece—and that's more than it really is, you know."

Aldagon acknowledged that, with a dip of her head.

"Well, that's thirty tons of dragon a year that they drain of blood. You weigh *eighty* tons . . ."

218

"And you drain thirty tons of me, I'll perish," Aldagon replied angrily.

"If we drained it *all at once,* it might kill you, yes, but suppose we bled you once a month, drawing blood equivalent to three one-ton dragons—three-eightieths of your blood."

"And how much would that be, in fact?"

Dumery shrugged. "I don't know," he said. "I've never done it before."

"And is there no variation with age and size? Does a ton of my flesh hold the same blood as the whole of a lesser dragon?"

"I don't know," Dumery repeated.

"You would have me, alone, compete with the entire farm?"

"Why not?" Dumery asked. "You're bigger than every dragon on the farm put together!"

She shook her head. "I am not convinced of that," she said.

"Well, then, you can steal some more dragons there! And we can bleed some of the ones you've rescued, the bigger ones, anyway—you can hold them while I do it, so they won't hurt me. And they can breed—or you can . . ." He stopped, unsure of himself, and a little embarrassed at bringing up something so personal.

"Mayhap it's still possible," Aldagon said, untroubled by the topic. "I've no idea. There's been none of a size to interest me these past two centuries. But yes, Prittin should be good for many a fine clutch of eggs, and there are more females to be had at the farm." She glanced at the blue dragon as she considered. "But what's to stop the farmers from breeding more of their own? What if they turn to slaughtering two score, or three, each year? Then I'll have suffered this bleeding for naught but your enrichment, Dumery of Shiphaven, and while I have no dislike for you, yet I see no reason to gift you so generously with the very blood of my body."

"Well, first off," Dumery said, "they don't have much room to expand on that mountaintop of theirs. And second, once there's another source of blood—yours—then the wizards won't need Kensher so much, and who's going to retaliate if you destroy the farm someday? *You'll* be the one with wizards for customers! And third, I could split the gold with you, of course. I don't have to keep it all. I wouldn't *expect* to keep it all."

Aldagon snorted, and gray smoke curled up from her nostrils. "Oh, surely, and what good to me is a fat purse? What is money to me? Am I to stroll into an inn and order a barrel of ale? Am I to buy gewgaws and playpretties, as if I were a female of your own species? Where would I wear such things, that they might be seen? And if we have customers among the wizards, and Kensher has customers, and I burn that stinking farm to the ground, will not his wizards be pitted against ours? Might we not provoke a split within the Wizards' Guild, or perhaps an outright war?"

"Well, what if we do?" Dumery said.

Aldagon blinked, and thought, and replied, "Aye, what if we do, indeed? You've no love for wizards, have you? And in truth, neither do I."

"And as for the gold, it can buy more than jewelry or wine. What if I spent half the money on cattle? I could bring them up here to feed you and the little ones." Dumery blithely waved an arm at the "little" dragons on the other side of the nest, the smallest of them larger than he was.

"Could you, then?" Aldagon asked, startled.

"Sure, why not?" Dumery said. "And anything else you want, I could buy it for you and bring it up here."

"Cattle?"

"Of course! You won't need to hunt any more, or steal from the farmers—no more worries about poison or magic or hunger, because you'll have your *own* cattle to eat! And seasonings for the meat, if you like. Sheep for variety, or anything else you fancy." He was beginning to pick up a trace of Aldagon's archaic phrasing.

"This seems too good to be true," Aldagon said suspiciously.

"Oh, not really," Dumery insisted. "I mean, I'll have to work hard, build up the business—I better start off by apprenticing myself to a merchant to learn the trade and make contacts. And you'll be giving blood every month or so, once we get going, you won't be just doing nothing. And you may need to free some more breeding stock from the old farm."

"I still find . . ." she began, then stopped. Then she asked, "How is it that a mere lad like you should bring this about, when I, after better than four centuries, had never managed it?"

"Age isn't everything," Dumery said. "You need determination, and ambition."

"And you, a child, have those in greater quantity than I?"

"Well," Dumery said, "back home in Ethshar, there's a saying that's used to describe someone who pushes hard, who won't be stopped—they say that he was apprenticed on his twelfth birthday." Aldagon looked puzzled, and Dumery explained, "That's the first day someone *can* be apprenticed; it's not legal to take on an apprentice before he's twelve. Most people wait a few months, to look around and think it over and see what they want."

"And were you, then, apprenticed on your twelfth birthday?"

"No," Dumery admitted. "I wasn't apprenticed at all. But it was on my twelfth birthday that I asked my father to arrange it; it's not *my* fault it didn't work out."

"Ah," Aldagon said, "and will this arrangement of ours work out?"

"If we're careful," Dumery said, "it ought to."


# CHAPTER 36


*T*hey talked for hours, well into the night, working out the details; when the sun dropped below the horizon they moved outside the nest, into a clearing where Dumery made a small pile of brush that Aldagon lit, providing a fire for light and heat.

They tackled such questions as how long it would take to get things under way, and how much of the arrangement they had made should be kept secret, and how many other humans would be hired to help with establishing a cattle ranch, selling blood, and the like.

Taking Dumery's age into account, they decided to build up slowly.

"After all," Aldagon said, "I'm in no hurry. I should live another millennium or so, if I'm careful, ere my body fails of its own weight and my heart bursts. I've learned patience."

The final discussion was over just how Dumery was to get back to Ethshar.

"You can't *walk* from here," Aldagon insisted. "It's too dangerous."

"Why?" Dumery asked, puzzled. He had survived encountering wild dragons; what worse dangers could remain?

"Why, you'll be passing within two leagues of the Warlock Stone!" the dragon told him.

"I will?" Here was a chance to confirm or refute what Teneria had told him. He asked, "So what?"

"Lad, don't you know?" Aldagon said, amazed. "That stone is the source from which all warlocks draw their power and which draws them in when it can, turning their own power against them. I don't pretend to understand it well, but I've spoken with a good many warlocks on their way to it—on their way to destruction, for none have ever returned. Ordinary mortals who go too near the Stone become warlocks themselves, but take no pleasure in the transformation, as they're drawn immediately to it. I'll not have you devoured by the Stone, whatever it truly is!"

"But I don't have *any* talent for warlockry!" Dumery pointed out. "Everybody told me that."

Aldagon considered.

"Well, 'tis possible," she admitted. "In truth, I've flown within a league or so of the Stone myself and felt nothing beyond a certain unease—but why risk it?"

"Because if I don't, how am I going to get home?"

"Why, go around, of course. And in truth, to be sure, I could fly you there. I've not seen Azrad's Ethshar in three hundred and seventy years, but I think I can find it. I could deliver you right into Westgate Market—if Westgate Market still stands."

"Oh, it does," Dumery said. Then he stopped to think.

The prospect of *flying* to Ethshar, on dragonback, was dazzling, both tempting and terrifying—and, after a moment, irresistible.

"All right," Dumery said, "but you can't fly me right into the city. Everybody would see you. Everyone would want to know what's going on. And someone might get frightened and throw a spell at you."

"True enough," Aldagon agreed. "Well, then, what if I fly you to the highway north of Ethshar, in the hour before dawn when all's quiet, and deliver you there, in sight of the walls?"

"That should be safe enough," Dumery agreed.

It was settled.

Then Dumery curled up in his blanket and slept, while Aldagon returned to her nest.

The following afternoon, when the time came to depart, a small snag appeared in their plans—just how would Aldagon carry Dumery?

"I can hold you in my claw," she suggested.

"It doesn't sound very comfortable," Dumery protested. "I thought I could ride on your back."

"But what would you hold on to?"

Dumery had to admit that she had a point; her back was far too broad to ride astraddle, as he might a horse. Still, he refused to admit defeat. Flying the entire way clutched in the dragon's claw like a sack of meal simply didn't appeal to him.

"What if I sat on your neck, just behind your head?" he suggested. "I think I'd have a pretty good grip there with a leg on each side, and I could hold onto your ears with my hands."

"And choke me and pinch me?"

"I'd be careful. And I really don't weight that much."

"True enough," the dragon agreed. "All right, then, we'll try it."

Dumery grinned. Aldagon lowered her head, and he clambered up onto her neck, swinging one leg over.

His seat was rather precarious at first—dragon scales were much more slippery than he had expected. Twice he almost fell off, and saved himself only by snatching at Aldagon's immense pointed ears at the last moment.

Finally, though, he found a position that seemed secure, with his toes hooked into the underside of her jaw, his body pressed forward along the back of her skull, and his hands hooked firmly around the bases of her ears.

"How's that?" he asked.

"Awkward," she replied, the movement of her jaw knocking his feet loose, "but 'twill serve."

"Don't talk," he said, "it pushes my feet out."

"I shall attempt to restrain myself," she replied. "Ready yourself, lad!"

Dumery crouched down and clung tightly while the great dragon leaped into the air.

The forests and hills fell away below with startling speed, the thick gray clouds above drawing nearer until they seemed to be almost close enough to touch.

Then Aldagon wheeled about, leveled off, and headed south.

They spoke very little; not only did Aldagon's jaw movements dislodge Dumery's toes, but the wind carried away the boy's words before the dragon could hear them, making conversation impractical.

He would have had little to say in any case, as he was too busy watching the World sweep by below.

The forest was no longer a thing made up of individual trees, with trunks and leaves, but was instead a vast green sea spilling down the hills and splashing up around the rocky mountaintops. He marveled at its beauty.

He marveled as well at his mount, her scales as green as the forest below and her wings as large as the mainsails of his father's largest ships. He could see her talons outstretched, the cruel, curving claws each nearly as large as he was.

Had anyone ever had so magnificent a mount? Even Azrad himself—neither the present Lord Azrad VII, nor the original General Azrad—had ever had so fine a ride as this. And he, Dumery of Shiphaven, was riding her!

Aldagon sailed on, blithely unaware of Dumery's egotisms.

He looked down at the ground below and realized that it all looked alike to him—he couldn't see any sign of where they had started from, or where they were going. How could Aldagon find her way, he wondered, with no paths to follow?

Presumably she was taking her directions from the sun and the few recognizable landmarks that thrust up through the general green.

The sun had been low in the west and the cloud cover dense when they took off, so it wasn't long before they were flying through darkness, the stars and moons hidden by the overcast. The forest below turned gray, and then black.

Now, more than ever, Dumery wondered how Aldagon knew where to go. Did she have some sense he did not that told her the way? She seemed untroubled as she soared steadily onward.

Then, after what seemed like and may in fact have been hours, Dumery glimpsed a faint glow, far, far ahead, on the horizon.

That puzzled him; it couldn't possibly be dawn already, and besides, how could they have turned east?

After staring for long moments he looked down and saw lights—faint and scattered, but lights. Campfires and lanterns and candles, surely; they were out of the forest and over inhabited lands.

Not long after they passed over lights that seemed to be oddly spread out and mobile, and Dumery realized they were boat lanterns reflected in the water of the Great River.

He looked ahead again and saw that the glow on the horizon was growing.

Ethshar, he realized. The glow had to be the city, Ethshar of the Spices, with its thousands of torches and lamps and braziers, lights lining the streets and burning in hundreds of courtyards, doorways, and windows.

He was almost home.

He watched, and the glow grew nearer and brighter and spread across a wider area—Ethshar was a league across, he knew.

"Boy," Aldagon said, "ahead I see naught but water between here and the city. Where does the highway lie?"

Startled, Dumery clutched at the dragon's ears and wiggled a dislodged foot back into place. "West," he shouted. "That's the Gulf of the East ahead; we want to circle to the west!"

He wondered how she could tell water from land; except where there were lights it all looked like undifferentiated blackness to him.

Then he had no time to worry about anything but holding on, as Aldagon banked into a long, swooping turn to the west. She descended somewhat as well, looking for landmarks.

They passed over a building with a torch burning by the

door, and Dumery thought it might be the inn where he had stayed the first night. Then they were over the highway, sweeping onward toward the city.

At last, as the city's glow spread across the entire eastern sky, Aldagon dropped to the ground.

"Behold, the towers that flank the gate," she said.

Dumery looked, and could just barely make out dim shapes on the horizon; there could be no doubt that Aldagon had better eyesight than he did. The great dragon lowered her head almost to the ground; Dumery swung his legs free, and dropped awkwardly down onto the hard-packed dirt.

He looked around, but all he saw was the city lights to the east and blackness everywhere else. He blinked, but it didn't help. He could hear the breeze stirring through grass, or possibly young corn, and he could hear his companion's breathing, like a strong wind in an open attic, but otherwise the night was silent. Not even crickets chirped.

"It strikes me," Aldagon said, shattering the quiet so suddenly that Dumery jumped, lost his balance, and found himself toppling into the ditch by the road, "that we have neglected an important facet of our scheme."

Dumery managed to land sitting up, with only a small splash.

"What facet?" he demanded, annoyed. The night was so dark he could barely even see Aldagon; only a faint glimmer of golden light reflected from her eyes was visible. He got carefully to his feet. His breeches weren't actually dripping, he was pleased to discover, just damp.

"The means for communication," Aldagon explained. "When you have all in readiness, and would summon me, or come to me, how are we to find one another?"

"Oh," Dumery said.

The dragon was quite right, they *had* neglected that.

Still, he had a ready answer.

"While I was away," Dumery said, "my parents contacted me twice by hiring a wizard to send me magical dreams. Do dragons dream? I mean, in their sleep?"

"Oh, aye, of course we do!"

"Well, then, when I have things ready, I'll hire a wizard and send a dream."

"Need you not know my location?"

"No—just your true name. Ah . . . it *is* Aldagon, isn't it?" The dragon was silent for a long moment.

"*Isn't* it?" Dumery repeated.

"Tell me, lad, if you can," Aldagon replied, "just what *is* a true name?"

"Oh," Dumery said. "Well. Ah." He stopped and thought.

He had heard magicians discussing true names when he had been unsuccessfully seeking an apprenticeship, and even before that, on occasion.

"I'm not sure," he said, "but I believe it means the very first name that you recognized as your own."

Aldagon sighed, and a pale flicker of flame emerged with her sulphurous breath, illuminating for an instant the muddy ditch, the dusty road, and the young green corn of a neighboring field.

"I was afraid of that," she said.

Dumery started to ask a question, then thought better of it. He waited.

Aldagon sighed again. "I fear, manling, that I must confess that the name Aldagon was not my first, though I've borne it these four centuries and more. Ere I could speak, however, I was known by another, and answered to it."

"Oh," Dumery said. "What was it?"

"You'll recall I had no choice, and was but a beast, in the service of Ethshar."

"I remember," Dumery said.

Aldagon hesitated, then admitted, "It was Yellowbelly. Yellowbelly of Third Company, First Regiment, Forward Command."

"Oh," Dumery said.

After a moment's silence, he added, "Well, at least it's easy to remember."

He couldn't see her face, but he heard Aldagon snicker. "Aye," she said, "it is."

Dumery waited for a moment, to see if she had anything more to say, then said, "I guess this is it, then."

"Indeed so, young man. From here you need but follow the glow, and you'll come to the city gates and your home. And when you've readied yourself, summon me to you with that spell of dreams, and I'll come. Readily I'll come; we'll put that foul family out of the business of butchering my kin and make ourselves wealthy in the doing!''

"Right!" Dumery answered, with a gesture of enthusiasm.

"Fare you well, then, Dumery of Shiphaven!"

Dumery's reply was lost in the booming of draconic wings as Aldagon leaped upward, into the black sky above.

When the wind of her departure had died away, Dumery turned and trudged toward the gate.

The next few years would be hard, he knew. He would take his father's advice and apprentice himself to some successful merchant; he would learn the arts of buying and selling, of transporting goods hither and yon. At fifteen, if he was lucky and worked hard, he might make journeyman—surely by eighteen!

Until he was a journeyman, though, he would be careful never to mention what goods he meant to trade in. He would hoard his earnings carefully.

And someday he'd be ready—at fifteen, or eighteen, or maybe twenty-one, if there were unforeseen expenses. But someday he'd be ready.

Then he would start his business—Dumery of the Dragon, Purveyor to Wizards. He would bankrupt Kensher and his clan and put an end to the abuse they inflicted on dragons. He would watch Thetheran and the other wizards fume and fuss, and then have no choice in the end but to pay Dumery's prices. He would send cattle to Aldagon and collect blood in exchange, and he'd be, in time, very rich indeed.

At first he might pretend to be a dragon-hunter, he thought as he stumbled, then reoriented himself and marched on. In time, though, once he was established, he could reveal his secret, show everyone that he had made friends with a dragon, rather than hunting or slaughtering the noble creatures. He didn't need to worry about competition; after all, where would anyone else find a dragon like Aldagon? And once found, who could befriend such a beast? His own encounter had been a fluke, a lucky chance—had he come upon the nest when Aldagon was in it, or when it was empty, she would probably have slain him, had he dared approach. Had he been armed with anything more than a belt knife, and therefore more threatening, or had the hatchling been too far away to grab . . .

He doubted he would have much competition even when his methods became known.

As he finally came close enough to see the open gates clearly, light spilling out from the torches and lamps of Westgate Market, he wished he had flown openly into the city on Aldagon's back. Think of the impression it would have made, he told himself. A hundred-foot dragon, landing inside the city walls, and he, Dumery of Shiphaven, Dumery of the Dragon, on its back! What a wonder! The city gossips would have talked of it for years!

He hadn't done it, of course.

But someday . . .

Someday, he promised himself, when his business was a going concern, he *would* do it.

# EPILOGUE

*Sella looked up as Teneria entered.*

"Good to see you back safely," she said. "Come for your things?"

Teneria nodded. She had learned years ago never to be surprised by Sella's conversational leaps. And she had, in fact, come to collect her belongings and move back to Fishertown—she could finish up her apprenticeship later. Right now she did not want to live under Sella's roof, where she would be reminded of her failure.

"Have you decided what you'll be doing with yourself, now that you're a journeyman?" Sella asked.

"But I'm not . . ." Teneria said, startled. "I mean, I didn't bring Dumery back!"

"Oh, nonsense," Sella told her, waving away such details. "You found him, and he got home safely, and he's given up his half-witted schemes and taken a respectable apprenticeship with a jeweler, so who cares if you didn't actually come home *with* him? And he says it was your magic that brought him home so quickly, though of course we both know that's not true."

"He said that?" Teneria stared.

Sella nodded.

Teneria considered that for a moment, then shrugged. The boy might have done it to make up for the trouble he had caused her, but more likely it was part of some scheme he had devised, intended to distract his parents from something. "Dumery," she said. "Ha. I'm glad to be done with *him*."

Sella smiled understandingly.

"Mistress . . ." Teneria began. Sella held up a hand, cutting her off.

"Not anymore," she said. "You're not an apprentice anymore."

Teneria smiled. "That's right. Sella, then. . . . Sella, do you know anything about warlockry?" As a puzzled frown crept across the older witch's face, Teneria noticed a pair of bulging eyes peering around a curtain.

"Or spriggans?" she added.

# ABOUT THE AUTHOR

Lawrence Watt-Evans was born and raised in eastern Massachusetts, the fourth of six children. Both parents were longtime science fiction readers, so from an early age he read and enjoyed a variety of speculative fiction. He also tried writing it, starting at age seven, but with little immediate success.

After getting through twelve years of public schooling in Bedford, Massachusetts, he tried to keep up family tradition by attending Princeton University, as had his father and grandfather. He was less successful than his ancestors and, after two attempts, left college without a degree.

In between the two portions of his academic career, he lived in Pittsburgh, a city he considers one of the most underrated in the country. It was at this time that he began seriously trying to write for money, as it seemed easier than finding a real job (he had previously worked in a ladder factory, as a feature writer for a small-town newspaper, as a sandwich salesman on campus, in a supermarket, and at other trivial tasks). He sold one page of fiction in a year and a half.

In 1977, after leaving Princeton for the second and final time, he married his longtime girlfriend and settled in Kentucky, where his wife had a job that would support them both while he again tried to write. He was more successful this time, producing a fantasy novel that sold readily, beginning his full-time career as a writer.

He now lives in Gaithersburg, Maryland.